STORYBOOK
HOUSE II
A SPIRIT'S REVENGE

STORYBOOK
HOUSE II
A SPIRIT'S REVENGE

Katie Jones

NEW
HOLLAND

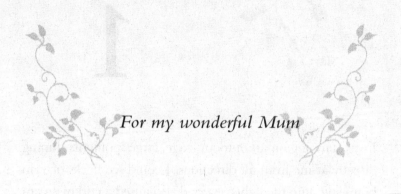

For my wonderful Mum

CHAPTER

1

I was standing on an outdoor stage, large spotlights shining directly at me from all directions. I could see flecks of rain bouncing onto the lights; every drop caused a curl of steam to rise off the round dish, giving a mist-like effect. Aside from the bright light of the spotlights everything in the distance was in darkness. I squinted to see the audience, but I couldn't make out their faces, only the blurred outline of shadows.

The sound of someone's voice made me turn: 'A glooming peace this morning with it brings; the sun, for sorrow will not show his head: Go hence, to have more talk of these sad things; some shall be pardon'd and some punished: For never was a story of more woe. Than this of Juliet and her Romeo.'

Who was saying that? I looked around me but staring at the spotlights had caused my eyes to fail when I needed them the most. I was completely disorientated, and the darkness crept towards me like a sinister shadow.

The audience stood and clapped loudly. I turned back in the direction of the applause but found myself again dazzled by the lights. I went to put my hand to my face to try to block the light, but someone grabbed it and pulled me forward to the front of the stage. I stumbled, catching myself before I fell, as my other hand was taken by another cold hand.

Both of my arms were raised in the air as the people either side of me took a bow. I just stood there, a deer in the headlights. The rain started to get heavier, and I looked up in the sky for the moon but either it wasn't there, or it had been blotted out by the clouds that were unleashing the downpour of rain.

I could see shadows moving in the darkness as each of the performers took individual bows. Abruptly the hands on either side of me released their vice-like grip and the two people who had been holding my hands stepped forward, bowing low to their applause, and then turned and ushered me to the front of the stage.

It was only then that I could see who had been standing either side of me: my beautiful dead friend Gus, one of the ghosts haunting the old mansion that my parents and I had moved into less than a year ago, and Charlie, the boy who lived next door to me, who I had been dating. Both of whom I happened to be in love with.

'Take a bow Sophie!' Gus demanded aggressively, pointing into the darkness. I stared at him in confusion, my mouth not connecting with my brain.

'What? But I'm not in the play,' I said, shaking my head, but he didn't appear to hear me.

'Yes, come on Sophie, can't you hear they adore you. And besides you are such a wonderful actress.' Charlie nodded his head, smiling at me with a manic-looking grin.

I shook my head again, looking from Gus to Charlie and then at the shadowy, faceless figures of the audience. They began chanting my name, 'Sophie, Sophie, SOPHIE, SOPHIE …' getting louder and louder. The heat coming from the lights, the rain that was falling in hard droplets, and the noise were all too much. It felt like the audience was moving closer towards the stage and there was a buzzing sound that was ringing in my ears. I needed to sit down.

'Stop it, please,' I said, but it came out as a whisper. I bent over double and closed my eyes to try to block out the noise and slow my breathing, but it didn't help. The rain fell harder on my back and the buzzing continued to ring in my ears.

'SOPHIE! SOPHIE!'

I sat bolt upright in bed. I had my eyes closed tightly and it took me a moment to re-orientate myself back into my room from the nightmare that I had just escaped.

'Sophie?' my mom called again, knocking on the bedroom door.

I realized the buzzing noise in my dream was coming from outside. It was the hedge trimmer that Gus's dad – our gardener Thomas – was using on the overgrown hedge that surrounded a sunken theater, on the other side of the property from my bedroom.

During the Halloween ball that had been held at our house five months earlier the drama representative for our year level, Sarah Forbes, had snuck away from the party with Toby Miller to make out and they had stumbled upon the garden. Once she had found out that the theater had hosted a number of local Shakespearean productions decades earlier, she had spent the rest of the evening begging my parents to allow her to host the school's production of *Romeo and Juliet* in the theater.

They had started preparing the site three weeks ago, coming most weekends to clean the moss off the stone steps that curved in a semicircle around the stage. Sarah planned to organize picnic baskets and had even recruited the art department to sew seventy-five pillows for the audience to sit on, marking out each spot.

The tickets had gone on sale a week ago and, as there were only seventy-five seats, (seventy-two if you didn't count the spots that had been reserved for my parents and me), they had already sold out. The night they had selected was a full moon, in the last week of the school year, at the start of June, to add an air of mystery and some convenient lighting to the evening, and I had been having nightmares about it ever since.

The full moon was the one night each month that the ghosts could roam freely around our house, when the key that I had hidden carefully in my bookshelf was turned in the clocks in each of the rooms in the haunted house in which I lived. I suspected that the drama department would not be interested in a couple of walk-on cameos from the spirits.

I had never seen any of the ghosts walk out of the house. When the clock struck 1 am they just seemed to disappear, so I didn't know if they could physically leave. Gus had told me not to let any of the ghosts leave the house in case they got stuck in some kind of ghostly limbo when the clocks were wound back, but I wasn't sure whether that meant they couldn't walk out.

Over the past five full moons I had come to know and be quite fond of some of the ghosts that appeared in the rooms of our house. The soldiers from the army that spent their evenings in the drawing room, recalling battles that they had won, and now and then some that had been lost, as well as places they had visited during the war; or the ladies and gentlemen in their evening finery who would sit down to a five-course meal in the dining room complete with butlers and ladies' maids clucking around them, attending to their needs.

I could just picture the ghosts roaming around the garden and onto the stage during the performance, causing the audience to scramble for the four small exits in the thick hedge that surrounded the stage and seating areas.

'Oh god,' I moaned and fell back down into my pillow with a thump.

'Sophie?' my mom's voice broke into my thoughts of ghosts appearing on stage during the performance and causing a panic.

'Mom?' I called back, remembering that she was standing outside the door. 'You can come in.' I pushed myself up into a seated position while trying to wipe the sleep from my eyes as my mom bustled into the room.

'I have to pop into the city this afternoon so I thought I would check if you wanted to come with me.'

'Absolutely!!!' I would happily throw myself out of bed right now to go back into New York City!

'Oh, and Alice is downstairs. I told her to help herself to a bagel while I checked on my lazybones daughter – it is after 11 am you know!' she looked at her watch and threw her hands up in the air. I groaned as I remembered that I already had plans for the day that didn't involve venturing into the city. Alice, my best friend also happened to be a witch with the ability to unseal the doors in my house that had been sealed shut with magic by her grandmother.

My dad had inherited the house from a distant relative, Poppy Farrell, who was another one of the ghosts that lived in the house. She spent most of her days sitting at her dressing table, looking out at the water and waiting for her husband who had died in the war, to return to her. My parents were doing up the old mansion with the aim of turning it into a bed and breakfast and I knew they would want access to all of the rooms in the house. When we first moved into the house, we discovered multiple doors around the house that we had thought were glued shut. Alice had managed to open two of the doors so far but there were five more to go and today we had decided to open the next one.

'Sorry Mom, I can't come this afternoon. I forgot that Alice and I have … an assignment that we need to work on. Next time, OK?'

Mom stopped opening the curtains and looked at me like I had rejected a free plane ticket around the world travelling first class.

'You don't want to come to your favorite place on this earth?' She made a big deal of walking over and putting her hand to my head to check that I didn't have a temperature. 'Wow, you are not sick, and you look like my daughter, but you couldn't possibly be. Sophie would never turn down a trip into the city.'

'Yeah, yeah, I just can't today that's all,' I said swatting her hand away from my face and flopping back down on my pillow again to stretch out my body.

'OK, raincheck then. Don't forget that Alice is waiting for you,' she reminded me, squeezing my foot as she walked out of the room.

CHAPTER

2

I took a few deep breaths and kicked off my duvet. After pulling on track pants and a long-sleeved top I dragged a brush through my hair and tied it into a ponytail.

When I walked into the kitchen Alice was sinking her teeth into a bagel smothered in cream cheese and reading out of an old journal of her grandma's while making notes into another small notebook of her own.

I poured myself a juice and sat down next to her, swiping a wedge of her bagel.

'OK, so we have decided on the downstairs guest room?' I said as though we were in the middle of a conversation, which it felt a bit like we were given we had gone over this discussion a million times in the past five months.

After the scary experience we had with a ghost that had been sealed in the study we decided to take our time to research who might have been in the other rooms of the house before we attempted to unlock another door. And neither of us were motivated enough to open the next door. Alice had been busy helping with her mom's restaurant, and for me, besides everything going so well with Charlie, my parents had been busy enough working on other parts of the house that they hadn't spoken about the doors that seemed to have been glued shut. I knew it wouldn't be long before they refocused their attention on them, and I wanted to be one step ahead.

We had a list of the five remaining rooms in the house that were deemed to have dangerous spirits. So dangerous that Alice's grandmother, Isadora, had sealed them shut so that no one could get in or out of them. The list read:

Downstairs guest bedroom – Fred Simpson

Clock tower – ????

Upstairs guest bedroom – H. Whitfield

Basement storeroom – ????

Servants' quarter's bedroom –????

We had listed them in order of urgency for unlocking the room – the first three being places that I suspected my parents would need access to for guests coming to stay – as well as the likelihood that someone might try to break down the door to get into them. We then had added the scant comments from Poppy's notebook and Alice's grandmother's journal, but they were generally light-on for details. We hadn't been able to find out much on H. Whitfield, and for three rooms we couldn't find any information about who the inhabitants were at all.

The clock tower entrance and servant's bedroom we had discovered locked, but they were not listed in either Poppy or Isadora's notes, while the basement was listed but we couldn't find where the entrance would be from the basement. There was only one door leading into the room.

During a previous full moon, I had brought up the names we did have with some of the spirits that had been in the house. Fred Simpson's name had rung a bell with the army group, and we had subsequently been able to verify that he had been a lieutenant in the US armed forces who had been sent to the Battle of Normandy in France at the same time as Poppy's husband.

I had thought about speaking to Poppy about Fred, but she had been increasingly absent from her room. I wasn't sure where she was going but I didn't feel right prying, so I asked Alice to speak to Isadora instead.

Alice finished writing down some notes on something that she had read and nodded. 'Yep, Fred Simpson sounds like the easiest candidate at this stage. From our research he doesn't sound that dangerous. I can't really see any reason that they locked him in here in the first place.'

'Well Poppy's memory from the last few years of her life was a little scatty so let's hold off on opening the door until you've had a chance to speak to Isadora. You still keen to go into the hidden safe this afternoon?'

A couple of months ago when we had unsealed Poppy's husband's office, we had found the ghost of Diana Faraday, who had murdered Poppy's older brother when he was just an infant. After we were able to calm her, she had revealed that she had been a witch just like Alice and she had also mentioned that she had knowledge of the magic required to seal spirits into the rooms. From the brief encounter with her it seemed that she had more information documented in her personal possessions that had likely been left in the house after she had been executed for the murder. Unfortunately, before we were able to gather more knowledge about her experience she had passed on, taking the valuable information with her.

Around the same time, Gus and I had found a treasure trove in a safe that was hidden in one of the secret passageways in the house, and Alice and I hoped that further inspection of the safe might uncover Diana's box of possessions.

'Yep, I'm still free if you are. No dates booked in with either of your boyfriends?' she teased.

I stuck my tongue out at her and stole another piece of her bagel. 'No but I did give up a date with the love of my life, the city of New York, so I hope this search is worth it!'

Alice's mention of my divided heart brought back memories of my dream. Obviously my subconscious was battling with the division as much as I had been. Since the ball and the profession of love from both Gus and Charlie I had felt like a piece of rope in a tug of war.

Charlie had not been completely surprised that Gus was still in the house, as he had suspected that he had seen his spirit once or twice when looking across into my bedroom from his. Charlie knew that I had feelings for Gus, but he didn't seem to see him as much competition, given he didn't have a heartbeat.

That seemed to be one thing that they both agreed on: Gus had convinced himself that the only reason that

I was still dating Charlie was because he was alive, and Gus wasn't.

Gus's dad, Thomas, was surprisingly happy knowing that Gus was haunting the halls of Storybook House. He had decided to stay at the house after his son had drowned, years earlier, falling off one of the sailing boats belonging to the house in a storm that had ravaged the area. I had been on the boat with him but had avoided the same fate, swimming to shore before the storm after the two of us had had an argument. The guilt of what had happened still ate at me, but I didn't regret telling Thomas about Gus's presence as a ghost in the house. The two of them spent long nights speaking about life before and after Gus's death. Each night, when he had finished talking with his dad, Gus would materialize in my room and stay beside me while I slept.

I felt like my heart was split in two. My days I spent with Charlie and my nights with Gus, and even though Gus was technically not alive and this should make my decision easier, I did not want to choose between them and risk losing one of them from my life. I needed them both. Charlie was my sun and Gus was my moon, both revolving around me, and I selfishly kept them both at a distance from each other. Both Gus and Charlie were keen to see each other but I had so far deflected all requests to this end.

I swallowed the piece of bagel that I had stolen and took the plate and my glass over to the kitchen sink to wash.

'Actually, I think Gus is going to come to the safe to

help us look,' I said not looking in Alice's direction because I knew that she didn't agree with what she perceived as me stringing both boys along. She remained silent but I could feel her dissatisfaction radiating from where I was standing.

For the next couple of hours Alice and I tried to do some more research on Fred Simpson, but we weren't getting anywhere. Just like Poppy's husband George, he had died while fighting for his country in France. He had one child, a daughter, and an ex-wife. On face value from the court documentation they were amicably divorced, and I could see no reason why he would have turned into an evil spirit worthy of being locked away in one of the guest bedrooms. I spent hours trying to dig up something that might have sent him over the edge or any indications in his early life that he may have been dangerous – maybe an apprehended violence order made by his wife indicating that their divorce was as a result of violent behavior – but there was nothing. After a while I conceded to Alice that I was probably spending so much time researching Fred because I was avoiding going back into the secret passage where our former chef Marcel had almost killed me months earlier.

After the school Halloween ball at our house had come to an end, and while my parents were seeing the partygoers off, our housekeeper Clara had gone back down the passageway and dragged Marcel out of the safe where we had trapped him and into the lounge room to await the arrival of the police. He had been remanded on $100,000 bail, which he couldn't afford, so had been languishing in prison to await his trial ever since. I knew that they would need me to testify, and I was dreading it. I never wanted to see him again or think about that night and I knew venturing into the passage would inevitably bring back painful memories.

Eventually I put the excuses behind me and we walked up to my room, where there was an entry to the passage. Gus was there waiting for us.

'Hey pretty lady!' he said, and when I rolled my eyes he added, 'Oh and hey to you too Sophie.'

'Hey Gus,' Alice said, waving her hand at Gus and chuckling.

He turned back to me with a serious expression on his face. 'You ready to do this?'

'I guess,' I said unconvincingly and shrugged my shoulders.

He moved to stand in front of me, looking into my eyes. 'We will be there with you Sophie,' he said with a reassuring smile. I could sense that he wanted so much to reach out and take my hand.

I tried to smile back but it came out as more of a grimace. I walked over to the bookshelf and pulled on the book that acted as the lock for the passage. Alice had never been in the passageways, and she peered into the opening with curiosity.

'You said that these are all over the house?' I nodded my head. 'Wow! That is so cool.'

I tried to match her excitement but couldn't. I looked

over at Gus and he smiled again and nodded, 'Nothing is going to hurt you Sophie.'

I took a deep breath and stepped into the passage. It looked just as it had the night that I had come in with Marcel but this time I could hear Alice and Gus talking excitedly behind me about what was in the safe and it made me feel a lot better. I had originally suggested that I would go into the passage alone and was immensely relieved that Alice and Gus had insisted that they come too.

I shivered as I glanced at the candlestick where Marcel had tied my hands but kept walking towards the familiar ripples on the wall that unlocked the entry. Alice watched in amazement as the door to the safe popped open and revealed the treasures inside after I ran my hands along the ripples. Thomas had been able to locate a couple of old kerosene lamps for us to take into the safe and the light they cast made the room look a lot bigger than the last time I had been in there with Gus and a failing flashlight. That felt like so long ago, but really it had only been a few months.

The shelves were piled high on both sides with treasures, so Alice and I split up, Alice going through the contents of the shelves on the left and me checking out what was on the right while Gus hovered behind us, making sure we didn't miss anything. I started looking through the contents on the floor, assuming that if they had kept all of Diana's stuff it would be in a large box or chest that would only fit on the bottom shelf, but Gus suggested that they could have broken it all up or just kept some things and not others, so we started searching all of the shelves, not just the large boxes at the bottom.

I picked up each of the items, marveling at how well everything had been preserved in the airless chamber. There were small statues made of jade and ivory, mountains of jewelry covered in priceless looking precious stones – rubies, sapphires, diamonds and several I couldn't identify.

I thought about Isadora's book that Alice had shown to me and scanned the shelves for large ornate-looking books. Towards the end of the shelf there was a collection of books but even though I flicked through each one, fingering the pages gently in case they fell apart, I couldn't find anything that resembled what I imagined Diana's spell book looked like. I looked over to see how Alice was going. She was holding up a beautiful-looking necklace, using the kerosene lamp to try and get a better look at it. I took the lamp from her and held it up.

'Thanks,' she murmured, her eyes focusing on the stone at the center of the pendant. She looked mildly concerned.

'What is it?' I asked her.

'I don't know. It's just that … I think … I mean I know this sounds ridiculous, but I think this necklace has some kind of power or is magic in some way. I don't know how to explain it but … well it's just …' She looked up at me shyly as though she was embarrassed about what she was about to say. 'I can feel it,' she said quietly.

'I believe you,' I nodded my head to make sure she

knew that I completely supported whatever it was that she was sensing. I turned and glanced at Gus to see what he thought but he just shrugged his shoulders and moved to have a look at another shelf.

'Why don't you take it. It won't be missed,' I said gesturing to the shelves laden with jewels and treasures.

I moved back to my side to finish checking the shelf with the old books. The last book that I looked at was even older and more weather-beaten than the others. It had a brown cover with an embossed image of a ship in the middle of the front cover. When I opened the cover the writing inside was all handwritten and it looked as though it had been done with a quill. I ran my hands over the words, feeling the indentations where the author had pushed a little harder. I couldn't make out the words very well in the dull light, but I thought it could have been some kind of historical archive of information. I could see what looked like maps and strange images. It seemed unlikely that it was Diana's – it had to be older than her – but I decided to take the book back to my room for a better look.

I glanced around the room again and ran my hand over some of the jewels that sat on the shelf next to where I was standing. How was I going to tell my parents that I had found this Aladdin's cave without mentioning Poppy's ghost?

'What am I going to do about this place?' I wondered aloud, shaking my head.

I had taken my parents to the safe in Poppy's room the night that Marcel had been arrested but I had conveniently used him as a scapegoat, saying that I wouldn't have known about the location of the safe had I not caught him trying to raid it. I knew I had to tell them about this safe too, but I didn't know how to explain it – this cavern of treasures wasn't something you could just stumble across.

My parents had been excited at the discovery of the money hidden in Poppy's safe, which she had gladly advised me they were welcome to, and when they had counted it all out it amounted to just over $250,000. So far the money had been used on re-plumbing and completely rewiring the house. The renovations had progressed quickly with my parents driving the improvements and the injection of capital from the safe and I sensed that the first guests of Storybook House would arrive imminently.

I was having one more look through the bookshelf to make sure that I had not missed anything when I spotted a corner of a piece of paper underneath the pile of books I had just checked. The corner that was poking out looked a little like blueprints.

'Alice? Can you give me a hand lifting up these books?' Together we lifted the books high enough so we could pull the large A3 sheets out from their hiding place. The pages looked very similar to the blueprints of the house that Poppy had given me earlier in the year. Poppy's plans were similar in every way to the plans my parents had apart from one key feature: they included the location of the hidden passageways.

At first, I thought these blueprints were the same as Poppy's version but on closer inspection there were additional markings coming from the basement. They marked the locations of several passageways that were not marked on either version of the blueprints that I had seen so far. I showed Alice and Gus and we made a plan to look into the locations on another day. After another fifteen minutes we conceded that if Diana's possessions were still in the house they were not in this room. I found myself thinking about Diana and her box of secrets. I wondered whether I would keep a box of things that was owned by someone who had murdered my child. I knew the likelihood of us being able to find any trace of her witch's notebook, spell book or whatever it was called was very slim, but I didn't mention this to the others in case it made them feel as depressed as it made me feel.

Walking back out of the passageway and into the warmth of my room I was happy that I had faced my fears and gone back into the hidden safe, but I was also very relieved to be out of there. I knew I would have to come up with a way to reveal the treasures to my parents but for the time being I was just happy not to think about it.

Alice went up to the room next to Poppy's to speak to her grandma and I ducked down to Thomas's cottage to see if he had any ideas on other areas in the house where Diana's box might have been stored. Gus knew where I was heading and had beaten me there. By the time I reached the cottage Thomas and Gus were deep in discussion about possible locations. Thomas nodded in my direction when I walked into the cottage without knocking.

'I know that there is a cellar in the basement that has

a large wine collection – it could be down there. I don't think anyone has been down there in decades because Poppy never really drank wine … oh, and there are also a few rooms up in the servants' quarters that it could be in. Another possibility, albeit an unlikely one, is the storage room under the stairs – you could check there. But to be honest there are secret passages coming off almost all of the rooms in the house so it really could be anywhere. That is probably not all that helpful, sorry,' he said, looking downcast. I put my hand on top of his and when he looked back up at me, I smiled encouragingly.

'It is more helpful than you know Thomas! Really. You have given us great ideas of where to look. Speaking of passages, did you know about the passageways that lead off the basement? We found blueprints of the house that indicated there were a few but I don't remember ever being in them or even seeing an entry point to them.'

He pulled his cap off and scratched the top of his head, trying to imagine where the entry to the passages would be, but when he pulled his cap back on and made eye contact with me he looked like he had drawn a blank. He shook his head and looked confused. 'The basement? There can't be. I can't think of an entry point for one passage let alone multiple passages.'

'Maybe they were concept designs, and those passageways weren't built into the final house.' I shrugged it off but made a mental note to check it out when we continued our search for Diana's belongings.

Gus and I came up with a plan of where to search

from the list of places that Thomas had provided as potential locations for Diana's trunk. We decided to have a quick look at the storage under the stairs when I got back up to the house. 'Race you,' Gus said, and, laughing, disappeared a second later.

'Hey! That's not fair!' I said loudly, hoping he could still hear me.

I looked back at Thomas who was sitting at his table with a smile on his face.

'Cheeky boy. It is almost like he never left,' he said, and a sad expression briefly passed over his face. When he saw me watching him nervously the smile returned, only some of the sadness in his eyes remained. 'Don't get me wrong Sophie, I don't regret a single day since the Halloween ball when you brought him to me. I feel fortunate to have him in my life at all. We have had some wonderful talks together, and he is getting pretty good with his practicing.' He gestured over to a smaller table which had a couple of broken coffee mugs, a book and some tissues sitting on it. I was confused and started to ask what he meant, but before I could say anything about the objects on the table, he continued his thought process. 'It's just that having him here, knowing that most of the spirits that have stayed around the house and not … you know, moved on, makes me wonder why my wife isn't here. Had she already found peace when she died?'

He looked confused and I couldn't help him; I was just as confused, my mind still stuck on what he had said about Gus and the broken objects – was he suggesting that

Gus could now move objects enough that they had fallen and broken? I was about to ask when the sound of a shrill voice and a hard knock at the door made me jump.

'Thomas are you in there? HELLO! HELLO? THOMAS?'

He looked at me and rolled his eyes. 'Here we go again. Excuse me Sophie,' he murmured and got up to open the door.

It was Sarah and half the drama committee, standing anxiously outside his door. She didn't wait for him to speak, instead launching into a tirade about needing Thomas's help with setting up for their afternoon practice. I waved goodbye and walked back up to the house to have a look under the stairs.

Even though I spent most of the walk thinking about how to raise the subject of the broken objects I had seen at Thomas's cottage, when I saw Gus's face, I couldn't bring myself to ask. I wondered if there was a reason that he hadn't told me. I was also preoccupied thinking about what Thomas had said about Gus's mom. Although I felt my mind wasn't properly on the task at hand, I ended the search fairly confident that Diana's belongings were not under the staircase.

By the time that I got back upstairs Alice had already left the house and Isadora was also nowhere to be found. I hoped that Alice had a chance to speak to Isadora about Fred. Unlike Poppy, who seemed to be stuck in our house, Isadora was able to roam freely between other locations that were haunted by spirits.

I sat down at my desk, hoping to get some homework completed. Study had never been a strong point of mine and with all of the distractions in the house, plus spending time with Gus and Charlie, I had definitely let my grades slip ever so slightly.

CHAPTER

3

The next day at school I steered Alice away from the lunchroom and found a quiet picnic table outside to eat our lunch where we wouldn't be disturbed or overheard. She had left the house before I had a chance to find out how her discussions with Isadora had gone. During literature she had been shooting me meaningful looks across the room like she had some information to share. The air was cold outside, but I was eager to know what she had discovered. I pulled my jacket tighter around me and breathed warm air into my hands.

'Did you speak to Isadora about the ghost in the guest room?' I asked picking at my sandwich.

She nodded as she sat down on the wooden bench, 'You are not going to like it.'

I rolled my eyes and groaned. 'What else is new! When am I ever going to like something about the ghosts that have been locked up in my haunted prison house for psychotic spirits?'

Alice snorted at my sarcastic comment but was quickly serious again. 'Gran remembered that she didn't agree with locking Fred in the room. In fact, it was the only ghost that she and Poppy argued about locking up. She said he wasn't violent or dangerous.'

'So why the locked room?' I asked, perplexed. I ditched my feeble attempts to eat my sandwich and studied Alice's features, willing her to reveal the mystery.

'She said that Fred had been trying to locate Poppy's husband and while he hadn't had any luck finding him, he had stumbled upon someone who knew of Poppy's husband and that ghost had told Fred that Poppy's husband was a double agent working for the Germans during the war.'

I gasped as Alice sat back and let her words sink in. 'NO!'

'That's what Fred told Poppy. Gran was there when he told her.'

'So … Poppy locked him in the room because he gave her information that she didn't like?' I asked dubiously, shaking my head. That didn't seem like her when it came to how she felt about her husband and how she pined for him still all these years later. Maybe I didn't know how far she would go.

'Yep. I think she was really angry, and she didn't believe him. Gran died not long after they locked him in the room so even if Poppy had regretted it, she wouldn't have been able to fix it.'

'Wow. Do you think he will be peeved when we unseal the door, and start throwing things at us?'

'From the way Gran spoke of him I think that is unlikely.' Alice shrugged her shoulders and took a bite out of her muffin.

'Maybe I had better speak to Poppy before we open the door and let old Fred out. Can ghosts harm other ghosts?' Alice shrugged again and waved at someone behind me. I turned and saw Percy walking towards our table. Percy was my first friend at my new school and Alice's boyfriend. I couldn't have picked anyone more deserving of my wonderful friend Alice. They had paired up at the Halloween ball and had been happily dating ever since. 'Let me know how you go with Poppy and when you are ready to open the room.' The conversation was officially over as Percy reached the table, wrapped his arms around Alice and nuzzled into the side of her neck.

'What are you lovely ladies talking about?'

'Math test,' Alice said at the same time as I blurted out 'Art assignment.' He looked from me to Alice and back again.

'Riiiggghhhttt ... So, what are you really talking about?'

Alice sighed and looked up with a guilty expression. 'I guess we had better tell him. You have kept it a secret from so many people all this time, but I think there is no point in hiding it anymore.' I shot her a look of confusion mixed with mild panic and concern.

'W-w-what?' I stammered.

She looked back at Percy and with a sincere look on her face conceded, 'It's Sophie's birthday this weekend and she has been trying to keep it under wraps.'

My expression of shock turned to one of embarrassment. How had she known it was my birthday? No one knew it was my birthday. I had kept it secret deliberately. When I was a child my parents had thrown me a disastrous roller-skating party. Two children had spectacularly collided, resulting in multiple broken bones, while another had vomited at the sight of all of the blood. After a trip to hospital and several sick bags I had avoided recognizing my birthday ever since. Percy clapped his hands and did a drumroll on the table as I stared at Alice with what I hoped was a seriously annoyed expression.

'Whoever told you that blatant lie obviously doesn't know me that well.'

Alice half coughed and muttered, 'Gus' under her breath and I groaned. Of course Gus would remember annoying little details like that and pass them on to someone who could do something about it.

'Who is Gus? Where should we have the party? Maybe we could do a dinner at your mom's restaurant?' Percy fired out, fortunately not seeming to linger on the first question that we couldn't really answer without blowing our actual secret.

'No, no, seriously I really don't want to make any fuss …' I started but was quickly cut off by Alice replying excitedly to Percy.

'That is a great idea, we could set up that small side room with some balloons and we have some beautiful wild roses that I can put in the middle of the table with some vines twisting across the table and …' they continued talking as though I wasn't there.

I lay my head on the table and focused on what

I was going to say to Poppy about Fred Simpson when I eventually found her.

I successfully avoided speaking to anyone else about my birthday for the rest of the day, but I suspected Alice and Percy had already decided on a course of action and all that was left was to bully me into attending. I was certain Alice would recruit my mom who would take pleasure in helping her organize the whole thing. It felt like I was standing on a train track and I could see the train looming large about to hit me, but I couldn't bring my legs to move so that I could get out of the way.

I walked up to the bike racks after the final bell had rung and stood there for a full thirty seconds, staring at the spot where I had left my bike that morning. I walked down the line of bikes, which didn't take long because it seemed most of the kids at the school received an expensive European car as a standard sweet sixteen present. I completed my search, but my bike was definitely not there.

'Damn it!' I swore, looking at the clouds and wondering whether I would make it home before it started raining. I pulled my backpack higher on my back and started walking down the pathway next to the car park.

'No wheels today?' I heard Charlie's voice on my right and looked to see him standing with a big smile next to his black four-wheel drive. I marveled at his looks for a full five seconds. When he smiled at me it made me go weak at the knees.

'Did somebody steal your bike? If that is the case,

I would of course like to volunteer my services to escort you home.' I smiled as I walked over to his car. Before I could hop in, he pulled me into his arms and kissed me, gently at first and then more passionately. When we pulled apart, he opened the passenger door for me and helped me climb in. As soon as I got inside, I turned and spotted my bike in his boot. He chuckled at my raised eyebrows and mildly irritated expression.

'Oh, when I said somebody, obviously I meant me. You know that you have had the same pin code since you were ten years old!' He made a tsking noise. 'Not very good security. Anyone could come along and figure that out!'

'It is easy to remember that way. And besides, no one is stealing anything from me. There is about $50 in my cheque account and my bike is the oldest and ugliest one on the rack. How do you remember my pin code?'

'I remember everything,' he tapped the side of his head. 'I also remember that this Saturday is a special day – your seventeenth birthday I believe.'

'Argh! How does everyone know that it is my birthday? I don't even think my parents have remembered this year so I was really hoping that it would just slide under the radar.'

'Why don't you want to celebrate? Birthdays are great. You get presents, eat heaps of cake and make a wish when you blow out the candles.'

'I don't like the fuss. I would be happy just hanging out with you and not mentioning the word birthday.' He took his eyes off the road momentarily to study my face.

'OK. Do you want me to take you into the city for the day?'

'Will there be motorbikes or helicopters involved?'

Charlie laughed. 'Would you like there to be?'

I thought for a moment back to the last trip we had into the city and involuntarily shuddered 'Um, no. I think I would like to be alive for my eighteenth birthday thanks.'

We pulled up in his driveway and he pretended to act insulted. 'I am a great driver, and you loved the helicopter!'

'Let's just pretend it is a normal day and travel in a normal way. We will be able to spend more time together that way too.'

He came around to open the door for me, but I had already opened it. I unbuckled my belt and he pulled me out of the car and back into his arms. He ran his fingers through my hair and then let them slide down my back leaving tingles all the way down my spine. With one hand he gently caressed my face and closed my eyes while his other hand traced its way down to my lower back. I waited with my eyes closed until I couldn't resist anymore and pulled him in to kiss me.

I could feel his mouth on mine was curved into a smile. He knew that he had been torturing me and could tell how much I wanted him. In the past few weeks each time that I had left him to return home I felt like he had done the same thing. I wondered whether he had seen Gus in my room at night from his room and was trying to cloud my head with my desire for him. If so, it was working. I also knew that Charlie could have driven his car into his family's huge garage when we got to his house, but I felt like he pulled up out the front of the house because you could see that part of his driveway from my room. I was positive he wanted to make sure that Gus could see us, and I tried to remain behind the car where I hoped he couldn't.

After I waved goodbye to Charlie I walked around the side of his house and down to the beach to get to the back of my house. I thought I saw movement in my window, so I decided to go and visit Poppy's room on the way upstairs. I knocked on her door and poked my head inside the room.

'Poppy?' I called out, glancing around the room to see if she was there. She was back in one of her favorite spots, sitting at her dressing table next to the window. She turned around at the sound of my voice and I softly closed the door behind me.

'Hello Sophie, is everything alright?'

'Yes,' I said uneasily. 'Um, I wanted to ask if you remember a spirit called Fred Simpson,' I asked her gently.

'I vaguely remember that name – who is he?' I didn't see any recollection on her face, so I pressed on.

'He is the ghost that you and Isadora locked in one of the guest bedrooms downstairs. Your notebook didn't have a lot of information about him or why he needed to be locked in the room. So, Alice spoke to Isadora and she said she thought he had some information about your husband.' I could see the memory begin to form in her mind. Her face clouded over and her lips pressed together in a thin line.

'Yes, I do remember now. He was helping me try to find George. One night he came to me insisting that George was involved with the Germans. A spy he said. Can you believe that? I couldn't let him walk around my house speaking to the other members of the armed forces spreading those lies.' She had been speaking with passionate venom but now her face softened, and she looked at me, her eyes pleading.

'You have to believe me Sophie. George would never have done that to his men. I am certain he would have been loyal to his last breath.'

I nodded my head and took a deep breath. This wasn't going to be easy so I would have to do it quickly, like ripping off a band aid. 'OK, well we are going to open the room because my parents are going to need it for guests, but I will speak to him and get to the bottom of his allegations, OK?'

She shook her head. 'We locked him in there so long ago, he is going to be angry and want revenge. Even if the allegations are not true, he might spread them out of spite.'

'It doesn't sound like he was an angry or vengeful spirit before. I'm sure he will understand, and even if he doesn't, I'll keep looking into what happened, but we are going to have to unlock that door sooner or later.'

She still looked unconvinced, but I pressed on. 'And if all else fails I'll tell him we will lock him in one of the toilets if he spreads false information! I promise!'

She seemed a little reassured. 'OK,' she said quietly,

but I suspected that she would be watching closely when we unsealed the room.

CHAPTER

4

After speaking to Poppy, Alice and I decided we would unlock the door on the Sunday afternoon after my birthday. Everyone else in the household would be occupied and out of the house in case something bad happened when we unsealed the door. My parents had plans to go to a nearby town to visit an antiques market to pick up some lamps to replace the old ones that were no longer working. Even though they knew what we were up to, Thomas and Clara were both busy. Clara was going to see a movie in town and the drama committee had booked Thomas in for rehearsals of their production on the Sunday afternoon, no doubt so Sarah Forbes could show him every errant twig that needed additional pruning.

I wasn't sure what I was dreading more; opening the door to unleash the ghost of Fred Simpson or the birthday celebration that Alice had planned for me at her mother's restaurant.

I felt like I would be better equipped to deal with any allegations that Fred Simpson presented if I had a chance to do something I had been putting off since we released the ghost of Diana Faraday. I had to go through

Poppy's husband George's study and see if I could find any information on what he had been doing in the war.

I walked back downstairs and into George's study. Besides cleaning up the mess that Diana had made when she had hurled every breakable object and then half the shelf of books at Alice and me, I hadn't spent time going through anything else. The room was designed to be a study and George's personal lounge. His desk was a beautiful dark oak with a matching chair and was orientated to look out over the stone driveway. There were two large bookshelves full of books on either side of a decorative marble fireplace, in front of which sat a couch with two smaller armchairs and an oriental-looking rug.

I suspected most of his important documents would be held in the study desk, so I decided to start there and work my way to the bookshelves and then the cupboards at the bottom of each bookshelf last.

In the desk I found some correspondence with various lawyers regarding George's will, dated around the time he went off to war, so it seemed he was aware enough of what was going on over there to get his affairs in order in case he didn't make it back. He also had some official-looking documents from the American forces about his position, and some correspondence from Poppy's parents regarding his engagement to their daughter. I flicked through the latter and was surprised at the formality of it all. It was such a different time to now. There were a handful of letters that had been sent to George from Poppy and I blushed at the thought that they could be love letters. As much as I was dying to read what would have constituted adoring words back then I felt that they were private and so I put them in my pile of information to take with me. I would ask Poppy what she would like me to do with them.

I put the letters from the armed forces on top, deciding to write to the relevant authorities and see if they could answer any of my questions.

As I was closing up the last drawer on the desk the cotton on the sleeve of my sweater got caught on a small metal lever poking out of the underside of the desk. I ducked my head under the desk and ran my hand along the edge until I could see where it started and finished, my mind whirring. I pulled the lever and heard a slight clicking noise. A hidden drawer popped out of the middle of the desk.

Eyes wide, I slowly pulled the narrow drawer out to reveal a handful of papers. The first couple were illegible to me. The words were faded and seemed to be in some sort of code – numbers and letters all jumbled together. The second document that I pulled out had writing in another language that looked like German.

I thought immediately of Fred telling Poppy that George could have been working as a spy for the Germans. One little document in his study wasn't exactly a smoking gun but it didn't look good, especially given its location in a hidden drawer. The next document made the case against George a lot stronger. It was mostly in German, but I could understand enough to tell it was a birth certificate for a male baby born in Austria at the same time as George would have been born. The name of the child was Gerhard Froese. Initials GF, just like George Farrell.

I sat down at the desk chair and considered my find. After deliberating over whether to report back to Poppy or not I decided to err on the side caution and, rather than alarm her, I would wait until I had gathered more information before speaking to Poppy about it. Now that I had another name, I would do a bit more research online and return to the study on another day to search through the bookshelves. At a glance the books looked unlikely to provide any additional clues.

I went over to the shelving on the left-hand side of the fireplace and tried to pull open the cupboard at the bottom. It was locked so I walked over to the other side but the cupboard there was locked too. Curiosity piqued I popped up to my bedroom to retrieve two bobby pins, which had always proved helpful unlocking the padlock on the old suitcase I had long ago lost the key for.

A couple of minutes later the cupboard doors were open and I was mildly disappointed. I wasn't sure what I had expected but the contents looked entirely unworthy of being locked away from prying eyes.

There were some books that looked a little bit like more albums. I pulled them out one by one and flicked through, the black-and-white images not revealing anything that I thought would be relevant to George's time at war. I sneezed as I pushed the albums back into their dusty shelves. Moving over to the right-hand side cupboards the contents looked a little more interesting. There were four boxes.

The first held a couple of vintage watches and some old spectacles, the second box held a handful of old diaries, which I put aside to have a look through later to see whether there was any valuable information. The third box had a collection of old coins, cufflinks and an old Bible with United States coat of arms. I flicked through the Bible and an envelope tucked into the back fell out. I picked up the envelope and glanced inside. There were several photos, each with George standing with various other people in uniform. I put these to one side with the diaries and pulled out the final box. There was only one item in the box. It looked like a case that held jewelry. Red velvet covered the outside of the case and I reached in and pulled it out. I wondered if it was a piece of jewelry that George had bought for Poppy but never had a chance to give her, and smiled at the thought. I needed two hands to pull the case out because it was much heavier than it looked. I glanced around the edge of the velvet for a latch or a lock but there was nothing. Reaching onto the desk I grabbed a letter opener and used it to pry open the lid enough that I could get my fingers inside to pull it open.

My eyes widened in shock as I took in the contents. It was silver but it was not a piece of jewelry. The inside of the case was also inlaid with the same buttery red velvet but lying inside was a silver revolver. I gingerly touched the cold metal of the outside of the gun. Glancing back in the box I had retrieved the velvet case from, I noticed another container that I hadn't seen. I reached in, pulling it out but, whether from the age of the box or the weight of the contents, one end of the container gave way and a dozen bullets fell into the larger box. At the same moment, I heard my parents walk in the front door excitedly talking about their latest find for the house.

As quickly as I could I closed the lid of the velvet case and half-heartedly pushed some of the bullets back into the box they had fallen out of. I replaced the gun in the large box and pushed it back into the cupboard that it had been sitting in for the past few decades. I threw the diaries and photos into my bag and took them upstairs before heading down to help with dinner.

CHAPTER

5

I don't know whether it was all the talk about unsealing the locked doors and the discovery of the new secret pathways from the house, or finding the gun, but the night before my birthday I had a terrible nightmare.

Alice and I stood at a giant door with a huge brass doorknocker. She knocked three times, each knock sending a vibration through my body. I wondered why she was knocking when she had been able to unlock the other doors simply with words. But before I could ask her the door began to slowly creak open, the hinges complaining from the lack of use. A mist came barreling out the door and wound its way around our legs.

As I watched the mist dissipate, I felt a growing sense of unease forming in my stomach and I reached out to Alice to stop her from going into the room, but my hands grabbed at thin air. Looking up again Alice's figure had disappeared and all that lay before me was a dark room. My mind screamed to flee but my legs disobeyed. I stepped forward, one foot in front of another until I was standing in the darkened room.

My eyes slowly adjusted to the darkness but not

soon enough. I heard a sound like something scratching, coming from the right and then a whimpering sound and my breath caught in my throat. Again, I seemed to have no control over my body as I walked over to the source of the noise. It was a large heavy brown timber wardrobe and it sounded like there was a small animal trapped inside. My hand reached out and clasped the handle and then pulled and twisted the brass until the door opened. The sound stopped as soon as the door was open, and I realized the cupboard was not a cupboard at all but a passageway. The faint noise of whimpering and scratching started again, and I continued to follow it.

The passage led me to a narrow, twisting staircase. I tried to see how far up the stairs went but the steps further up blocked my view. 'Alice?' I called out but it sounded like a whisper. I looked back down the passage I had just walked down, wondering whether to continue or go back, but I had already come this far so I decided to keep going.

Up and up and up the staircase wound, my thighs screaming in protest until I thought I couldn't take another step, and then I saw light coming from underneath a door at the top of the landing. I pushed the little door open and was blinded by bright light. It looked like I was standing on the top of the house; I could see the tops of the houses to the left and right and all of the trees. Turning around I realized that I was in the clock tower at the top of our house. The whimpering and scratching was coming from above me where the bell sat. I climbed up onto the rafters to get a better look and saw a small bird stuck on the chain leading to the roof. I gently pulled the little bird's wing from where it was stuck on the chain and tried to release it into the sky but instead of flying to freedom it turned around and tried to swoop me. I cowered down as its sharp claws began to dig into my skin.

'No!' I screamed as the claws tore at my flesh. 'STOP!'

I sat bolt upright in bed, my heart racing as I rubbed my body, still feeling the sensation of the bird's claws digging into my shoulders, back and head. I turned around and looked at the clock on my bedside table. It was 3 am on the day of my birthday.

I glanced around the room but for once Gus wasn't in his spot on my window seat.

'Breathe,' I whispered to myself, willing my heartrate to return to normal.

'What a horrible nightmare,' I mumbled. I buried my face into my pillow and rolled around in bed trying to get comfortable again, willing sleep to come, but it was elusive.

At 3.30 I climbed out of bed and sat on my window seat, reading a book in torchlight until my eyelids again felt heavy. Instead of clambering over to my bed I pulled a blanket over me and rested my head on one of the throw cushions, at last surrendering to sleep.

CHAPTER

6

With the nightmare still lingering in my mind, I woke up on the morning of my birthday with mixed feelings. My parents still hadn't mentioned anything about it, Alice and Percy had organized some sort of dinner that they assured me was not going to be big and Charlie was picking me up at 9.30 am to spend the day with him in New York City. I was a bundle of emotions, apprehensive, concerned but also happy that I was going to have the whole day with Charlie.

Gus was there, right next to my face when I opened my eyes. He looked really excited and, having already realized the day, I wasn't surprised when the first words out of his mouth were, 'Happy birthday beautiful Sophie!'

I smiled and stretched out my arms above my head.

'I have something for you,' he said quietly, and I turned back to look at his face, my eyebrows raised. He looked nervous.

'Really?' I asked with unconcealed surprise. 'Umm … how did you do that?' I asked. I couldn't picture him heading to the shops.

'My dad helped,' he conceded, ducking his head.

'That is so sweet Gus. Tell me where it is and I'll get it.' I looked around my room with curiosity wondering if Thomas had snuck something into my room while I was asleep.

'No, I want to give it to you myself.' I looked at his face again, but he was no longer looking at me, instead his eyes were focused on something on my desk. He raised his hands and something on the table moved up into the air and, after being suspended there momentarily, floated over to me and landed next to me on the window seat.

'You can move things?' I said in shock, and he smiled. I slowly opened the lid of the little box and examined the silver bracelet inside. It looked vintage and had a small diamond sitting in a circle on a solid silver band.

'Oh, it is so beautiful Gus! I love it. Thank you!' I looked up at his face with tears in my eyes. I wanted more than anything to kiss him and I wondered if my desire was heightened because I couldn't. Charlie's kisses ignited my body and left me craving him more, wanting to go further, whereas I had only had the chance to kiss Gus once and I wondered whether it would be the same, whether I would be as desperate to kiss him if I had the option to all the time. I thanked god that Gus was not looking at my face as I studied his lips, thinking about Halloween night when we had kissed. I bit my bottom lip and wondered whether he would ever be able to touch me. He took his eyes away from the bracelet rescuing me from my thoughts as he smiled.

'It was my mother's; she had the same birthstone as you – diamond.'

I slid it around my wrist. I wanted more than anything to hug him, but I knew I couldn't, and it would make him feel bad. He had obviously been trying so hard to be able to move objects. Instead I smiled at him with a curious look on my face.

'Since when can you move things?!'

He grinned from ear to ear, clearly very proud of himself, 'Just something that I have been working on. What are you doing for your birthday?' he asked, changing the focus back to me.

I didn't want to ruin the moment by mentioning Charlie, so I decided not to tell him the complete story. 'I'm heading into the city for the day and then Alice and Percy have organized a dinner for me at Alice's mom's restaurant. Which to be honest I'm sort of dreading. I can't stand being the center of attention, so I'm hoping that it is just a small group of people.' I climbed off the window seat, my back groaning in protest, and started to sift through my wardrobe for something to wear for my date with Charlie.

'Will Chucky be going?' I ignored Gus's grumpy reference to the movie about the creepy doll and continued pulling clothes out of my cupboard. With my back to Gus, I pulled some clothes on being careful not to flash him and give him the wrong idea.

'Actually, aside from Percy and Alice I'm not sure who will be there. They have been very scant on details.'

He seemed pleased with my response but pushed further. 'Now that he knows about my ghostly presence

and nightly haunting of your house, your bedroom in particular, when will you bring him over to say hello?'

'I don't know, I haven't really thought about it,' I answered evasively. I could hear my parents clanking around downstairs in the kitchen and I wanted to see them before I headed off to the city with Charlie. 'I'd better go downstairs and see whether my mom and dad even know it's my birthday. Thanks again for the beautiful gift Gus, I won't take it off.'

He waved his hand at me, but he looked a little disappointed that I couldn't stay with him. As I walked down the stairs, I felt guilty leaving him in such a hurry when he had made such a huge effort for my gift.

When I got to the kitchen my parents turned and looked at me as soon as I walked into the room. 'Morning,' I said politely.

'Oh, good morning Sophie,' my dad said cheerily.

'Did you have a good sleep?' my mom asked casually.

I could smell a rat from a mile away and I looked at them both suspiciously.

'Whhaatt's going on?' I said slowly, pouring myself a juice and a bowl of cereal.

'We know you're heading to the city with Charlie today, but would you mind helping us bring in the firewood from the front porch quickly before you go?' Dad asked with a side glance at Mom.

'Sure,' I said slowly. Obviously, there was something out on the front porch that I was supposed to get a huge surprise from, so I quickly gobbled down my cereal and walked with them to the front door. As soon as my mom opened the door, I saw it. A little old Toyota Corolla sitting in the driveway with a big red ribbon on it. Even though I had suspected something would be waiting for me outside I had definitely not expected a car and I squealed with excitement and turned around to look at my parents.

'Thank you, thank you, thank you!!! I love it!'

They both looked so happy that I was so excited, they reached out and hugged me between the two of them.

'Happy birthday Sophie!'

'There is another little surprise sitting inside the car Button,' my dad said, calling me by the nickname he had given me when I was two. He held the keys out to me, which had a big shiny brass S on the key ring.

I took the keys from his hand and started walking towards the car. I couldn't believe that it was mine. When I was halfway over to the car I realized that all of the windows were down. I paused, unsure, and looked back at my parents who smiled with excitement. When I was even closer, I started to hear little whimpers and my mind flashed back to my nightmare. Could I still be dreaming? I secretly pinched myself. No, I was absolutely awake. Was there a small creature that was going to attack me waiting in the car? I took deep breaths; there was no way that my nightmare was going to come true I reasoned with myself in my head. I was less than four feet away from the car when a little head popped up out of the passenger window and I almost jumped out of my skin. It was a caramel-colored furry face. With its tongue poking out of its mouth it barked three short barks at me and then started panting with its tongue out of its mouth again.

'A PUPPY???' I turned to look at my parents who were both nodding enthusiastically, my mother with her hand on her mouth like she was trying not to laugh, or possibly cry.

Reaching through the window, I scooped the dog out and into my arms. It happily licked my face with its huge tongue. 'Are you a girl doggy or a boy doggy?' I cooed to it as it smothered me with more slobber.

My parents had walked over to where I stood. 'It's a boy of course, I can't be outnumbered,' said my dad, ruffling his ears. 'The furniture shop that we went to yesterday had them sitting in a pen in the corner. One of the owners had a caramel cocker spaniel that had a litter of pups around ten weeks ago and there were only two left. This little guy and another one that they had promised to another customer. We had already bought you the car, but we thought he might be good company for you since we have been going away a little bit.'

The puppy planted several more licks on my face. 'What should we call him?' I asked trying unsuccessfully to escape his lapping tongue.

'When I was little, we had a very similar little dog called Milo,' my mom said, rubbing the dog's back.

'What do you think of that little puppy? Do you like the name Milo?' He agreed with me by smothering me in more licks until I put him down on the stone driveway.

He walked over to one of the trees and lifted his leg. I ran backwards down the driveway and then knelt down, calling out to him, 'Come Milo!' he ran towards me with his giant ears flopping around his face and leapt back into my arms, knocking me over.

'Do you always let strange animals lick your face the first time you meet them?' I heard Charlie's voice and squinted into the sun to try and make out his features. He smiled and pulled me up, tickling Milo behind the ears to allow me to extract myself from his constant puppy licks. Milo responded by pushing his backside against Charlie's legs for a scratch.

As I let go of Charlie's hand I took a moment to brush off any pebbles that had stuck to my clothes and subtly checked him out. He was wearing jeans and a dark blue hooded sweater with a white T-shirt sticking out from underneath.

'Happy birthday Sophie,' Charlie said smiling, pushing a lock of hair behind my ear before kissing me softly on the mouth. He was obviously conscious of my parents though and the kiss ended too soon, leaving me wanting him more badly than I had when he pulled me up off the ground. I glanced back down the drive and my parents were politely focusing on Milo. I could have taken the opportunity to pull him back to me, but I figured we would have the whole day for that and I wanted to make sure I gave my full attention to the gifts from my parents before Charlie and I headed into the city.

Dad ran me through all the safety features of the

car ad nauseam, until he was sure I understood every last button and warning light. Milo was sitting on my lap trying his best to distract me with licks and puppy bites, so it probably took a lot longer than it needed to. By the time we were finally able to tear ourselves away it was closer to 10 am and I could tell Charlie had something scheduled by the way he was glancing at his watch every five minutes.

We decided to go in Charlie's car, which was a relief to me. I would have liked to drive my own, but I was feeling tired after my average sleep and I didn't want to drift off behind the wheel. With Charlie's hand resting on my thigh, his car seat warmers and the music on I lasted twenty minutes before my eyes closed and I drifted off to sleep.

I was woken by the feeling of Charlie gently rubbing my arm. When my eyes finally focused on his face, he looked as confused as I felt. I looked around and realized we had already arrived in the city. I glanced back to Charlie, but he was now staring off in the distance looking mildly annoyed. I must have been asleep the entire drive and I rubbed the side of my mouth self-consciously wondering whether I had drool running down the side of my face.

I put my hand on his and said softly, 'I'm sorry that I slept the whole way. Is everything OK?' He deflected my question by asking a question of his own.

'Did you know that you sleep talk?'

Oh god what did I say? I nodded my head, 'Yes I have been told that.' Mostly by Gus. Oh crap did I say something about Gus? Charlie looked away again and then back at me with a confused look on his face. He opened his mouth to say something, seemed to change his mind and closed it again. I squirmed uncomfortably in my seat trying to think of something to break the silence.

'Where are we?' I asked looking outside the car at where we parked.

'Oh my god!' I said excitedly when I realized that I already knew the answer. We were parked outside Ample Hills, my absolute favorite ice-cream shop, which my parents had taken me to every birthday when I was younger. I glanced over at Charlie; it seemed his mildly irritated mood had dissipated, and he wore a broad smile. The next couple of hours were a tour of all of my favorite places in Brooklyn and Manhattan. I was amazed at the effort he had gone to, researching and crafting a plan for the day. We went to Stinky Bklyn cheese shop, Levain Bakery and Gourmet A'Fare and bought cheese, bread, meats, dips and dessert then Charlie took me to Cherry Hill in Central Park where I had spent a lot of time doing sketches before we moved away.

Charlie pulled out a picnic blanket that he had in his car and we sat down and started tucking into our feast.

'Thank you so much for today Charlie, it has been so special,' I said as I licked some of the runny cheese I had been eating off my finger. 'I have to say though it seems like an unusual strategy to take me to all of my favorite places in a city that I am considering moving back to if you don't actually want me to move,' I said, chuckling.

'Interesting you bring that up,' he said mysteriously, reaching into a tote bag that he had carried the picnic blanket in. 'Another small gift,' he said, pulling out a box and handing it to me with a glint in his eye. What more could I possibly want from this birthday?

'Should I open it now?' I asked and he nodded his head.

I tugged the ribbon until it was loose enough for me to pull the lid of the box off. Inside there was a soft purple hooded sweatshirt. I pulled it out of the box and saw the letters HUNTER in yellow on the front. He had bought me a hoody to the art college I wanted to go to. It was beautiful but again I was surprised that he was enthusiastically encouraging me to leave the Hamptons, and even though it was only a couple of hours in the car, it felt a little like he was pushing me to leave him. He picked up on my confusion and touched his hand to my knee.

'What's wrong? Did I pick the wrong college? I asked your mom and she said you have been set on going there for the past three years. You don't want to go there anymore?'

'No, it's not that, I really do want to go there but … I didn't realize you were so keen for me to leave.' He surprised me by laughing. I looked up again in confusion and he pointed at my gift box.

'There is another gift in there that might make you feel better.'

I reached back into the box and felt another soft object. This one was a navy-blue color with white writing that said Columbia curving across the front, and I looked up at him for an explanation. My mom had been right, the only college I had wanted to go to for the past four years now was Hunter and I didn't remember ever even mentioning Columbia.

'Ummm … is this like a back-up in case I don't get in?'

He took it from my hands, and I realized how big it was. As he pulled it over his own head it dawned on me that it wasn't for me to wear.

'You got into Columbia?' he nodded his head and I practically leapt into his arms. I couldn't believe it. He was going to go to college in the same city as me. I laughed with happiness and pressed my lips to his as he fell backwards onto the picnic blanket.

CHAPTER

By the time Charlie delivered me home I only had twenty
minutes to get ready to go back out again to Alice's
mother's restaurant. Charlie had to go to a training session
with the football team so wasn't able to come. I still wasn't
a hundred per cent clear on the guestlist or what Alice had
organized so when I got there I was pleasantly surprised.
It was a nice small group of our friends from school, Alex,
Megan, James, Emma, Percy and Alice. Alice's mom Sally
gave me a warm hug and a small box which had a name
tag for the restaurant with my name on it. 'For when I open
the restaurant in the city,' she said and gave me another
hug. The first time I had dinner at Alice's we had talked
about how much I wanted to move back to the city. She
had told me about her plans to open another restaurant
in New York and I had happily volunteered to be her first
employee.

Percy and Alice had organized the party for me so
I told them they had done enough and shouldn't get me
a gift, but they still gave me a framed picture of all of our
friends wrapped up with a beautiful silver ribbon and Alex,
Megan and James gave me chocolate and a candle. Even

Emma had signed the card, which was a surprise, given the two of us had not got along since the first day that I had started at the school. Alex, who she was interested in, had shown an interest in me, and even after I had started dating Charlie she still hadn't warmed to me.

Alice's mom had kindly allowed our group to take up a big table in a semi-private alcove where Alice and Percy had stuck a happy birthday banner up on the wall and lined the table with flowers and candles. In the corner was a beautiful round birthday cake with 'Happy Birthday Sophie' written in icing, and flowers decorating the top that matched the ones on the table.

I wasn't one for birthdays and making a fuss, but this birthday had been so special, and I felt so lucky. More than once I looked around the table and had to pinch myself at how fortunate I was to have made such good friends.

At the end of the night when everyone else had left and it was just Alice and me, Alice pulled out another small gift box from inside her pocket.

'Alice you really didn't need to get me anything, you have gone to so much trouble tonight. I feel so spoilt!'

'This isn't really a gift but more of a return,' she said, gesturing for me to open the box. As soon as I opened it, I recognized the ruby-colored stone from our trip to the hidden safe when Gus, Alice and I had been looking for Diana's box of witchcraft. Alice had given back the necklace that she had found in the safe.

'I thought you wanted to keep it,' I said, studying the markings again. It was a truly unique piece of jewelry.

The chain appeared to be just an ordinary silver chain but when you examined it closely it was clasps that looked like tiny interlacing hands and the glass bulb that hung from the chain seemed to have blood-red ink floating in a clear liquid. I also noted, the sliver that connected the glass bulb to the chain looked like a key hung down into the deep red.

'There is something about it,' she said, her eyes on the necklace, looking warily like it was going to jump up and bite her but also a little in awe of it. 'I really do think it could have special powers. I know it sounds strange, but it is almost as though I can feel protective magic coming out of it.'

I tried to laugh it off, but Alice's face stopped me. Alice and I assessed the necklace one more time before Alice's mom brought us out of our thoughts.

'Right girls! We are officially closed for the night. Do you two want to help me finish the clean-up and we can toast Sophie's big birthday with a cheeky little limoncello?'

'What is that?' I asked laughing as Alice immediately scrunched up her face and shook her head at me. I put the necklace back in its box on the table and picked up some rubbish, tossing it in the bin and clearing the plates off the table.

'It tastes like gasoline and lemons mixed together.' She imitated throwing up and I laughed more as her mother smacked her on the bottom.

'It is an Italian specialty Sophie and I insist you try it. How often does a girl turn seventeen?'

After cleaning up the restaurant and forcing down two sips of Sally's limoncello, which burned all the way down my throat, I begged sleep and headed home to my waiting bed.

Milo pounced on me as soon as I walked through the door. After taking him outside to go to the toilet I scooped him up and carried him upstairs to my room, laying him in his little dog bed that my dad had bought. The bed was made out of a caramel-colored faux fur so when he lay in it he was almost invisible save from his two chocolate brown eyes that looked perpetually sad and hungry at the same time.

Gus was sitting on my window seat that looked out over the water and he turned around to look at me as I walked in the door.

'Cute dog. Is that from your bestie next door?' he scoffed.

I stroked Milo's soft coat and rolled my eyes at his tone. 'No, he is from my parents.'

'How was your party?' he asked, as he focused on a glass of water on my side table. It lifted up into the air by itself and moved towards me, stopping just in front of my face. I laughed and lifted it out of the air with both hands, taking a long drink.

'Why thank you!' I said and sat down on the edge of the bed. 'It was great actually. Percy and Alice went to a lot of effort and it ended up being really fun.'

I watched Milo walk around his bed and scratch up the fur in an attempt to get more comfortable. After a couple of minutes he gave up and jumped onto my bed.

'What did you get?' he asked, gesturing towards the gift bag that I had thrown all my presents into to transport them home.

'Flowers, chocolates, jewelry, dogs, cars, you know, the usual,' I smiled, lying back and watching Milo throwing his teddy around. I wondered whether he could see Gus but when Gus sat on the bed, he made a little rumbling sound that had to be a growl and then moved to my side of the bed, spreading his body over the top of my feet so that I couldn't move without him knowing.

'Jewelry?' Was that just from me or did you get some from someone else?' I knew he was talking about Charlie just from the way his eyes moved inadvertently towards his house. I ignored the inference and looked in my bag for the box the necklace had come in.

'Yeah, I did get something else. Alice gave me back that necklace we found in the hidden safe the other day. I'm not sure if that is a good thing or a bad thing. She seemed ... I don't know, I guess a little in awe of it and she thinks it has magical abilities.' The box wasn't in my bag, and I could picture it, sitting on the table in the restaurant. 'Oh crap, I just realized I left it at the restaurant. I'll have to grab it from her tomorrow.'

CHAPTER

When I woke the next morning to the sound of birds and the bright sun shining into my room, I couldn't believe the time. I had slept through two alarms and it was already 10 am. The terrible sleep the night before my birthday had taken its toll and my body must have needed to catch up. Gus was not there when I woke up and I wondered whether he had gone to visit his dad.

I knew Alice would be arriving at any minute to unseal the room holding Fred Simpson hostage, so I quickly ran myself through the shower and came back to my room wrapped in a towel. I turned to look at Charlie's window to make sure that I wasn't visible from his house and saw him standing in his room. He waved and I waved back then hid behind the cupboard door so he couldn't see me getting changed. I was just about to drop my towel when I heard a noise from behind me. Gus was sitting on the bed clearing his throat.

'Uhhhh, Gus! What would you have done if I had dropped my towel before you cleared your throat'?

'I don't know. Can a ghost die of a heart attack?'

'You're an idiot. Turn around or I will ask Alice to

figure out how to send you to hell,' I said viciously, and he obliged, turning his back. I changed into my jeans and a T-shirt while ensuring I was hidden behind my cupboard door to make sure neither Gus nor Charlie got an eyeful of me in my birthday suit.

I was just pulling my hair into a ponytail when I heard the doorbell ring. I turned around to see Charlie still standing in his window and Gus sitting up in my bed, both with their arms outstretched in almost the exact same pose. I wasn't sure whether to laugh or cry, so I just said, 'See you later' to Gus and waved to Charlie, rushing down the stairs. It was almost a relief to have to focus on something other than my confusing love triangle.

Fred Simpson had been locked inside one of the guest rooms on the ground floor of the house for the past five years. The room was down the western end of the house that was away from the main living spaces of the kitchen, lounge and dining rooms, past the glasshouse entrance. Unusually, the door to the room came off one of the lounge areas rather than the hallway. I think this was part of the reason that Poppy and Isadora had decided to lock him in that room. Because it was tucked away my parents had yet to try too hard to access the room, but I knew they would want to use it at some point to accommodate guests.

When I opened the front door, Alice looked a lot calmer and more relaxed than I felt. I was so nervous I completely forgot to ask her about the necklace I had accidently left at the restaurant.

'Ready?' she asked me, looking excited.

'No!' I said, and she laughed.

'From everything that we have found out about him so far he doesn't sound half as scary as Diana. It will be completely fine,' she said, making me feel a little better. 'Besides, we don't have to let him out.'

'No, but we will be stuck in there with him,' I mumbled, opening the door to the lounge room antechamber of sorts that connected to the room Fred was sealed in. Alice sealed the doorway leading to the hall behind us in case Fred decided to try to make a run for it as we had discussed. My nerves must have been wearing off on Alice. We glanced at each other nervously as she locked it, wondering whether we would be able to get out again if Fred decided to go a little crazy like Diana.

The entry to the guest bedroom was through a concealed doorway camouflaged by a full wall of books.

'*Aperio!*' Alice said clearly, and I felt my breath catch as I pushed the door open. The door was positioned in the middle of the room, a large four-poster bed sat on the wall to my left, aligned with the bay window looking out over the water on my right. Other than the bed, furniture in the bedroom was scant, just a small desk and set of drawers as well as a large ornate fireplace opposite the doorway that we stood in.

Almost as soon as we had opened the door the spirit of Fred Simpson rushed towards us and moved through the door that we had just walked in.

Alice and I glanced at each other with raised eyebrows, our suspicions confirmed. He wasn't here to attack us or negotiate with us. He just wanted out. He didn't look much older than the two of us I realized sadly as I took in his translucent form in his uniform. His dark brown hair was neatly combed into a side part, there was a dusting of freckles on his face and his wide olive-colored eyes took us in suspiciously.

As soon as he realized the door to his freedom through the lounge room was sealed, he spun around with a confused and angry expression on his face. Medals clinked together as he turned, so obviously he was a decorated member of the armed forces, and that alone made me feel confident that we would be able to discuss his current predicament in a rational, non-violent fashion.

'Who are you and why am I still a prisoner?' he asked cautiously, obviously noticing that we had also locked ourselves in with him.

'We are friends of Poppy.'

His face turned a rose-colored shade and he looked angry again. 'That crazy woman locked me in here after I did exactly as she asked and passed on some information regarding her husband that she didn't particularly care for.'

'Yes, I know,' I said calmly, 'And we are here to negotiate your release,' I said gently, trying to calm his rising aggression, gesturing to the couch in the lounge room for us to sit and discuss in a civilized, relaxed manner. Alice and I sat down on the couch, hopefully appearing to be a lot more relaxed than we both felt inside. He was still miles away from Diana in terms of threatening, violent behavior, but who knew what he was capable of after being locked in the room for several years.

'And what, pray tell are the terms?' he asked, refusing to move away from the door and join us on the couch.

'You tell us everything that you found out about Poppy's husband, George. You tell us and only us and we will let you out of this room and help you, if required, to pass on.'

'What do you mean pass on?' he asked, sounding concerned.

'Most of the spirits who are bound to the living world are only here because when they died there were things that were left in a way that prevents them from moving on. Unfinished business so to speak. We can help you with any unfinished business that you have that is preventing you from leaving,' Alice explained carefully.

'Why do you want information about Poppy's husband?' he asked suspiciously.

'We are trying to help Poppy,' I said, matter-of-factly. 'She was happy for us to help you so long as you were not going to spread misinformation about George.'

'Well that is convenient,' he snapped sarcastically, but he no longer looked aggressive and after looking out onto the water he let out a big sigh and conceded.

'Fine, I will tell you what I know, which is not much, mind you, and then my lips are sealed.' He moved from his position next to the door and came to sit down beside me on the three-seater couch.

'Poppy asked me to try to locate his spirit. I have been

able to move around a lot as a ghost. Most spirits seem to be tied to one place but not me. Maybe it's because I moved around a lot as a child, my spirit has no fixed address so to speak. So, I found another spirit in the United Kingdom that knew George. He said that the last time he had seen him was at a POW camp in Austria.'

'He was a prisoner?' I interrupted.

'No, that's the thing. He said that George was decked out in Nazi clothing and was wearing badges of a high-up official so he must have been working for them long enough to earn those badges. That is all I found out and when I told Poppy she coaxed me into that room and another woman appeared at the door. They locked me in.'

I turned to look at Alice. His story checked out with what we had been told by Isadora and Poppy. Alice nodded her head and I turned back to look at Fred.

'OK. And you didn't tell anyone else about this?'

'No. I barely had a chance to tell Poppy,' he said defensively.

'And you promise you are not going to tell anyone else if we let you out of this room?' I cautioned.

'Why would I tell anyone else? I don't mean to sound spiteful but no one else cares, do they?'

'Just promise us that you aren't going to speak about what you just told us to anyone,' I said sounding mildly threatening.

'Scout's honor.' He crossed his heart and pointed towards the sky.

Alice nodded again at me.

'OK. So how can we help you?'

'I don't know about unfinished business, but I do have regrets,' he said softly, eyes welling up with tears. 'Well, only the one really. I have had a lot of time to think while I have been locked up in that room and the only thing that I can't stop thinking about is my child.' He wrung his hands together.

'Your daughter?' I asked, thinking about the documents I had read from the divorce court records.

'Yes,' he nodded, 'my baby girl, Clare. She was only three when I left to go to war. Her mother and I were not on good terms long before then. I made a mistake … I … I had an affair,' he said looking down into his hands, his face a picture of anguish.

'There was nothing about that in the divorce papers,' I said gently, and he looked up, shaking his head, sadness etched into his eyes.

'No, there wouldn't have been. As I said, her mother and I hadn't loved each other for years before I slipped up. We hadn't been sleeping in the same room for over a year before, but when we divorced, she told me that if I challenged her for custody of Clare, she would make sure that I never saw Clare again.'

'That is terrible,' Alice said sympathetically.

'The divorce was finalized just before I was shipped out. I was supposed to see Clare the Sunday before I left but my ex-wife never showed up at the park where we had arranged to meet. I was shipped out the next day. I need to know that she didn't feel like I left her by choice, and

I want her to know how much I love her. She is … she was my everything.' His face collapsed again, and he buried his head into his hands and sobbed.

Alice and I sat there, wanting to comfort him but not knowing what to do or say. The only thing I could think of was to distract him with the task at hand.

'OK well let's start with where you were living before you went to war?' I asked, hoping that it wasn't the other side of the country.

'Not far from here. We were on the edge of Brooklyn and Queens.' I felt relief wash over me. At least it was an area I was familiar with, and I was always happy to have an excuse to go back into the city.

'Would your wife have kept Simpson as her surname?'

'I would say that would be highly unlikely,' he said, looking dubious.

'OK, what was her maiden name?' I thought back to the divorce court records. I suspected that I would be able to locate this information as well as her last known address and contact details on the court documents.

'Ramsey. Audrey Ramsey.'

'OK. Anything else that we should know? Do you have any idea where she might have taken Clare?' Alice asked gently.

'There is a chance that she might be in the Hamptons. Her family had a winery, I think it was in Sag Harbor. It was one of the reasons I ended up in this house. I was hoping that maybe one day Clare might just walk through the front door.'

He must have been able to read the doubt on our faces because he nodded his head and chuckled to himself. 'Yeah, I know, bit of a stretch, right?'

'Stranger things have happened,' I said, trying to stay positive.

'We will go and do some research and see if we can locate Clare. We won't lock you back in here so long as you promise not to spill any of the information that you received in relation to George,' I said firmly, reminding him of our deal.

'Who am I going to talk to?' he said, shrugging his shoulders. 'Actually ...' he continued, and I threw a nervous look at Alice. We had threatened to lock him back in the room, but would we really be quick enough to get out the door ourselves and then lock him back in? I strongly doubted it.

'Actually what?' I pressed him.

'Do you think Poppy would mind if I spoke to her? I won't upset her. It would just be nice to have someone to talk to while I wait around, you know?'

I glance over at Alice again, trying to hide my lack of enthusiasm.

'Um, I'm not sure. Why don't you let us go and ask her first? And please also remember that my parents have no idea that you, or any of the ghosts in this house actually exist. So, I would be much obliged if you didn't go roaming around the house. Perhaps I can suggest to Poppy that she come down to this lounge room?'

'Thank you. That would be wonderful.' Fred

looked extremely happy with the prospect of having some company as well as the thought that we may be able to return to him with some information about his daughter Clare. I thought back to our encounter with Diana Faraday. She had been so thrilled to be able to see photos and hear what her son had done in his life. I wondered whether Fred would be content with the same.

'I will go and speak to Poppy now,' I said, as Alice and I headed towards the door.

As we were walking, I saw a movement next to the door out of the corner of my eye and spun around expecting something or, worse, someone to come flying across the room. Alice turned in surprise to check what it was that had given me a fright. It took me a moment to realize what I had seen because there was nothing moving in the room, but as my eyes adjusted, I saw the figure standing there as still as stone. It was Poppy. She must have been there the whole time, invisible to the naked eye, listening to our exchange. I expected her to be angry or at least a little argumentative but her expression was contrite. I glanced over to look at Fred who hadn't noticed Poppy in the room as he had his back to her, looking out the window to the water.

Poppy turned to look at me and I threw her a questioning look, wondering if she was happy to speak to him. I assume she wouldn't have made herself visible if she hadn't wanted to speak to him, but she gave me a quick nod and smiled at me, and I took this as permission.

'Fred?'

'Yes?' he said not moving from his position by the window. When I didn't immediately respond he turned around to look at me and noticed Poppy standing nearby.

'Poppy?'

'I am so sorry about locking you in the room Fred!'

'I understand,' he said quickly, allaying her guilt somewhat and moving towards her with an outstretched arm, beckoning her to sit down with him on the couch.

Alice and I took this as our cue to leave and give them some privacy for Poppy to make amends. Both looked contented to have company and I was relieved that everything had turned out so well when I had built it up in my mind to be a potential disaster.

CHAPTER

9

For the next week I searched every possible angle I could to locate Fred's daughter. I noted every bit of information from the divorce court papers – his ex-wife's full name was listed on the documents as Audrey Elizabeth Ramsey from 15 Fairbanks Street in Brooklyn. I used the location and contacted the local schools to ask about whether they had a Clare Ramsey or a Clare Simpson on their records but most of the schools didn't have records back that far and the ones that did had no record of a student by that name.

I checked the marriage records that were available online for the following five years after Fred and Audrey's divorce thinking that maybe she could have been remarried but the online records had a disclaimer that not all of the records were complete, and I suspected that was a vague way of saying that they had more holes in them than a piece of Swiss cheese.

I popped my head in to visit Fred a couple of times during the week but each time I did I felt progressively worse as his expression slowly went from one of excitement and hope to one that was politely just happy to see me and have a chat while watching Milo clamber up on the couch and sleep. I suspected that he was trying to make me feel better, but he seemed to suggest if I hadn't found her yet it was unlikely that I was going to find her at all. If I was being honest, I was starting to lose hope in finding his daughter too but each time I left with a promise to keep looking.

In the back of my mind I was also conscious that I hadn't progressed my search for information on Poppy's husband George. I made a mental note to try to contact someone in Veterans Affairs to discuss what I had found in George's study.

On the Thursday afternoon when I went to visit Fred, Poppy was already in the lounge room speaking to him about times gone past. They had grown quite fond of each other's company during the week since we had unlocked Fred's room and I had to admit I was happy to see Poppy somewhere else apart from staring morosely out of her window waiting for George to come back.

Fred raised an eyebrow and smiled politely, if not a little sadly when I shook my head and mouthed 'sorry'. Poppy noticed the exchange and put a comforting hand on Fred's. 'It is never easy not knowing where your loved ones are. Sophie will do her best to locate your daughter.'

It was lovely to have Poppy giving me her vote of confidence, especially when I had yet to find her husband. I wondered briefly whether I should mention some of the things that I had found in George's study, but I decided against it and held my tongue.

'I'm so sorry I haven't found her yet Fred.'

'It's OK Sophie. I really am grateful for all of your efforts. You know, after she didn't turn up for our appointment the day before I shipped out, I did wonder whether Audrey might have worried that I would try to take Clare and maybe she made a run for it. It is very possible she moved away from the area and changed her name. That might make it a little difficult for you to locate her.'

I thought about what he had just said. It was an interesting idea and it gave me a new avenue for my search too. 'That gives me another idea Fred. I will contact the police stations around where her family were to see whether they lodged a missing person's report.' He beamed at me.

'What?' I asked, surprised at his joy.

'I am just happy that I could contribute to the search. It also helps me to stay positive and a new search avenue is always a good thing, right?' His enthusiasm was contagious, and I nodded and smiled back, but deep down I felt a nagging worry about what I was going to do if I ran out of ideas and I still couldn't find her. What if he couldn't move on and it was my fault because I had failed?

I left Poppy and Fred cheerfully discussing other potential ways that I could try to locate Clare's whereabouts. When I left the room, I took a moment to lean my head against the wall in the passageway outside. I was feeling a little overwhelmed by the responsibility of finding Clare for Fred and George for Poppy.

These two people were bound to the living because they hadn't been able to find their peace and move off to be with others that had passed. I knew that it was silly, but I felt so responsible for them finding that peace. I turned around and pressed my back up against the wall, sliding down into a seated position, and let the tears fall down my face as the emotion overwhelmed me. After a couple of minutes, I started to feel like I couldn't breathe properly. I needed to get outside, to get some fresh air. I pushed myself up the wall, walked through the house and out the glasshouse doors into the sun. As soon as I was outside I felt the vice-like sensation across my chest lessen. I closed my eyes and hungrily gulped in the cold, salty air that blew across my face. Within minutes I felt my heartbeat return to normal.

I could hear familiar voices to my left in the direction of the sunken theater and I followed the sound, walking through the new archway that Thomas had carved into the side of the hedge. My parents were standing with Thomas, Charlie, Sarah Forbes and some of the drama committee who had been spending a great deal of time at our house. I hadn't been in the sunken theater for weeks and I had to admit they had done an amazing job getting it ready.

The first time I had walked into the space the green hedged-in walls had felt haunted and eerie. The hedge had been horribly overgrown, the green leaves encroaching from both the sides and reaching a canopy across the top and making the area seem small and suffocating. Now that Thomas had tamed the foliage it felt a lot larger, the sky easily visible while it still felt intimate and almost a little magical.

I felt a shiver run down my spine as I recalled my dream the previous week. The sound of the audience screaming at me reverberating around my head, and I looked at the now neat rows of stones, marking the spots where the drama committee would allocate seats with cushions.

Charlie spotted me first and walked off the stage, wrapping me up in a big hug before kissing me gently on the mouth.

'What's going on?' I asked sounding a little confused and glancing over at the collection of people gathered on the stage. 'Are you part of the play now?'

'God no, no one wants to see me try to act,' he chuckled weaving his fingers through mine. 'I came over to your house to see if you wanted to work on the English assignment together this afternoon.' He gestured towards the stage. 'Your parents saw me walking up the beach and asked if I could help with some of the work for the play. Sarah wants me to build a concession stand.'

'Oh, OK.' I glanced around Charlie's shoulder again at the group that had gathered and caught Sarah eying off Charlie. 'Just make sure she doesn't ask you to build her more than a concession stand,' I said with a raised eyebrow. Sarah realized that I was watching her check out my boyfriend and quickly turned her attention back to my parents.

I had felt better when I had walked out of the house and away from Fred and Poppy but now I was beginning to feel uneasy. The more I thought about the play the more

I felt sick about it. I wasn't sure why, but I just had a feeling that something bad was going to happen the night of the play and I would be powerless to stop it.

I left Charlie in the garden while I went to retrieve my notes for the English assignment from my room. Milo jumped on me as soon as I walked through the door. I picked him up and tickled him behind his ears.

'I can see why they use animals for patients with depression,' I mumbled, losing my hands in his soft fur. It felt so calming. I had almost recovered from my moment of self-loathing. I clipped on his lead and walked him up and down the driveway so that he could go to the toilet and then left him in his bed in the kitchen with a chew toy.

By the time I returned, Sarah had drawn Charlie a diagram of what she was hoping to achieve and was standing next to him giggling flirtatiously, touching the side of his arm. I was happy to see that for the most part Charlie just looked uncomfortable. I made sure I got right up close to Sarah before I loudly asked, 'READY CHARLIE?' which made Sarah just about leap out of her skin.

'Yep, let's go,' he said, draping his arm around my shoulder and pulling me in to kiss the side of my cheek. This will never get old, I thought as I snuggled into his arm and felt all the senses in my body tingling. I could feel Sarah's envious stare on us as we walked back through the archway and out of the sunken theater.

As we walked through Charlie's living room, we said hello to his mom, Felicity, who was sitting at a desk working on her laptop. She had been working as a guest editor for an interior design magazine, which didn't surprise me at all given her beautiful taste in her own house. I thought we would probably hang out for a few minutes downstairs before going to work on our assignment, but Charlie had different plans, taking my hand and pulling me in the direction of the stairs up to his room.

'You are welcome to stay for dinner Sophie,' Felicity called out to me as we started walking up the staircase. Charlie's mom not only had fantastic taste in interiors, she was also an amazing cook. I had been lucky enough to have dinner at their house a couple of times since we had started dating. I also suspected my parents would be helping the drama committee for a while yet. Charlie looked at me quizzically and I nodded, starting to walk back down the steps to accept her invitation.

'She would love to, thanks Mom,' Charlie called out pressing his lips to mine and not letting me move past him. I was like putty in his hands and he knew it. I could feel his lips curved into a smile as he pressed me up against the side of the staircase and moved his hands from the top of my spine all the way down to my hips. My body felt like it was on fire and I was disappointed when he pulled away from me. I tried to pull him back to me, making a noise to object to him stopping. He smiled and winked at me, taking my hand in his to pull me up the rest of the stairs. As soon as we were in his room, he pushed the door closed and pulled me with him onto his bed. I laughed, pressing my lips back onto his.

My lips parted and I felt his tongue gently caressing mine, sending tingles all over my body. I moaned in pleasure and ran my fingers through Charlie's hair causing him to do the same. We were lying side by side with our legs interlocked and our bodies pushed up against each other. His hand went up underneath my T-shirt and he traced his fingers across my back. I arched and he followed my cue, moving his lips down onto my neck, kissing the soft skin there and back up to my face.

'Can I take this off?' he asked, pulling the hem of my T-shirt. I nodded, moving my body so that Charlie could pull my top off. I helped him take his off and we lay there kissing passionately and breathing heavily.

'Can I touch you here?' His hand moved from my back around to my bra.

'You can touch me anywhere,' I replied and blushed. Everywhere he touched my skin tingled.

The kissing, touching and breathing were causing me to experience sensations all through my body that I had never had before, and I wondered how far I was willing to let this go. Right at that moment all I wanted was him and I could tell that he wanted me. His hand moved again from its position on my bra down to the top of my jeans and he started unbuttoning each of the buttons, slowly, still intensely kissing me. Just as he was sliding down the zip on my jeans and I thought I might pass out from desire I heard his mother's voice echo down the hallway.

'Charlie? Sophie? Dinner is ready.' As soon as I heard

Felicity, I sprung off the bed like I had been electrocuted, in my haste to pull my top back on I pulled it on the wrong way around.

'Be down in a minute Mom,' Charlie said with a chuckle, not moving from his shirtless position on his bed. 'Don't worry, she won't come in,' he added for my benefit.

'Oh my god! Well then it's lucky that was your mom and not mine. Mine would have barged into the room and demanded you leave our house immediately and never come back!' As my heart rate slowly returned to normal, I looked at him suspiciously. 'Done this with a lot of girls have you?' I asked, feeling a mixture of embarrassment and irritation.

'Ha! No, I just have two older brothers and she learned the hard way with them that it's best to knock when a door is closed.'

'Oh, right.' It made perfect sense, but it did make me wonder how far Charlie had gone with other girls he had dated. We hadn't talked about it, but I assumed he hadn't been single in the years that I had been away. Based on the past ten minutes alone I would say he definitely seemed to have more experience than I did. Charlie pulled his sweater back on as I rearranged my top, feeling a little self-conscious. I had no experience at all in this area and I knew I should have been able to speak to Charlie about it, but I was too embarrassed. He wrapped his arms around me and kissed the top of my head as I walked out of the room in front of him.

Sitting at dinner with Charlie's parents my mind

wandered to what I was going to say when I called the police to ask about Audrey and Clare. I obviously couldn't mention what had prompted my search into their movements. I wondered whether they would only release that kind of information to immediate family.

A couple of times during dinner I realized that I had been asked a question and had to ask for it to be repeated. After a while they stopped asking me questions because they could all see I was a little distracted. I feigned stress over the assignment that we were working on, thanked Charlie's mom for dinner and we headed back up to his room to study for a bit longer. I was doing my best to focus on my study while Charlie tried his best to start back where we left off. Curiosity got the better of me and I decided to ask about his previous experience.

I swatted away one of his hands advancing across my legs. 'You are pretty good with your hands there.'

'Oh, you have no idea,' he said trying to pull me back down onto the bed with him. I rolled my eyes and pushed him away, managing to stay upright.

'That is a terrible line,' I said as he sat up and tickled me gently. I pushed him back down and sat on top of him, my notepad sliding off my lap onto the floor. I wasn't going to get any of my assignment done between Charlie's distracting behavior and my constant thoughts about Fred's family.

'Now who is the expert?' he asked, laughing when I pinned his arms above his head and squeezed his sides with my legs to tickle him.

'Seriously though, how far have you gone with a girl before? Have you … you know …' I couldn't bring myself to meet his eyes, glancing nervously above his head at his duvet cover. I don't know what I had expected him to say but it wasn't what came out.

'Yes.'

'Seriously?' I had to admit I was a little disappointed and I sat up, releasing my grip on his hands. 'With who? Someone at school?' I asked, hoping that the answer was no.

He sat up too and put his hands on either side of my face making me make eye contact with him. 'Does it matter?'

'No … Yes … I don't know.' I was so confused. Talk about a buzz killer. I climbed off him and sat next to his desk.

'Hey, come back over here,' he said patting the spot next to him on the bed. I stayed obstinately where I was sitting. He looked for a moment like he might insist I sit with him but instead sat up opposite me.

'She was a friend of my brother's. Andy took me to a college party, it was the first one that I had ever been to, a couple of years ago. I got a little drunk and one of the girls there pulled me into a bedroom. I have no doubt that it was an underwhelming experience for her but the next party I went to she approached me again. We had sex only once more and she gave me some pointers. I think she saw me as being a little bit of a project.' He glanced away from me and laughed at himself then glanced back at me.

'Did you two date?' I asked wondering whether she was still friends with Charlie's older brother Andy.

'She transferred to a college on the west coast not long after that and we didn't stay in contact. We never even discussed dating. I don't think she ever saw me as a potential boyfriend.'

'What was it like?' I asked, sitting beside him on the bed.

'Truthfully, my first time was not great. I had too many drinks, she was an older girl that I didn't know' He wrapped his arms around me and rested his chin on my shoulder. 'I don't want it to be that way for you. It should be special. You need to make sure that it is with someone you trust, someone that you feel a connection with.' I lay down on the bed and pulled one of his pillows over my face. I had to admit I did feel a little relieved. She didn't sound like a great love of his life. But did I want my first time to be with someone who was experiencing their first time too so we could experience it together? Probably not, I conceded, but I had never thought about it before.

'Are you alright?

'Yeah, I'm OK.'

'I feel like it's not just the sex thing. It seems like you haven't been here for some of the night. During dinner and when we came back upstairs, I feel like you've been somewhere else. He pulled the pillow off my face and studied my features. 'You have been all up in here,' he touched the side of my head.

'I can't stop thinking about Fred.'

He laughed, obviously not expecting me to confess to thinking about another guy while in his arms. 'OK, should I be jealous? Who is Fred?'

'He's a spirit occupying one of our guest rooms. He asked me to find his daughter and I haven't had any luck so far. Every time I go to visit him, I can see his heart breaking a little bit more because I keep coming up empty. I saw him this afternoon before I came down to the theater and I thought maybe I could call the police to see if they have any records of a missing-person report being lodged for his ex-wife and their three-year-old daughter.'

'Why don't you call them now? That way you know that you are doing everything you can.' He looked down at his phone then passed it to me with contact details for the local police station.

I called the police stations in Brooklyn, Queens, New York and the local stations in the Hamptons area. All of them assured me that their systems were all linked, up to date, and went back a number of years before the year that I was asking about, 1942. Not one of them had any records for a missing woman and her three-year-old daughter around that time. Charlie sat next to me on the bed, pretending to do his homework but glancing up often. Each time I was told there was nothing matching my search I deflated a little more.

Charlie stretched back on the bed, his head on the pillow, and pulled me down next to him, leaning my head against his chest. I should have been in a state of bliss, lying next to him, but all I could think about was the next time

I would see Fred and his expression when I told him his idea had been a bust. I buried my head into Charlie's chest and let out a frustrated groan. Charlie pulled my ponytail back gently so that my chin rested on his chest.

'You said you had an address of their house in Brooklyn, right?'

'Yeah, it was on the divorce papers.'

'So, we could do a title search and find out the registered address of the vendor. The ex-wife would have had to provide a forwarding address to the lawyers that handled the legal work. Also have you thought about visiting the house? Maybe the current owners or some of the neighbors could have some information.'

It might have been a bit of a stretch but at least it was a new avenue to explore, and I didn't have to go back and see Fred empty-handed just yet. I pushed myself up the bed so that I was looking into Charlie's face. 'Thank you.' I leaned down and our lips met.

'You're welcome. Do I get to meet Fred?'

'Maybe,' I said evasively. I pushed myself up and started sorting out my English notes to take home. I knew that he wasn't really asking to meet Fred but actually to see Gus.

'Speaking of spirits …' Here we go, I thought, just as I predicted, 'I feel like now that I know I wasn't imagining Gus before, I see him there a lot more.'

'Yeah?' I said non-committal.

'Yeah,' he hesitated slightly before continuing. 'It's weird actually, it is usually at night when I'm going to bed.

When I look over I think I see him in your room.' I held my breath and glanced sheepishly at him. His handsome face was tilted on the side, studying mine, and waiting for my response.

'Yeah, he does spend a bit of time up there. We talk at night before I go to sleep and I guess he sometimes kind of … sleeps there.' As soon as I'd said it, I wished that I hadn't. Charlie's face registered surprise and also a little bit of hurt. I wasn't sure what he had expected me to say but obviously that wasn't it.

'Our dead friend who also had a huge crush on you comes to your room at night for deep and meaningful talks and then sleeps there, with you?'

I shrugged my shoulders. 'It's not like that.'

'OK but if we had a really close dead friend that was a girl that you and I both knew was almost definitely in love with me would you be comfortable knowing that she was coming into my room each night and sleeping beside me?'

No. Absolutely not, I thought but didn't say.

'He is lonely Charlie. It's not just me. He spends a lot of time with his dad too.' I knew how the excuse sounded. I could tell from his expression that Charlie didn't buy it.

I knew that if I was in Charlie's position, I would feel the same. I was jealous of Sarah Forbes just asking Charlie to help out with the play because I could see she really liked him. I could understand how he felt but I couldn't bring myself to tell Gus not to come and spend time with me. Maybe I could ask him to sit where Charlie couldn't see him? No that wasn't the answer either. I sighed and finished packing up my books.

'Well at least you know I haven't slept with anyone else,' I blurted out defensively.

He looked like he had been slapped. 'You left me here alone and I had no way of knowing whether you were ever coming back.' This argument wasn't going anywhere, and I knew that I had overstepped the mark.

'I'd better go home.' I walked towards the door and turned around when Charlie didn't say anything to stop me. He was looking over to my bedroom, his eyes narrowed. I hoped that he would volunteer to walk me back to my house, but he didn't, and I didn't push him. I walked down the stairs slowly, again expecting him to appear, but again was disappointed.

'Goodnight Felicity and Nick. Thanks for dinner,' I said to Charlie's parents as I left.

'You are always welcome Sophie,' Charlie's mom said as they both waved goodnight from their positions on the couch where they were watching TV. I let myself out the back door wondering if I was in fact still welcome. Charlie had seemed really upset and I had to admit that I couldn't blame him. I had been petty with the whole sex thing, and I knew how he felt about Gus.

When I got upstairs to my room I looked over at Charlie's, hoping to wave at him and reassure myself that we were OK, but his blinds had been drawn. I looked towards the water feeling sad, like something I had never even started was finished.

'Trouble in paradise?' Gus said from the direction of my bed. He was sitting against the pillows looking a little smug. I wondered if he had been watching or, even worse, if he had somehow heard our argument from my open window and I pulled it closed with unnecessary force, causing it to slam.

'None of your business,' I snapped, unfairly blaming him for my argument with Charlie. Something told me that he wouldn't have cared that we had been arguing about him, in fact he probably would have enjoyed it. I was glad that Charlie didn't know that we had kissed at the Halloween ball, but it made me think about what secrets do to a relationship.

CHAPTER

10

During school the next day I spent my study period in the library looking up how to do a title search online, but the records online only went back as far as 1966. To find information on property transfers before this date I would have to go the City Register's office in New York to check them on microfiche. The office was closed on weekends and only open between 8.30 am and 4.30 pm during the week. Fortunately, the school had a planning day for the teachers organized for that Friday and I had nothing planned for the day aside from clearing some of my backlog of homework and helping my parents with the house. I was sure they wouldn't mind me taking a break from sanding the floorboards in the ballroom to test out the mileage on my birthday present. I thought about asking Charlie to come with me but the football team had been on a heavy training regime for a big game scheduled for the coming Saturday night so I didn't see him at school or around the car park at the end of the day, and his curtains had remained firmly closed.

I hadn't heard from him or seen him since our argument, and I wondered whether he was annoyed with me or just really busy. By the time Friday rolled around I still hadn't seen him. I got up early on Friday morning and took Milo out for a walk then worked on a history paper until it was in a good enough state for me to finish the next day. I then spent the next couple of hours on the sander while my dad cut new floorboards to replace the ones that were too far gone. By 11am the room looked better than new again and I got Dad's blessing to head into the city. I had told my parents that I was going to walk through the galleries and maybe pop into my favorite bookstore.

I glanced down nervously at my phone directions, winding my way through familiar streets into unfamiliar territory to the City Register's office for Queens, which was located further north in Jamaica.

When I walked into the office a helpful lady behind the desk took me to a bank of screens and showed me how to find the information. Two bad coffees from the vending machine and an hour and a half later I found what I was looking for. The records indicated that Audrey had transferred the property to the new owners but when I searched for the address that she had listed as her new address I discovered that it was for an old post office in Sag Harbor that was no longer there. I almost cried with frustration. Every time I felt like I was getting close, that I was within arm's reach of Clare, the trail dried up. I resisted the urge to bang my hand down on the table, instead throwing away my coffee cup and walking out the front door, away from the musty smelling records and into the fresh crisp air.

'Damn it!' I muttered to myself. I wondered whether I was feeling lightheaded and moody from my failure or whether I was just hungry. I walked around the block and found a cozy cafe where I ordered a sandwich and a peppermint tea, which helped.

It was almost 3.30 and I decided it was probably time to head back home. Instead of going directly there I punched in the address of the house that Audrey and Fred had owned together, arguing that there was no harm in driving past, even if just to tell Fred that I had made the effort. I wondered whether the house would still be standing but when I got to the address the house looked exactly as I imagined it had back when Fred and Audrey lived there. It was a pretty little brick house with roses planted along the low brick fence. I climbed out of my car and peered into the garden. There was a patch of lawn in the front nestled behind a metal gate that had white paint peeling off the top of it. I could almost picture a little girl playing in the front yard.

I thought about what Charlie had said about the possibility that the current owners might know Fred and Audrey. It was such a long time ago that I seriously doubted it, but given I was here I figured I may as well ring the doorbell and ask. I walked up the little pavers to the front door and listened as the doorbell rang inside. I could hear the sound of a chair scraping back from a table but then silence again.

'Hello?' I called out, ringing the doorbell again. I cupped my hand against the pane of glass and peered into the darkened house.

An older woman came hobbling down the hallway and I felt my breath catch in my throat. Maybe Audrey and Clare had never really left. I listened to her heavy footfalls as she made her way to the front door, wondering if Clare herself would be behind it. The wooden door opened, and the woman glanced through the security door at me standing on her front door mat.

'Hello?' she repeated, observing me cautiously.

'Clare?' I asked hesitantly; although now that I could see her face, she didn't look much like Fred.

The confused expression remained on her face and she shook her head. 'No, sorry. There is no one here by that name.'

'Oh, sorry to bother you. My name is Sophie. Have you been living in this house long? My grandmother was friends with the people who used to live here. She recently passed away and I wanted to let them know.' The confused expression on her face cleared and she shook her head.

'I'm sorry dear,' she said sympathetically, 'but I've only been in the house around seven years.'

'Oh OK, never mind.' Yet another dead end I cursed to myself. 'Sorry to bother you again and thank you for your time.'

I turned to leave but I heard the sound of the security door opening and the lady cleared her throat behind me. 'If you're looking for information about the people who used to live here, you should speak to the lady next door. She's lived here for over fifty years, and she is the self-appointed neighborhood watch.' She rolled her eyes and continued, 'Just don't agree to have a cup of tea with her or *you* will be in there for the next fifty years!' I thanked her and she smiled before going back inside, locking the security door behind her.

I was certain that the woman next door would probably be another dead end, but I had nothing else to go on and I was here already so I figured I may as well ask. I knocked on her door as I eyed off her garden. Her house was very similar to Fred and Audrey's – the same red-brick house and low-lying fence but instead of grass and rose bushes her front garden was covered with all different little trinkets. There were collections of shells and groups of cactus plants bunched together, little gnomes stood in pairs turned towards each other as though they were speaking about the weather.

When the woman opened the door, I tried and failed to wipe the smile off my face and be serious, but I couldn't. 'You have the most fascinating garden I've ever seen,' I told her, and she smiled and puffed out her chest, looking very proud.

'I've been collecting it all since I was a child.' I assessed her, feeling excited. She definitely looked older than seventy. I repeated the story that I had told the woman next door. My compliments to her garden and knowledge of her former neighbors must have made her feel comfortable about me and she invited me in for a cup of tea. Remembering what the woman next door had said about her long-winded cups of tea I politely declined and brought the conversation back to the people who had occupied the neighboring house.

'Were you here when there was a young girl and her parents living next door – their names were Fred and Audrey.'

Her face clouded over and she seemed a little sad. 'Oh yes, I remember them. They used to have the most terrific screaming matches. Their little girl, I think her name was Clare, she would come over to our house to play in the garden. It wasn't as full of things as it is today, but it was still more enjoyable here than it was over there.' She gestured towards the house I had just come from. I nodded my head solemnly and she continued.

'When I was in my teens, I heard they got a divorce. Just after my parents told me that Fred had gone to war and died. Such a tragedy! The couple may have fought like cats and dogs but both of them adored that little girl.' Her eyes misted over as she remembered the family. I couldn't believe that I had stumbled upon this wealth of information. There was just one piece of the puzzle missing and I wondered whether she would be able to fill in the blank space for me.

'Do you know what happened to Audrey and her daughter?'

'Oh, they moved away. Not far mind you. To the Hamptons area, I think. Her aunt and uncle had no children and they owned a vineyard there. She was going to help them run it she said.'

I nodded my head encouragingly. I couldn't believe

it – they had gone to the Hamptons, just as Fred had suspected. That also correlated with the address that was provided in the records of the house transfer. Now I just needed an address or some way to narrow down where they might have gone.

'Do you remember the name of the winery?' I asked and held my breath as I watched her face pinch in concentration.

'Oh yes, I'm sure I can remember it if I try. Let me see ... it was something like Valley View or Hill View. Something like that.' I plucked my phone out of my bag and punched 'Hill View winery' into the search bar.

I started to read some of the names that appeared in the search results: 'Seaview, Sandhill, Hillcrest ...'

'Yes, Hillcrest – that's it! Sounds idyllic doesn't it!'

'Thank you so much for your help. You're a lifesaver!'

'Not a problem. You sure you wouldn't like to pop in for a cup of tea? I just put the kettle on before you knocked.' I felt bad saying no but I really had to start heading home, so I wasn't driving in the dark.

'I need to be getting home for dinner and I have a long drive. I'm really sorry I can't stay.' I smiled and waved as I walked out the front gate and climbed back behind the wheel of my car. I couldn't believe it! I actually had a lead for once. I prayed that Audrey hadn't sold the winery and Clare was still there, or at the very least whoever was there now had contact information for them.

By the time that I arrived home my mom had made a lasagna and after gobbling down a big bowl I decided to bite the bullet and go and see Charlie. I walked up the back way from the beach entrance. Charlie's mum Felicity was standing at the island bench in the kitchen, sifting through some client plans, and she waved me in when I knocked on the glass doors.

'Hey Felicity, I just wanted to say hi to Charlie.'

'Sure Sophie. He's in the library,' she replied, gesturing to the entryway from the kitchen. 'All the way down the hall and on the right. It's the dark room with lots of books.'

I thanked her and followed her directions to the only room in the house that didn't seem to get much natural light. It seemed deliberately designed to feel like a cozy den. Charlie was sitting behind the desk next to the window. Every wall was covered from bottom to top with bookshelves holding thousands of different books. The ones lining the top shelves looked ancient while the ones at the bottom seemed to be brand new. I tapped my knuckles gently on the door and Charlie glanced up, with a surprised look on his handsome face.

'Hey you,' he said, putting the pen that he had been spinning around between his fingers down onto the notepad in front of him.

'Hey you.' I smiled and glanced around the room again. 'This room is cool. Do you usually study in here?'

'Sometimes … when I want to get away from things or I need to concentrate. It's less distracting than my bedroom. No beautiful views.' He said smiling back at me.

'I just wanted to come over and thank you for giving

me the idea to visit Fred's old house in Brooklyn. I think I might have a good lead.'

'Oh yeah?' he said, looking interested. 'The current owners?'

'No actually, the next-door neighbor. But if you hadn't suggested going to the house then I never would have spoken to the neighbor so thanks. I have the name of a winery that I think his ex-wife and daughter moved to. I'm going to check it out tomorrow.'

He nodded his head. 'That's good. I'm happy you found something.'

'Also, I wanted to say sorry about the other day. The things that I said were … unnecessary.'

'Yeah, I said some things that were unnecessary too.' He paused and stood up from behind the desk, walking over so that he was standing only a foot away from me. I could feel the warmth coming off him and I felt an overwhelming urge to reached out and wrap my arms around him, but he clearly had things that he wanted to say, and I felt that I should give him a chance to say them.

'To be honest, it's been months since you told me about Gus. I feel like you are trying to keep the two of us separate for some reason and I don't really understand why. And the other day, on your birthday, when you fell asleep in the car on the way into the city you said his name in your sleep.' My cheeks flamed red and I shook my head.

'That is really strange, I have no idea why I did that.'

'It doesn't matter.' He looked back to the desk with his notepad sitting on top.

'I better get back to my assignment. I left it to the last minute which is another reason why I'm bunkered down in here.' I felt like there was more that needed to be said but I didn't want to push so I nodded my head.

'Sure, OK. I'll see you at school then,' I said, turning to head back into the hallway. As soon as I turned around, I felt Charlie's warm hand take mine and he spun me back around, catching me off guard. His other hand went to my face and he pressed his lips against mine. My lips parted in surprise and his tongue traced mine. After the initial surprise I kissed him back, passionately, for seconds, minutes, decades. I never wanted him to stop, so of course all too soon we broke apart.

'Just wanted to make sure that tonight you have dreams about me,' he said smiling. 'Do you want me to come with you to the winery tomorrow?'

I knew that he had training and I needed some time to get over my disappointment if I didn't find Clare.

'No, it could be another dead end. But I appreciate the offer,' I said, burying my face in his chest as he moved his hands across my back. I felt so safe in his arms I wished I could stay there forever.

CHAPTER

11

When I saw the sign for the exit to Hillcrest Vineyard my heart started beating faster and I felt my mouth go dry. On the fifteen-minute drive to the winery I had come to the realization that I had been so preoccupied with my objective to locate Clare in order to find peace for Fred that I hadn't even considered what Clare might want. If I were in Clare's position would I want a total stranger coming along and opening a can of worms, decades down the track? What if she had been brought up with her mother feeding her mistruths all this time and now I was about to go and spin her world around on its axis. Would she believe me? Would she even care? What if she wasn't here anymore?

I pulled into the driveway and wound my way up the gentle hill and into the visitor parking. The house was a beautiful old single-level white weatherboard with a sweeping, faded grey porch wrapping around the whole house, and outdoor tables and chairs scattered around for visitors to enjoy the view. A couple of tables were occupied with people sipping glasses of wine and sampling cheese platters. Climbing out of the car I dropped my keys in my haste. I knew I needed to calm myself, so I didn't just blurt out the story and sound like a crazy person to Clare. I retrieved my keys from the gravel and took three deep breaths.

Although I felt a little calmer as I made my way up to the front door, I could still feel butterflies doing flips around my stomach and I immediately regretted not accepting Charlie's offer to come with me.

I walked up the three steps to the front door where there was a welcome sign that directed visitors around to the other side of the property for wine tasting. I wove my way through the tables on the deck and stood for a minute taking in the beauty of the view on the other side of the house. The lush green grass spread in front of the house gave way to vines crisscrossed over the surrounding paddocks up to a long line of gigantic pine trees. In between the large trees and green paddocks there was even a small glimpse of the water.

'Beautiful, isn't it?' I heard a voice behind me and turned to see who was enjoying the view with me. A young woman who I thought would have been eight to ten years older than me was standing next to me taking in the beautiful view. She didn't look how I envisaged the usual wine-tasting type to look. She was wearing jeans, caramel-colored work boots and a long-sleeved grey sweater.

I looked back out to the vines. 'Breathtaking,' I agreed with her.

'Is this your first time to Hillcrest?'

'Yes, this is my first visit to a winery full stop. I'm only seventeen.' I smiled at her politely. 'Have you been here before?'

'Many times – I live here.'

'Ahhhh!!!' I wondered whether she had been sizing me up, probably due to my age, unsure as to what I was doing there. She probably wanted to make sure I wasn't going to try to buy alcohol underage. But if she lived there, I wondered if she was related to Clare. I was more curious than nervous now. This could be another relative of Fred's. Studying her face, I fancied that I could see a vague resemblance but maybe that was just wishful thinking.

'Do you know a Clare Ramsey? I was looking for her and her last known whereabouts were listed as this winery.'

'Sure. I'm Amy Hannaford, her granddaughter. What did you want to speak to her about, er …?'

'Sophie, Sophie Weston. Actually, it's probably best I speak with her directly about it sorry. I know that's a little vague, but it is a bit of a personal matter,' I replied evasively.

She raised her eyebrows and considered my request before making her mind up. 'OK, well that is a little mysterious. She's up at the homestead. Let me give her a call and see whether she is up for a visit.' Amy wandered into the wine-tasting room and reappeared ten minutes later.

'She is very cautious but also curious about what you want to speak to her about. You aren't selling anything are you? Bibles, the elixir of life, entry to a cult?' I laughed and shook my head.

'OK, I can take you to see her if you want. Follow me. We can go in the Land Cruiser.' I followed her to a dusty, beaten-up four-wheel drive and she opened the door for me to climb in. She jumped in beside me and fired up the engine, taking us down a service track and across several paddocks before we came to a house even more beautiful than the cellar door. Amy led me to an outdoor table where a woman sat, sipping on a tea. Although the weather was cold the sun warmed the space where she was sitting.

'Hello,' she said politely, trying not to be too obvious in her study of me.

'Clare?' I asked and she nodded, again struggling to hide her curiosity, but I had to be sure before I opened my mouth and said something that I couldn't take back. 'Clare Ramsey?' she tilted her head to the side.

'No one has called me that in a long time. My married name is Clare Hannaford. Please, have a seat. Would you like some water?'

I nodded. My mouth was so dry I was unsure whether I would be able to tell her what I needed to if I didn't accept her offer. I sat down on one of the seats, looking nervously at her granddaughter who had brought me to see her. Amy looked at Clare, and she waved her away with her hand.

'I am sure you have plenty to do over at the cellar door Amy, thank you for bringing Sophie over to me. I will take her back to the visitor car park after we have had a talk.'

She looked uncertain but took one last glance at me and nodded, clearly unsure of my motives but content in my non-threatening appearance.

'Nice to meet you Sophie. Come back and sample the wines when you turn twenty-one! They are even better than the view.' I smiled at her and waved goodbye and she headed back to the Land Cruiser.

I turned back to look at Clare who was pouring me a water. I took a couple of grateful sips and tried to rearrange my thoughts so that they made sense.

'I'm really sorry for this strange intrusion Clare. The truth is I … I … wanted to talk to you about your father.'

I wasn't sure what she had been expecting me to say but it clearly wasn't that.

'My father? Max Crawford?'

'No, Fred Simpson, your birth father.' She put down the jug slowly and deliberately, taking the time to moderate her feelings. 'He left my mother when I was only three. He died in the war. I don't know a lot more than that. My mother remarried and I always saw her new husband, Max, as my father.' She glanced off towards the rows and rows of vines, avoiding eye contact.

I had come up with several different strategies to convey the message that Fred wanted Clare to receive without sounding like a crazy person claiming to be able to speak to dead people, but it all went out the window, and after taking another sip of water I just plowed straight in.

'I, um, have a message from Fred. He wanted you to know that he loved you more than anything else on this earth and he would never have left you by choice. He told me that things were strained between your mother and him and he was very sorry that you were caught in the middle of that.'

She looked at me for a minute with a pained expression on her face, a deep furrow in her brow, and then buried her face in her hands. I wondered whether she was crying but when she moved her hands away from her face, she looked furious. She pushed back from the table, knocking one of the glasses, which rolled off the table and smashed onto the sandstone tiles underneath. The sound of glass smashing seemed to anger her further.

'You need to leave,' she declared, stabbing her finger in the direction of the paddocks that Amy had driven across. 'Right now!'

'What?' I asked, surprised.

'I specifically asked my granddaughter if you were here to sell something to me and you said no so I invited you up to my house. And now you are here trying to sell me some bogus story about my father. Is this what you do for a job? You just go around looking up people that have long lost relatives and try to extort them?' her face was a mask of anger. The calm, refined woman whom I had introduced myself to moments before was now a ball of fury raining down on me.

'What?' I asked again. 'You think I want money? I don't want any money from you ...'

'You need to leave,' she repeated, turning her back to me, effectively closing the conversation.

I opened my mouth to try to explain but closed it again and started to walk back towards the cellar door

to the vineyard where my car was parked. My brain was screaming at me not to leave her thinking I was some swindler. After walking a dozen steps, I turned around and stalked back up the path. She was standing in the same spot, her hand covering her face, back to me.

'I really don't want anything from you Clare. Your father is one of the spirits trapped in limbo in our world, not moving on, and the one bit of unfinished business he said he had was you. He wanted to make sure that you knew that he never wanted to leave you. That he loved you until his dying breath. That is all.'

She didn't turn around, but I heard her say in a choked voice, 'If what you are saying is true why would he come to you and not just come to me himself?'

I couldn't answer her question without telling her about the house and I couldn't do that. My own parents didn't even know about the spirits that haunted the rooms of Storybook House. I glanced at her once more, but she didn't move from her position, frozen in her memories or lack thereof. I had no choice but to leave. But I would come back. I just needed some proof, some evidence that I had spoken to Fred – and I knew where to get it.

I didn't see Clare's granddaughter Amy when I reached my car, but I suspected that Clare would have spoken to her after I left her house, and I could almost feel her watchful eyes on me as I drove away from the vineyard. I wondered if she regretted taking me up to see her. Probably, I decided, she seemed to have a protective way about her.

As I drove back towards my home my conviction that I should go back to Clare with proof waned. Who was I to force-feed her a message she didn't want to hear? Maybe I could just lie to Fred. He would never know what had transpired between Clare and me and surely it would be the right thing to do if it gave him a little peace in his afterlife? To help him move on.

As soon as I got back to the house, I went to see Fred, but my prepared lie unraveled as soon as I saw his face. He was ecstatic that I had found her but seemed a little sad that she did not accept his message as genuine. Unlike me he wasn't quite ready to give up.

'Can you try one more time? Please?' His eyes looked like a sad puppy. I opened my mouth to try to convince him to let it go. I just couldn't see Clare being convinced that I was not trying to sell her some fanciful story, but I couldn't bring myself to crush his hopes, so I gave in. What a pushover! I thought back to my original idea.

'OK,' I conceded, 'but I can't go there empty-handed. Maybe you could tell me something about the two of you. Something that only she would know. Maybe something that you shared or something about your life together?'

He looked doubtful. 'I don't know, she was only three. I doubt that she would remember anything about me.'

He looked towards the roof slowly shaking his head. I groaned internally, picturing myself standing in front of

an angry-looking Clare to try to appease Fred's decades-long guilt trip. Suddenly, he snapped his fingers and shouted, 'I've got it!'

His eyes were glowing with excitement. 'I had a necklace made for her; it was a locket with a photo of the two of us inside. I gave it to my parents to give to her with a letter that I wrote to her. The only problem is that I'm not sure whether it would have ever reached her, but I have to believe that my parents would have found a way. They loved her as much as I did you see.' It sounded like a bit of a stretch, but he looked so hopeful that I made myself smile and nod encouragingly.

'OK, that's great. So, there's nothing else? Because I don't even know if I am going to get to speak to her again but if I can and she doesn't believe me again I sincerely doubt there is going to be another chance. So just put it all out there on the table.'

He shook his head. 'That is all I have. I understand if it doesn't work. You can let it go after this. I am so grateful for your help and I know that you will give it your absolute best shot. Thank you so much Sophie.'

Poppy came into the room and I took it as my opportunity to leave. The relief of being able to find her was crushed by the feeling that even though I had located her physically I may not be able to truly deliver the message Fred wanted her to hear. I had a sinking feeling, based on my last visit, that it was decades too late.

I walked up to my room and collapsed on the bed, pulling Milo up next to me so that I could wind my fingers through his fur. What was I going to do? It was unlikely Clare would want to speak to me again and to be perfectly honest if I put myself in her shoes for one minute, I actually couldn't blame her. I was selling something, pure fantasy, and the price I was charging was the emotional toll it would take for her to believe me.

'What has he done now?' I opened my eyes and sat up to see Gus at the end of my bed gesturing to Charlie's house. 'If he is going to upset you all the time then perhaps you shouldn't spend so much time with him.'

I rolled my eyes and lay back down, staring at the ceiling. 'This has nothing to do with Charlie. I tried to help Fred Simpson to move on by finding his daughter. It took me forever to even locate her, but I did, and she doesn't believe a word I am saying. He's asked me to try to speak to her again, but I really don't see the second attempt going any other way, unless you count her calling the police and reporting me as a deviant.'

'So why don't you just stick a note in her mailbox telling her to come and see for herself?'

'I can't do that. My own parents don't know about you and the other spirits. What if she turns up asking them about Fred?' I shook my head. 'Besides, she doesn't believe me. Unless she believes he is there I don't think she will be able to see him.'

I moaned, wanting to think about something else for a change.

'Well, I guess you will have to just go to her, tell her exactly what Fred wants you to say and that is the best you

can do.' I looked at Gus's face and laughed but inside I was extremely dubious.

'Easy as that huh?!'

CHAPTER

12

I couldn't go back to see Clare until the following weekend. When I walked around the front of the house, I spotted Clare's granddaughter Amy whom I had spoken to the last time I had come to the vineyard. Amy saw me coming from her position pulling bales of hay off the tray of a utility. She cut me off before I could open my mouth.

'No, no, absolutely no, we are not looking for any more spirit readings John Edwards or whoever you are. Don't waste your breath.' She threw the last two bales of hay off the tray, jumped off the vehicle and walked inside the shed next to the big weatherboard house. Discussion over.

I hadn't driven out here to give up that easily, so I followed her into the shed. It was darker and it took my eyes a minute to adjust to the darkness. There was a long, large bar set up against the back wall with several bottles of wine sitting in three different spots along the bar ready for tasting. Wooden chairs were scattered throughout the room, which matched the beautiful, exposed beams crisscrossing the big open barn. She realized I had followed her into the room and shot me a look of mild irritation.

'So, she told you what I said?'

'That you spoke to the ghost of her long dead birth father?' She snorted, 'Yeah, she told me. I felt like an ass for taking you up there and making her listen to that rubbish. Do you get many people buying your ghost stories?'

'Actually, I have only ever told a couple of people and one of them is your grandma. Believe me I know how kooky it sounds. I didn't even believe in ghosts before I moved into the house that we live in. I'm not going to try to convince you that they exist.'

'Then what brings you back here?'

'I just want to make sure that Clare believes me when I tell her that her father loved her. He asked me to try one last time. It's his only wish. I think that he will cross over if she just believes that is how he felt. That is all.' I could see she was starting to wane ever so slightly. 'Please Amy. I know that you have absolutely no reason to trust me. I know that. Really, I do. You don't know me, and I don't know you, but I am begging you. I need to speak to Clare just one more time.'

She opened her mouth to argue with me, but I could see her hesitating just a little and I used her moment of weakness to push as hard as I could. At least then I could go back to Fred and tell him I gave it my best shot with a clear conscience.

'I really am not looking to take anyone's money and I promise you; I promise you! If she doesn't believe me and she doesn't want to listen to what I have said today

I will never come back.' That last pledge pushed her over the edge and her defenses crumbled.

'OK, but if I am disowned because I have delivered you to her again, I am going to have to come live with you in your haunted house!'

I was so excited I jumped up and down and gave her a hug.

'Whoa, whoa, calm down there. I said I'll take you up there. There is a good chance she is not going to listen to you. She was pretty shaken up last time you visited.'

'I'm sorry about that.'

The last time we had driven up to Clare's house we had driven in silence. This time, armed with the knowledge of what I had spoken to her grandmother about, Amy was a little more inquisitive.

'What exactly do they look like?' she asked, testing me a little.

'Like human jellyfish,' I said honestly, and she laughed.

'How many of them are there?' We hit a pothole and my head grazed the roof.

'Most of the time there are only a few – your great-grandfather, an old woman who lived in the house before me and a boy my age.'

'A boy your age? How did he die?'

I looked off into the distance so that Amy didn't see my eyes well up. 'He drowned.' She didn't have to see my face to know my feelings; she could hear the sadness in my voice and didn't pry. I took a couple of deep breaths and

continued. 'But on the full moon there can be a lot more. I'm not sure why, but they seem to be attracted to the house. It's like a ghostly meeting place I guess.' I shrugged my shoulders.

'That is kind of cool.'

I snorted. 'You think?'

'What is he like? My great-grandfather?' I felt her mood shift from skepticism to curiosity.

'I haven't known him for very long,' I protested, but her pleading look made me reconsider. 'From what I can tell he is a really kind man. I can see that he loved his daughter, your grandmother, very much. It took me forever to find you and it broke his heart every time I would go to see him and had to tell him that I hadn't been able to find Clare and then when I did find her and she didn't want to listen to anything that I had to say … he begged me to come back, to try one more time. I told him this would be the last.'

She looked deep in thought as we drove up to the house and parked around the back. I held my breath as we walked around the house to the outdoor table that Clare had been sitting at the last time I had visited. But when the table came into view she wasn't sitting there. She wasn't in the house either. I waited while Amy walked through the house calling her name, but she came out empty-handed.

'Do you think someone at the winery told her that I was coming and she left?' I asked, concerned.

She shook her head, 'No, no one else knows who

you are.' She glanced out at the rows of vines and her face cleared as a thought came to her. 'There is one other place that she could be.'

Amy drove carefully through the vines and towards what looked like the furthest corner of the vineyard, where a bench seat sat shaded underneath a huge oak tree. As we moved closer, I could see the blue flash of clothing worn by a woman sitting on the bench and I felt the butterflies start to build again in my stomach. What if I had caused the poor woman to have a nervous breakdown?

When we reached the tree, Clare glanced in our direction and then looked towards the house we had just come from. I turned to Amy and she shrugged. Slowly I climbed out of the car and walked towards Clare wondering whether she was going to be furious at Amy for bringing me to her. I stopped when I was a few yards away, waiting for her permission to engage in conversation. She closed her eyes and sat very still for thirty seconds and then turned in my direction. Her face looked peaceful, and I wondered whether she had been meditating.

'Hello Sophie,' she said calmly.

'Hello Clare,' I responded, again waiting for her, giving her an opportunity to tell me to go away, but she surprised me by patting the spot on the seat next to her. I walked over and sat beside her, taking in the breathtaking view. Although the weather was cold the tree provided shelter from the wind, and I could understand why she came up here. There was something so serene about it. I couldn't put my finger on it, but it was like the deep green leaves acted as a weighted blanket over any negative emotions or anxiety.

'Do you have something that you would like to say to me?' she asked gently without looking over at me, and I wondered whether she had decided to hear me out before she got angry and told me never to come back, or whether she had changed her mind. Either way, I didn't want to look a gift horse in the mouth, so I threw myself into my prepared speech.

'I spoke to your father again. He told me about a couple of things that perhaps were not common knowledge to try and persuade you that he really is in my house and I have actually spoken to him. He told me that he gave his parents a locket with a photo of the two of you and a letter that he wrote to you, but he wasn't sure whether you would have received them. I want you to know, and this hasn't come from him but from me, I really believe that he is stuck here because he feels he was never able to tell you how much he loved you and he never knew what happened to you. He was supposed to see you just before he was shipped out but your mom didn't turn up to the meeting spot. He seems like a really good man, and I just thought that you should know. That is all.'

She had sat still, glancing up towards the arching branches above us during my speech, not interrupting or acknowledging what I had said, and I wondered if maybe she had tuned me out but after a full minute, I noticed her eyes had welled up and a couple of tears escaped and tumbled down her cheeks. I didn't need her to say the words to know how she felt. It was time for me to go.

'I'm really sorry to have bothered you again, I will leave you now and I have promised Amy that I won't come back. Thank you for hearing me out.' I exhaled and stood up, starting to make my way over to Amy who was waiting in her car, but I stopped midway when I heard Clare's voice behind me.

'He didn't mention anything about the acorn?'

I turned back to look at her, confusion etched across my face. 'Acorn?'

She didn't answer my question but again glanced back up above her at the canopy of green and took a couple of deep breaths before she spoke.

'My mother always told me that my father left us. That he never wanted children and he left because of me. You can't imagine how horrible that is to hear day after day. Don't get me wrong Sophie, she was a wonderful mother in every other way except when it came to my birth father. I believed her and stopped asking about him but deep down I always wondered. She stopped talking about him at all when she met her second husband and they married when I was seven. One day when I was ten my mother and I drove to town to go shopping. I was waiting for my mother outside the change rooms and this strange woman came running up to me, a total mess. She was practically incoherent with excitement. She claimed that I was her long-lost granddaughter, and she wouldn't stop hugging me, telling me how much my father would have loved me, how amazed he would have been to see me, but he had died. I told her that my mother had told me my father didn't love me. Hated me in fact. She was horrified. She pulled an envelope out of her bag. She said she had been carrying it with her for years. It looked like it, although it looks much worse now.' Clare pulled a well-worn piece of paper from the pocket of her linen pants. It was the letter that Fred had been talking about. I couldn't believe that she had it.

'The woman pushed the envelope into my bag and made me promise not to tell my mother.'

Clare continued her story while I stood still looking at the letter, my eyes popping out of my head. 'She made me promise to hide it from my mother. She told me that everything I needed to know was in the letter. And then she disappeared, and I never saw her again.' More tears formed in her eyes and made pathways down her face. After a full minute she took a deep breath, her face grew angry, and she continued.

'But I did tell my mother. Not about the letter but about the woman I had met, my grandmother. Until that moment I wasn't completely sure that the woman wasn't just a random crazy person but as soon as I saw my mother's reaction I knew. I knew that she had been who she said she was. My mother and I had a huge argument and I ran away.' She chuckled to herself. 'I didn't run very far mind you. Just to the edge of the property where the fences met each other. To here.' She gestured to where she was sitting.

'And so, we return to my question about the acorn.

I am guessing after seeing your confusion that it was my grandmother, his mother, whom I met in town that day who put the acorn in the envelope otherwise you would have mentioned it when you said he had told you about the locket and the letter. The night I ran away I opened the envelope and along with the letter inside a necklace and acorn fell out. I planted the acorn and the tree that shades us now is that tiny acorn over fifty years later.' I looked up at the branches in amazement. Clare's voice brought my attention back to the base of the tree where a glint of light caught my eye. I scanned the wide trunk and saw a silver locket hanging off a small branch at the base of the tree.

'Over the years any scraps of memory that I had clung to all but disappeared, but I always had my tree. It gave me more comfort than any teddy could. If I was ever feeling sad or alone, I would come here.'

My eyes welled up, but I smiled and nodded my head. She knew, she had always known because of that fateful meeting with Fred's mother. I didn't know the contents of that letter, but I knew that I could go back to Fred and tell him that she knew how much he loved her, and he could happily move on.

'When you came here the other day I really did think that you were a con artist and somehow you had figured out my little secret but then I realized that not even my family knew and there was no way that you could have known. I am sorry for accusing you Sophie.'

I waved off her apology 'To be honest I probably would have done the same thing in your position. I'm glad that I could pass on his message. I know that he will be able to move on now. Thank you for sharing your place of peace with me, he will be so happy to hear that his memory lives on.' I looked back up at the beautiful green and brown of the majestic tree and smiled. 'I had better go. Goodbye Clare.'

I started to walk away but again her voice stopped me in my tracks. It was barely more than a whisper, so I thought that I had misheard her.

'Excuse me?' I said, turning around. She looked up again at the mighty oak tree, then looked at me with a searching expression on her face and repeated what she had just said.

'I want to see him.'

CHAPTER 13

I shook my head, immediately picturing my parents asking about my random visitor, 'Oh yeah, she is just here to visit her long dead dad who happens to be a spirit that is haunting our house because he never got to make sure she knew that he loved her. Oh, by the way did you know that our house is often infested with ghosts?' No, no, no. That couldn't happen.

'Please Sophie? There is so much that I need to know. You may have sorted his unfinished business, but I have some of my own.'

'I can't,' I responded, my voice pleading. 'My parents don't know about the spirits in the house. There are only a couple of people who know about them and I want to keep it that way. I need to keep it that way.'

'I won't breathe a word of it to anyone. I promise. Please Sophie,' her eyes searched my face, 'you asked a favor of me and now I am asking one of you.'

I had to admit I really didn't enjoy a woman over the age of seventy begging me for a favor so I probably would have folded then and there but her next words were the proverbial nail in the coffin. 'Don't you think if he had an opportunity to speak to me, to tell me these things that you have said to me himself, that he would?'

That was it. She knew that she had me. She jumped up from the seat and practically danced over to the car. Amy looked surprised and a little alarmed when Clare jumped into the back seat and informed her that she was going to go for a drive with me. I shot her a nervous glance as I got back into the car. Amy knew immediately what her aim was, and she seemed just as unsure as me.

'Are you sure this is a good idea Nan?'

'No. But I do know that from what Sophie has said this will be my only chance. I know in my heart that if Sophie goes back to her house and he hears that I am just fine and dandy thank you very much he is going to poof into oblivion, or whatever it is that they do, and I will never have the chance to say the things that I want to say.'

'I am coming with you then,' Amy said in a firm, this-is-not-an-option kind of way.

'Fine,' Clare said happily, surprising us again.

Amy and Clare dropped me back at my car in the parking lot of the visitor center and I drove back to my house with them hot on my tail. I hadn't given them the address so I guess Amy felt if she lost me it was likely they wouldn't be able to find me again. By the time we had reached the house I had concocted a story about Clare being my history teacher who was curious to see the historic house I had written about in my assignment in case my parents asked about the surprise visitors, but when I drove down the driveway my dad's car was noticeably absent, and I breathed a sigh of relief.

It was highly likely that I would have to tell my parents about the ghosts at some point, given they were turning it into a bed and breakfast where visitors may encounter them, but for the time being, I was happy with them being oblivious. Amy and Clare climbed out of their car and looked up in awe at the house. I turned and looked at it as if seeing it from their eyes. I was so proud of the work that my parents had done. When we had first come it had been so dark and run down. Like a tired old vintage car, but they had restored it bit by bit back into the grand dame I was sure it had been when it was first built.

'Ready?' I asked Clare, pulling her out of her review of the house and back to the task at hand. For a moment she seemed unsure, but she looked over at Amy and then back at me and nodded her head, walking in long strides across the driveway and following me through the front door.

Clara was filling a vase of flowers in the front entrance as we walked in and she mumbled an awkward greeting at the visitors. Clare smiled at her and mumbled her own nervous greeting in response, and I led them down the hall and to the entrance of the lounge room where Fred likely was waiting for news. When I turned to look at Clare she was wringing her hands and breathing erratically.

'Do you want me to go in and speak to him first?' I asked gently.

'Um I don't … I am not sure that I … What do you think is best? This is going to sound strange, but I feel like you know him better than I do,' she replied, her eyes glistening.

I thought for a minute and remembered back to Thomas seeing Gus during the night of the Halloween ball. I knew how much Fred loved this woman standing next to me and I knew there was no way that his reaction was going to be bad but just in case I thought I might just give him a quick heads-up. I took her hand in mine and looked into her eyes. 'Give me one minute, OK? Just one minute. Come in in one minute.' She smiled and nodded her head.

I eased the door open and walked through, closing it behind me. At first, I thought that Fred wasn't there but then he walked through the door of books from the next-door room.

'Sophie!' he greeted me with a smile as he always did, and I smiled back. 'What stories do you have for me today?' he said in a joking manner but stopped suddenly when he realized I was not sporting my usual sorry-I-have-bad-news face.

'You talked with her again, didn't you? What did she say? Did she believe you? Tell me everything. I want to know every detail down to her face. Can you describe her expressions? I should have asked for you to take a photo of her. I bet she is lovely.'

I nodded my head. 'She is lovely. Would you like to see?' I asked nervously.

He nodded his head enthusiastically, 'You have a photo of her?' He reached his hand out.

'No ...' I started to explain but was cut off by the sound of the door to the hallway opening. I spun around and watched Clare's expression carefully as she walked into the room and searched around for her father. I looked back to see what Fred's reaction would be, but he had vanished. I looked again at Clare and her excited expression had been replaced by a pained and confused look. Oh no! He must have disappeared not knowing who she was, thinking that they must have been guests of the house that I had told him must never see him. Now she was really going to think that I had lied to her. I had to get him to come back!

'Fred?' I called out loudly, not worried about who could hear us but more concerned at this point about getting him back in the room. I walked over to the hidden door to the guest bedroom and pulled it open. He was standing next to the window looking nervous.

'Have they gone? I don't think they saw me. Did they see me? I'm sorry Sophie,' he spluttered out in a rush.

'Fred, stop, it's OK. I told them they could come in. What I was trying to explain to you before they came in ... The woman that walked into the room. She came to see you. The woman is ...'

'Clare?' Fred gasped and his hand went to his mouth.

Clare had been standing behind me listening as I spoke, and she moved closer behind me and touched my back. As she did, I moved aside so that she could see into the guest room. So that she could see her father. She took in his translucent appearance and fresh tears filled her eyes before her mouth turned up in a broad smile and she let out a short laugh. 'Dad?'

Tears ran freely down Fred's face as he nodded his head and when he finally brought himself to say something the only words that came out were, 'Oh my beautiful girl I am so very sorry.'

Clare reached out to hug him, but her hands ran through the air that was his body instead.

'Oh Clare! What I would give to hug you.' He reached his hand near her cheek where tears were running down her face. 'I love you so much. You have grown up to be a beautiful woman. I hope that you know … that you knew you meant the world to me. Did you get my letter?' He looked up at me and I nodded.

'I will leave you two to talk. I think there is a lot to say.' I turned to walk back through the lounge room and stopped when I saw Amy standing watching the exchange between her grandmother and great-grandfather. I smiled and patted her arm. 'A little strange seeing them for the first time. Do you want to stick around, or do you want to come to the kitchen for a coffee?'

She turned to look at me, eyes still wide, and nodded, mutely following me to the kitchen, and sat there quietly while I boiled water and made two cups of coffee. She remained silent as she helped herself to milk and sugar and then sat looking out towards the water.

'Are you alright?' I asked after we had sat there for a full fifteen minutes in silence. I was slightly nervous that she might tell other people what she had seen at our house, and I didn't want my parents' bed and breakfast out of business before it had even started.

She glanced down at her coffee before looking at me. 'Yeah ... yes. I mean it is just so weird. You always wonder what happens when you die but you never really expect to see someone, like that, as a ghost. Where is the young guy?'

'He mostly hangs out in my room.' I took a sip of coffee before I realized how strange that sounded. 'I mean, before he died, he was a friend of mine, so we still spend time together now.' I blushed and looked away. Amy didn't pry. We finished our coffees and I checked my watch. Clare had been speaking to her dad for around thirty minutes and I ducked my head in to check how they were going but they seemed engrossed in each other's company, so I decided to leave them talking a little longer. I had left Amy sitting in the kitchen, but I found her standing behind me looking shyly into the room.

'Why don't you go and speak to him?' I asked, reading her expression. She glanced at me nervously and I smiled encouragingly. Clare and Fred heard us talking and stopped speaking, glancing in our direction. Amy took a small step into the room and Clare reached out her hand.

'Dad, I would like you to meet my granddaughter, Amy.'

Fred stood up from his position on the window seat and did a small bow. 'It is an absolute pleasure to meet you Amy.'

Amy continued walking into the room and managed a quiet 'Hello'. She sat down on the arm of one of the couches and looked nervously at Clare. Clare nodded encouragingly at her and tried to explain Amy's apprehensive behavior to Fred, who was looking back and forth between the two women.

'Unfortunately, Amy's father was raised to think that my mother's second husband was his grandfather. When Mom passed away, I told him the truth, I showed him the letter, but I didn't explain any of this to Amy and her brother. She grew up never knowing that you existed so I think she may be a little confused by the whole situation. When Sophie came to the house it dropped a bit of a bombshell on the family.' She glanced at me looking apologetic. 'Not that I mind now of course. I am just grateful to have the chance to see you. I had memories of you in my mind, but I was so little when you left …' She paused to correct herself. 'I mean, when you died, that I never knew if they were real or whether I had created them in my mind.'

'I am so grateful that I had the chance to see you too,' Fred said smiling proudly at Clare and then at Amy. 'Both of you. Thank you, Sophie, for finding them for me and for bringing them to me. I feel like I have had a weight lifted off me and I can move on now.'

Clare nodded her head understanding his meaning and tried to stifle a tear but gave up and openly sobbed. Amy moved over to the couch to hold her, and she put her hand on hers.

'Don't forget me,' Fred said quietly, tears rolling down his face.

'Never,' Clare said softly, managing a smile through her tears. 'You have always been and will always be with me when I sit under the oak tree.'

'Goodbye until we are together again my darling daughter. I love you.'

'Goodbye Dad. I love you too.' The tears continued to run down her face, but she also wore a determined smile. And then he was gone. And all that remained in the room were the three live humans and an overwhelming feeling of sadness, but also hope. Amy sat with Clare for several minutes as she collected her thoughts, taking deep breaths. I wondered whether she would feel better or worse for coming to the house, but she seemed to have a light in her face that wasn't there before. When she stood up to leave, she came over to me and took both of my hands in hers.

'Thank you for giving him peace. And thank you for giving us this time together.' She collected her bag and left the room. Amy, who looked like she had just witnessed something as equally beautiful as it was terrifying, gave me a lopsided smile and an awkward wave.

'You were right about the jellyfish thing. Nice to meet you Sophie.'

'Bye Amy. Take care of her.'

She nodded and followed her grandmother out the door. I knew I should see them out the front but instead I went and sat on the window seat looking out over the water. Another ghost had left the house. As much as I had

thought this time it had not been as traumatizing as it had been with Diana, I was coming to the realization that it may have been worse. Locating Clare and then convincing her to believe me and bringing her to the house, having to watch the heartache that came with watching her say goodbye after just finding her father again was far more draining than the experience had been with Diana. I wondered whether it was entirely necessary to unseal the rest of the rooms in the house or whether I could just leave them as they were, trapped inside.

CHAPTER

14

The next day at school I made a point of running Alice through what had happened. She had volunteered to help me find Clare and come with me to see her, but I had pushed back. It felt like unlocking the doors was enough of a burden for me to place on her.

We sat on the top of the bleachers watching the running team doing laps of the track. Alice sat back at the end of my story and dabbed her cheeks with a tissue, wiping away the tears that had flowed while she had listened to my account of Fred and Clare meeting again. We sat there in silence for a couple of minutes. I was enjoying the gentle tugging of my hair in the wind. Getting all of it out had actually felt cathartic and I was happy that I didn't have to go through all of the house's spirit issues alone.

After several minutes Alice looked at me and said the words I was quietly dreading, 'I guess we should probably start thinking about the next room we should open.'

I groaned. Unlocking the clock tower was down the bottom of my priorities but we still had four rooms to go, and I had overheard my parents talking about whether they would allow the house guests access to the viewing platform located on the roof that was accessible through the clock tower. They were planning on assessing the safety railings to see whether they would need an upgrade, or whether it was just too risky to allow visitors to go out there, so I suspected they would be trying to unlock that door soon.

The room that housed the clock was accessed by a narrow wooden staircase that led off the hallway in the servants' level. The entry to the wooden staircase was concealed behind a false wooden panel. I had told Clara the day before that Alice and I were planning on unlocking the door and she had seemed unconcerned. She couldn't remember any details of who was locked in the room or why and neither could Isadora or Poppy. Isadora had mentioned that several times a year she had done a sort of all-encompassing spell on the house in case there were evil spirits lurking in some of the rooms that they had missed, so it was possible the room was locked accidentally during one of those cleansing periods. It was also possible the structure was unstable so we would have to be careful when we went up there.

Alice arrived full of nervous excitement late on Sunday afternoon. Although the spring air was crisp the sun was out, so we had something to eat next to the fountain in the secret garden before setting our mind to the task at hand.

'I wonder who is locked in there,' Alice said quietly, as she glanced to the top of the roof from where we sat in the garden.

'Can't be worse than Diana throwing things at us, surely. I thought she was going to kill us when she ran out of vases and started throwing books.'

I chuckled as I cleaned up the plates from our afternoon tea. We dropped the dirty dishes in the kitchen and then walked up the stairs to my room. My parents were in the house, working on the interiors, so we snuck up to the servants' level through the secret passageway coming off my bedroom. I pressed in the panel on the wall as I had seen Clara do months ago and it popped in and then slid along the wall to reveal the opening to the narrow staircase.

'It sure is steep,' I said, looking at the steps in front of me that went almost vertical before hitting a landing and then turning around to the right. I led the way up the steps with Alice following closely behind. When we hit the landing, we turned to the right and up a final set of stairs. The steps gradually widened until they hit another landing where the door to the inside of the clock sat. Once we reached the top landing, we found that it was wide enough for us both to stand together on the top step.

As we had in the past, Alice and I took one more look at each other to check that we were both ready and, as had been the case with the other three doors, we both looked mildly terrified about what we might find on the other side. We still hadn't found Diana's box of treasures that we were hoping would hold the answers to several questions we had around controlling the ghosts, and again I mentally questioned whether we should wait until we had exhausted all possible locations that the box could be, but we were standing at the door now so it felt a little late to back out.

'*Aperio!*' Alice said with a lot more confidence than I felt, and we heard the familiar sound of the lock waking from its slumber. We both held our breath as I turned the handle and stepped into the room.

The room itself was not large, it must have been around twelve feet by ten and the walls were all inlaid with wood paneling. In the middle of the room sat the mechanism of the clock and in front of us was the glass window of the clock face. The glass was dirty, letting in fragments of smudged light. The stationary black arms marking out the minutes and hours were peppered with rust.

To the right of the clock face there was another small door which I assumed must have led out to the viewing platform, as there were no other doors in or out apart from the one that we had entered. The handle on the door to the balcony was hanging at an angle as though it had been broken in the past, but the door appeared to be firmly shut.

I involuntarily shivered as I realized that the room was almost identical to the nightmare I had the night before my birthday. Had my subconscious been trying to tell me something? I didn't recall ever being in the clock tower before so I was unsure as to how my mind would have known what it looked like. I immediately glanced at the big bell in the middle of the room that had been still for so many years, half expecting to hear the flapping of a bird trapped inside, but it was as still and silent as the rest of the room.

Our eyes searched every inch of the space as they adjusted to the muted light that was coming through the clock face.

'Empty,' Alice stated, and I could tell that she was relieved, as was I, but she also seemed to have a note of suspicion in her voice.

'Yeah,' I agreed, 'it doesn't look like anyone has been here in a while does it.'

I walked over and twisted the loose handle, opening the door to the roof outside, and was immediately blinded by the light. Once my eyes had a chance to adjust, I stepped gingerly out onto the roof. It was less of a balcony, more like a small walkway that went a couple of feet out on either side of the roof and narrowed in front of the clock face. The walkway looked solid, there was no cracking, and it didn't feel as though I was going to fall through the roof at any point.

I carefully examined the railing on each side, and it also looked to be relatively sturdy. My dad might have to replace a screw here and there and the doorknob obviously needed to be fixed but given the state of the rest of the house when we had arrived, I was pleasantly surprised. I took in the view from the front of the clock, which looked out over the water. I hadn't fully appreciated how high up the top of the house was. You could see for miles across the neighboring properties and over the water.

'Wow,' I exclaimed under my breath as Alice stepped through the door and joined me on the balcony. She took in the view and whistled in appreciation.

'This is incredible!'

'I know,' I agreed, shaking my head. 'Who knew this was up here!'

'Actually, now that you mention it, I remember some of the deadbeats at school started a challenge last year to break into the big old mansions and take photos as evidence. It's possible someone came up here. This house would have been a prime target, given there were rumors about it being haunted,' she rolled her eyes in disgust.

'Really?' I was more than a little surprised. I looked down over the edge of the railing. I couldn't see where their footholds would have been, but I guess it was possible. 'I doubt anyone would climb up here.'

'Maybe the front door wasn't locked, and they came in through the house. It's possible Poppy didn't always lock up, given it didn't seem like there was much to steal.'

'So that's got to be the easiest room we have opened so far.' I smiled, more than a little relieved. Again, I got the feeling that Alice was not entirely convinced.

'What are you thinking?' I asked noting the furrow in her brow.

'I don't know. There is just something not quite right about it.' She paused to collect her thoughts. 'OK, this is the only way that I can explain it. This is the top of the house, right?' I nodded, agreeing with her. 'And what is the temperature today, say around 65 degrees?' I nodded again, following where her thoughts were going.

'But it is really cold inside that room,' I finished her chain of thought.

'Yeah. And not just coolish but freezing cold.' I glanced back towards the door and then back out over the water. The bay was like a pond today, the still, glassy water reflected the blue of the sky and the puffy clouds like a gigantic mirror. I wondered whether Poppy ever came up here with her husband. The thought made me involuntarily glance over to Charlie's house.

'Aside from the cold room it is actually a little romantic up here.'

Alice laughed and followed my gaze over to Charlie's house. 'Well, I better get back to help Mom with the dinner prep. Do you want to come down with me or are you going to stay up here for a bit?'

'I think I'll stay and watch the sunset. When you're at the restaurant can you check with your mom if she found the necklace you gave me for my birthday? I left it on the table when we were cleaning up.'

'Sure thing. See you tomorrow at school.'

Alice walked towards the door and I called out, 'Hey, thanks again for your help.'

'Yeah, no worries I guess,' she called back, her light response not matching the concern on her face.

I watched the sun sink into the water and then wandered back into the small room that housed the clock. I was walking over towards the door to the stairs when I saw the glint of something shiny poking out from the clock mechanism in the middle of the room. I walked over and looked underneath. There was a vodka bottle lying on its side. Next to the bottle there was a black, soft woolen blanket that had been pushed right down underneath the bottom beam of the clock mechanism. I knew I would have missed it if I hadn't seen the light reflecting off the bottle. I reached for my phone in the back pocket of my jeans to call Alice before realizing I had left it downstairs in my room.

I felt around a little more under the beam to see if there was anything else that I had overlooked but my hands touched nothing aside from the wooden and steel components of the clock. I looked again at the bottle and throw rug and tried to see if there was a label attached to the blanket with a name, but the light had all but gone and I could barely see my hand in front of my face.

I wrapped the bottle in the throw so that if I accidentally fell on the way back down the stairs it wouldn't smash. I took one last look at the room as I closed the door behind me and I gingerly felt my way down the stairs, wishing that I had brought my phone or a torch to help me find my way.

When I got to my room, I still couldn't solve the mystery of who might have left the rug and the bottle up there. The bottle was not old. It looked like any other vodka bottle that you would find down at the liquor store, but the label still looked new and there was a tiny bit of liquid at the bottom of the glass, which suggested that it hadn't evaporated over a number of years of sitting in the clock tower. I figured that it had to have been left there within the past year or two.

I thought back to what Alice had said about the kids

from school breaking into the houses and taking pictures. It was definitely a beautiful spot to take a photo, but I couldn't imagine how they would have gotten up there. I picked up my phone and tried a couple of hashtags on various social media channels to see whether I could figure out who was up there but none of the images looked like our house and I figured if it was last year it could take a while to find anything recent.

I picked up the throw rug again and spread it open on my floor. I found a label attached with cleaning instructions, but no brand. Speaking of cleaning, I wondered whether the owner had ever cleaned it. Now that I could see it under light there were several marks spread across both sides. A long, brown-colored stain on one side looked like it might have come from grease on the clock mechanism. There were a couple of white marks scattered across one side, a small rust-colored stain that could have been dried blood and the top edge looked frayed. I wondered if the rug and the bottle were owned by the same person but there was literally nothing else in the clock tower so I assumed it would have to have been.

I wrapped the bottle back up in the rug and hid the two of them in the bottom of my cupboard.

15

That night, I had another dream that I was unlocking the clock tower with Alice, but when we opened the door the animal stuck inside was not a small bird but a tiger, walking around and around in circles. When it spotted me and Alice standing at the doorway it bared its teeth at us and snarled. I turned to Alice in fear, but she had a mask over her face, and I couldn't see her eyes.

I sat up in bed, sweating. Gus was sitting at the window seat that looked into Charlie's bedroom and turned to look at me in surprise.

'Sophie? Are you alright? What is it?'

I shook my head, trying to rid the images from my memories. 'Nothing,' I mumbled, 'Just a bad dream.' I rubbed my eyes and stretched my arms up towards the ceiling. 'What's the time?'

'6 am – the sun is just coming up.' He nodded to where he was looking out the window. I pulled back the covers, figuring that there was no way I was going back to sleep after that horrible nightmare so I may as well go and enjoy the sun that I had watched go down the previous night coming back up again. There was no stopping the world from spinning I thought ruefully. I wrapped a blanket around my shoulders and sat down on the cushioned window seat, my back to Gus, staring out at the sun peeking out from the water. Milo looked up from his bed, where he was curled in a little ball, gave me a look of fatigue and lay back down. I smiled at him and then looked back out the window. The water was like a pond again, not a ripple on the surface and the sand looked grey in the half-light.

'Beautiful, don't you think?' Gus said, looking at me and not the sun.

I turned to look at him, a smile creeping onto my face. No matter how bad I felt, he always knew what to say to cheer me up. I rolled my eyes at him, and he winked at me. At that moment I felt so drawn to him. I wanted to lean my back against his chest and feel his heart beating and the warmth coming off his body as we watched the sun coming up together.

I looked into his eyes and desire coursed through my body. I bit my lip when he looked back into my eyes with the same expression on his face and I knew that he was thinking the same thing as me. For that second, we both forgot that he was dead, our faces moved together at the same time, but this time I felt his lips on mine. It wasn't the same as kissing a real living person, but it was better than my lips passing straight through his. Not the same, I thought, for instance as when I kissed Charlie.

I jerked backwards as though I had been electrocuted. Gus looked at me in confusion as I turned to look straight into the next-door house that shared the same view as mine. I prayed that the blinds were drawn but this morning I had no such luck. The blinds were wide open in Charlie's room and he was standing in his window, with a similar expression to Gus's, complete and utter confusion. Gus turned to follow my gaze and I saw Charlie looking at Gus and Gus looking at Charlie. They had both seen each other and neither of them looked happy.

'Crap!' I said and leapt off the seat. I ran around the room throwing on whatever clean clothes I could find and pulled my hair into a messy bun. Gus stayed sitting on the window seat looking mildly annoyed at the carry-on but also occasionally glancing at his hands looking amazed.

'So what if he saw. Do you know what this means? I can touch you now! Like a normal, living person!' I looked at him with an exasperated expression. 'Well not quite like a normal living person but you know what I mean. That was amazing. Come on Sophie you felt that too!' he argued. I continued trying to get myself into a semi-respectable state.

'What are you doing?' Gus said, sounding mildly amused but his eyes looked disappointed. 'He was bound to find out eventually.'

I paused in my search for a missing shoe. 'Find out what exactly Gus?'

'About us.' He stood up and I glanced behind him, but Charlie was no longer standing in the window and I worried that he had already taken off.

'There is no us,' I said a little bit too aggressively.

I could tell by Gus's face that this stung. I found another pair of shoes but one of them had been used by Milo as a chew toy. I threw them back on the floor and kept searching.

'But I love you. And I know that you love me too. Does he make you feel the same way as I do?'

I resumed my search for the missing shoe, which also allowed me to avoid eye contact and pretend to be distracted to avoid answering Gus's question. I needed to get next door and try to salvage what I had done.

'Sophie?'

'What? What do you want me to say? You are not going to hear what you want to hear Gus. Yes, I do love you and yes, I love him too. It's different the way that I love you and the way that I love him. But I don't know how I could ever have any kind of normal relationship with you. We can't go to the movies together or go out for dinner. I can't introduce you to my parents.'

'Your parents already know me,' he said, his voice hoarse. He had turned away from me and I could tell he was upset.

'I need you Gus, please don't be mad with me.' I was almost pleading with him now and I knew that I needed to stop talking. Nothing I was going to say was going to make him happy. I spotted the missing shoe and pulled it on just as he turned around. His eyes looked cold, distant and it made me feel sad and alone.

'You need me do you.' It wasn't a question. 'You know what Sophie, I think it would be best if I gave you

145

some time and space for you to work out what or who it is that you really want. For the next three weeks I won't be haunting your room every night and making you feel something if you don't want to feel it.' His face was unreadable. I couldn't tell whether he was angry or sad and the tears started rolling down my cheeks before I could stop them.

'Wait!' I called out but he had vanished. I smacked my hand into the bed, wiped the tears from my face and ran out into the hallway and down the stairs almost colliding with Charlie as I ran out the front door.

'I can explain,' I blurted out just as he was saying, 'What the hell was that?'

'I … I didn't mean for it to happen. It wasn't even a real kiss.'

Charlie looked at me incredulous.

'It looked like a pretty real kiss from where I was standing. Is this why you have been keeping us apart? You didn't want me to see him in case he told me that you are having some sort of weird ghostly relationship? Is that what this is?'

'No! It was a mistake.'

'Have you kissed him before?' I couldn't lie. Not to him, so I just stood there looking at his face and wondering if what I was about to say would spell the end of our relationship.

'Yes. Once before. But it was before you and I were actually dating, and it was a life and death situation and … and … and … I'm sorry.' I looked down at the pebbles on the driveway, feeling as small and as heartless as the tiny little stones.

I heard Charlie's intake of breath as he took this new information on board. He turned and walked several steps down the driveway and then walked back to me. I looked up at his face. His handsome, wounded face.

'I love you so much Charlie. I'm so sorry. I told Gus what I feel for him is not the same as what I feel for you.'

Charlie looked at me with suspicion. 'What did he say to that?'

I figured it was better to tell the truth at this stage rather than be caught in another lie. 'He told me I need to choose between the two of you and he is going to avoid being around me for the next three weeks while I decide.'

Charlie looked towards his house and then up at mine. 'Then I think it is for the best that I do the same. I still love you Sophie, but I won't compete with a ghost.' I closed my eyes to try to stem the tears. I heard him turn and walk back towards his house. I stood frozen in the same spot; my eyes closed until I could no longer hear the tread of his shoes on the pebbles. I opened my eyes again and he was gone. When I saw the empty driveway, my heart dropped, and I collapsed onto the ground and burst into tears. I had never felt more alone in my life. It was like there were little needles being repeatedly stuck into my heart.

Clara found me sitting in the same spot an hour later, my face streaked with tears, and helped me up to my room. Milo clambered up onto the bed, licking the salty tears cascading down my face. My room felt so quiet and empty knowing that Gus wouldn't be visiting me in the near future, if ever again. He and Charlie were both angry with me and rightly so. I knew that I couldn't have both of them, but I couldn't breathe at the thought of losing either one of them. From the beginning, when I had told Alice what had happened on the night of the Halloween ball, she had warned me this might happen, but I hadn't listened and now I had blown up both relationships.

I looked over at Charlie's room, but the blinds were pulled closed. I lay back down on my bed and buried my face into my pillow, sobbing until I had no tears left.

CHAPTER

16

For the next couple of days my parents let me get away with claiming illness. I would drag myself out of bed only to go to the toilet, not eating or showering. Clara brought meals up to my room, leaving them on my desk only to come back again in a couple of hours to take them back down to the kitchen untouched. My only consolation was the dog. As if he could sense my sorrow and neediness Milo was my constant companion, curling up in a ball against my legs so that he would know if I left my refuge and follow me.

I suspected that Clara may have spoken to my parents because by Thursday my mother called time on the illness, took my temperature and sent me off to school.

Alice was waiting for me on the top step of the entry when I got to school. I wondered whether my parents may have had a quiet word to her.

'Hey you,' she said gently, assessing my face, which was swollen from crying.

'Hey you,' I said weakly, trying and failing to smile. I was sure it looked much closer to a grimace, and she pulled me in for a hug, which made me feel like crying again.

Fortunately, she didn't say the words that I was sure she was thinking – I told you so. Instead, she was my constant companion the whole day, even ensuring that I sat with my back to Charlie in the cafeteria at lunchtime. But I couldn't help myself. I had to know whether he had asked about me at all or made any kind of inquiry into my whereabouts.

'Has he come over at all during the past couple of days while I have been away?' She shook her head. I fought the urge to look over at his table, to see whether he had noticed me sitting there. As we left the cafeteria, I snuck a glance towards his table and immediately wished I hadn't. Sarah Forbes had one of her arms draped over his back. He looked up and made eye contact with me at the exact moment that my eyes filled with tears. Before they could spill over, I swallowed the lump that was rising in my throat and moved quickly out of the cafeteria to my next class.

During English, I struggled to focus on what the teacher was saying. Instead I was working my way through the grieving process. My sadness had quickly turned to anger. I knew that I was totally in the wrong but come on Charlie! Sarah Forbes? Seriously!!! You have got to be kidding me! By the end of the class I was ready to charge out of the classroom and end his vow of silence, but Alice was waiting for me at the door. As we walked together to our Art class she gently talked me off the emotional ledge that I was teetering on.

'You didn't actually see them kissing or anything?'

'No,' I said, hesitating.

'So, she was just putting her arm on his back then?'

'I guess,' I conceded. Alice was right; I hadn't actually seen him interacting with her at all. It was a completely one-sided, comforting-looking move rather than a romantic interaction.

'To be honest Sophie, I actually think it is a really good idea that you don't speak to either of them for the next couple of weeks. Distance always brings with it some clarity.'

By the time we reached the art room I did feel a little better. Alice and I started setting up our easels next to one another. We had dawdled a little bit on the walk over so most of the class had already set up and were starting their work. Just as I finished setting up my paints and canvas a thought came to me through my fog of sadness.

'I forgot to tell you I found some things inside the clock tower that were strange. I'm going to go back up there after school and have another look while it is light,' I whispered to Alice and was immediately shushed by the teacher.

'I have to go home straight after school to help Mom but let me know what you find,' Alice whispered back even quieter, but the art teacher still heard and threw us a scathing look that immediately silenced the two of us.

True to her word Alice packed up and left as soon as the bell rang and dashed out of the class after motioning for me to call her later.

As I packed up, I glanced out of the rounded windows that looked towards the trees and realized that it had started raining. I was grateful that I no longer had to rely on Charlie to give me a lift home on days like today when the weather was average, or else get soaked riding my bike. It would just make the hurt of being cut off from speaking to him even worse.

When I got home I took the dog for a walk in the misty rain, not bothering to take a rain jacket. By the time Milo and I got back we were both soaking wet. I walked into the kitchen and grabbed a towel from the washing pile, drying myself and then Milo. My parents had left a note that they were meeting with someone about fixing the boat dock. Knowing that I couldn't go and see Charlie or Gus made me feel isolated and lonely, which made me think of Poppy and how lonely she was.

I had spent so much effort finding Fred's daughter. Maybe, I argued to myself, I could now channel that effort and keep myself distracted from my miserable love life at the same time by trying my best to help Poppy find George. Since Fred had left the house Poppy had returned to her vigil, sitting at the desk in her room watching over the water, and I found her there after I had come up with a plan of attack to try to find some answers. I knocked on the door and she ushered me in.

'Hi Poppy, I wanted to let you know that I had a look through George's study and found a few documents that look like they might be connected to his time in the army.'

'Really? Does it provide any information about where he might have been when he died?' She looked excited and I imagined what her reaction might be if I told her that I had also found a weapon and some documents that supported the connection with Germany.

I shook my head, 'No I couldn't see anything that indicated where he might have died but I thought I would send the documents to the US Veterans Affairs office and see whether they can provide me with any additional information. Are you happy for me to do that?'

She looked uncertain but having seen Fred reunited with his daughter must have given her the push that she needed, and she nodded. 'Do whatever you must Sophie. I want to know what happened. I need to know.'

I smiled encouragingly and nodded. 'I'll do everything I can,' I said. 'There were also what looked a little like love letters,' I said sheepishly. Although I hadn't read them, I still felt a little self-conscious having them.

'Oh yes, George was a wonderful wordsmith. You are very welcome to read them if you like. I think the historical society in town may like to take a look at them too.' She smiled and her eyes glinted, which made me more curious to have a look at what he had written.

When I left Poppy, I headed straight to my room to draft up a letter to the US Army. After several discarded versions I came up with something that I thought gave enough information to hopefully elicit a response.

To Whom It May Concern,

I am writing to request some information on behalf of a relative of mine, Mrs Gladys Farrell. Her husband was Lieutenant George

Farrell of the United States Army and we understand that he was sent to war to fight in the Battle of Normandy.

From the information we have been able to find he also seems to have had another alias, Gerhard Froese, and we believe he may have been involved at some point with the Nazi forces, but we are unsure in what capacity.

Lieutenant Farrell's widow would be very interested in any additional information that you can provide.

Thank you in advance for your assistance,

Sophie Weston

I had taken copies of the official-looking documents that I had found in his office, and I added these to the envelope then popped it downstairs with a pile of other mail to be sent out.

I wandered into the kitchen and made myself a grilled cheese sandwich and chopped up some apple, putting it all on a plate to take back up to my room to work on my assignment for an hour. After I had finished my snack and my assignment, I headed up to the clock tower to see whether there were any more mystery objects that had been left in the room.

Even though it was still lightly raining outside the air temperature was a mild 70 degrees, but when I walked into the clock tower the temperature dropped at least 10 degrees. It was still light and clear outside, but the inside of the tower seemed dim and dark. I had brought up a torch this time and I scanned every corner of the room before moving into the center where I had found the rug and bottle. That all seemed clear too and I stood up and dusted myself off. So much for my efforts to solve that mystery. I wasn't sure what I was hoping to find to try and solve the riddle of who had come up there and why.

I walked outside onto the small balcony and took in the view again. I could almost picture a man sitting up there, rug wrapped around his shoulders as he took swigs of the vodka bottle. I hoped that the person hadn't drunk the whole thing by themselves and then tried to climb back down the way that they had climbed up. Three stories with no alcohol under your belt was one thing but with a whole bottle of vodka it was suicide. My body involuntarily shuddered, and I turned to go back inside but again my eyes were drawn to something before I could leave.

It looked like a small piece of red fabric tucked under one of the eaves. I leant down to have a closer look and realized that it was more than just a piece of fabric that had been caught on an edge. I pulled at the red leather and slowly but surely a small red wallet came out. Could this hold the answers that I was seeking? I studied it as I turned it over in my hands. It didn't look like it was very good quality, the stitching coming apart in a few spots, but it had survived being tucked under the roof, partially exposed to the elements for god only knows how long. The light was fading quickly but I opened the single button holding the contents inside.

There was a credit card in the name of a Mr Stuart Waters along with a New York state driver's license for a Miss Mia Thompson. She looked around the same age as me and I wondered whether we were at the same school.

She didn't look like the people that I hung around with, nor did she look like she would fit into the nerd group or the jocks. She had jet-black hair, dark eye makeup and looked a bit goth. But you could tell that she had an attractive face underneath the black makeup. I squinted in the fading light to get a better look. It could have been my imagination, but her face looked sad. There was no cash inside and a couple of other cards in the wallet, none with a name. I wondered whether the wallet belonged to Stuart or Mia. It looked a little bit feminine suggesting it was more likely to be Mia's, but I couldn't completely rule out Stuart. I made a mental note to check out both names.

I had another thorough search around the room as well as the outside deck and felt under the other eaves in case there were any other objects hidden up underneath, but I couldn't find anything else.

When I got to my room I was about to climb up to the shelf where I hid my other treasured objects but before I could get a chance, I heard a voice behind me.

'Hello Sophie.'

CHAPTER

17

I spun around to the sound of the voice and dropped the wallet that I had been clutching. There was a female spirit I didn't recognize standing a few feet away from me, a sinister sneer on her face. She was obviously enjoying catching me unaware.

'How do you know my name? Who are you? What do you want?' I asked, alarmed. The look on her face was making me nervous. I tried to move closer to the door, but she moved so that she was in between the door and me. Now that I knew Gus had developed the ability to touch me, I wondered whether she might have the same ability, which made her seem even more threatening.

'You don't know who I am? Think about it for a minute. I'm sure you will be able to figure it out. I've been watching you the past few days and from what I've seen I thought you were smarter than that,' she said in a patronizing, sarcastic tone.

It was not a full moon and the only ghosts that I had seen in the house were the ones that had died here or had some connection with the house. Or, I thought, dread building slowly in my stomach, the ghosts that were stuck in the sealed rooms. And the one who was standing in front of me looked just like the driver's license that I had found in the wallet upstairs. Dark hair, slightly goth-looking makeup.

'The clock tower,' I said, my words sounding raspy, as my mouth went dry.

'Well done!' She clapped, slowly, deliberately, like a teacher clapping a four-year-old who had finally figured out how to count to ten.

My mind was racing. Who was Mia and what had she done that had resulted in her being locked in the clock tower? Why hadn't she revealed herself as soon as we had unsealed the room? I thought about Alice and I going through the room and me being up there twice more by myself, and a shiver ran down my spine at the thought of her watching us.

'But … but … the room was empty. And that room is a tiny box. There is nowhere you could have hidden.' As soon as I had I uttered the words she vanished and then reappeared in the same place she had been seconds before. I had seen Poppy and Gus do the same thing and I kicked myself for not suggesting it to Alice when she sensed that something was off about the clock tower.

'You can make yourself invisible.' It was not a question, just a statement of fact, an acknowledgment that I had not seen something that I knew I should have. She smiled again, that same sneering, threatening smile.

'Well done, clever girl. You know I was never very studious at school. But I am realizing it is not because

I am dumb. No, no, I just never applied myself. But when you are stuck in an airless little box for months on end with nothing to do, well then you figure out you can do all sorts of things. You know I even had a little mouse that came to visit me. I discovered the most amazing thing with this little mouse. The human spirit really doesn't need much space. I guess because we are essentially like air. The only thing I couldn't figure out was where the little mouse came in and out of the room.' She was moving closer and closer towards me as she was telling me her creepy story about the mouse, and I nervously tried and failed to move further and further away. My legs hit the edge of the window seat. I knew there was nowhere left for me to go.

'What did you do to the mouse Mia?' My voice was too high pitched. It sounded wrong in my ears, and it made me feel even more scared than I was already.

Her menacing smile grew larger. 'Tsk, tsk, tsk, Sophie, again with the obvious questions. Think about it really hard. No? Can't figure it out? Well, you will soon.' She was so close to me now she was whispering in my ear.

'I have a little unfinished business that I need to sort out and I'm going to need to borrow your body to do it.'

I gasped as my body went rigid. It felt like ice water was being poured through my veins. My head moved down to look at my arms, but I had not moved my head or my arms.

It slowly dawned on me that somehow Mia was inside my body, controlling my limbs but not my mind, and I had absolutely no power to push her out. I was trapped in my own body. She walked my legs slowly over to the full-length mirror that was inside my wardrobe. She moved my arms and legs like a baby giraffe getting used to its body.

I started to panic. How was I going to get her out of my body? I needed help but how could I tell my friends and family that Mia had control if I couldn't control my body? I had to tell someone, somehow, I had to find a way to get her out. I focused again as she looked at my reflection and lifted up my breasts with my hands. 'Nice body Sophie. Yes, I think I picked well. I will absolutely be able to get my revenge with you as my vehicle!'

Stop it!!! I screamed inside and then watched as my mouth twisted into an evil smile.

'Ohhh, what's the matter Sophie? Afraid I might have a little bit too much fun in this body of yours?'

You can hear me? I thought in my mind, and she nodded slowly back at my reflection. *Shit!* I swore to myself, thinking of my earlier thoughts of getting rid of her – why couldn't I hear her thoughts when she could hear mine though. That hardly seemed fair. My eyes narrowed in the mirror and my mouth turned down in a frown. She tilted my head to the side, which made it look like she was listening for my thoughts. I couldn't hear what she was thinking, but I could sense that she was angry.

'Am I going to have to teach you a lesson Sophie?'

No. Please don't do whatever you are thinking of doing.

She smiled again, the evil smile, and turned my body around, walking to the door and making her way upstairs to the clock tower. Once she was in the small room, she turned to the doorway leading out onto the balcony, twisted the handle and walked outside. She didn't stop there. Outside, she climbed over the edge of the little balcony that sat on the top of the roof like a topper on a cake. I felt the fear in me rising as my feet slid out from underneath me on the roof tiles. Mia felt it too and steadied herself with the banister that wrapped around the balcony to prevent anyone from doing exactly what she was currently doing in my body.

'This is how I died; did you know that Sophie?' she said in her sing-song voice as I whimpered internally. She must have committed suicide, I thought sadly, and I heard her hiss at my thought.

She found her balance and took one slow step towards the edge of the roof and then another. Mia looked out towards the driveway and I noticed that we were level with the top of the big tree that Gus had tried unsuccessfully to climb when we were children, resulting in a broken arm and an extremely swift reprimand from his father. But Gus had only climbed ten feet up the tree and right now we were on the top of the house, level with the top of the tree. I knew perfectly well, if I fell from where I was standing it would not end with just a broken bone.

I felt Mia's hand let go of the railing around the clock tower and I held my breath. Her hands moved out on either side as she stretched out like a bird and looked up at the stars in the sky.

'Why do you think God made us so we couldn't fly?' she wondered out loud.

Mia please! You made your point don't go any further! I begged her in my mind.

'Because you are not a bird you foolish girl. What are you doing?' I heard Clara's voice behind me as she took my hand and pulled me back to safety on the other side of the barrier. *Clara! Thank god!* I thought, but then I wondered nervously if Mia might try to push Clara off the roof. She stood there for a minute, perhaps debating whether to act on my concerns and then laughed bitterly, pushing past Clara on her way back down to my room.

Once we were there, she left my body and stood in front of me, her face twisted in a cruel smirk. 'Now don't you get any ideas about telling any of the people in this house or any of your friends about me, particularly that witch friend of yours, or we are going to have to take another trip back up to the tower. And if you make me mad, the next time we go up there you will not be using the stairs to get down, do you understand.' It didn't sound like a question and I could tell that she knew her meaning was crystal clear.

CHAPTER

18

When I woke up the next morning, I had a couple of seconds of control over my body before Mia woke up and took over. She waltzed into the kitchen, helped herself to all of the breakfast goods that Clara had laid out on the island bench and promptly inhaled it all within the space of ten minutes.

Dad came into the room, obviously returning from taking Milo for a walk because he came barreling in after him. Milo padded over in my direction but before he could reach me, he paused and sniffed the air, his tail went down between his legs, and he began to whimper and ran back to my dad. Dad, who hadn't noticed, picked up a croissant, poured himself a cup of coffee and came to sit at the table to read the paper.

I wondered if Clara, who had been arranging flowers in a vase and watching out of the corner of her eye had noticed how the dog had reacted to me. There was no way it was a coincidence; in the short time I had Milo he had only ever been excited to see me. Mia didn't seem too concerned however and poured herself a second cup of coffee, which I was not certain my body would handle.

'Aren't you going to be late for school kiddo?' Dad asked without lifting his head out of the paper.

'Oh, I have a free period on Tuesday mornings Dad, don't sweat it,' she said, but grabbed an apple from the fruit bowl and headed off anyway, probably to avoid additional questioning. I wondered whether she was going to keep up the pretense of going to school when she obviously had no interest in it, but she packed up a bag and drove to the campus.

When we got to school, I actually thought that she was going to go to classes but instead she walked around the back of the gymnasium where there was a large pile of old bricks from the construction of the building. She picked up two of the back bricks and pulled out a cigarette packet that was hidden in a void underneath. That answered one question. Obviously, she had attended my school when she was living. There was a lighter inside and after lighting up the cigarette she took a long drag. My body immediately went into a mild seizure, coughing and spluttering until I felt like I was about to cough up one of my lungs.

Your mind might be addicted to smoking Mia but my body will not handle it so you may need to forget about that filthy little habit, I thought, irritated by the way she was taking control of my body and poisoning it. She deliberately took another long drag, I was certain just to spite me, but again my body vehemently rejected the nicotine, coughing so much that she ended up stubbing out the cigarette in frustration. She walked around the gymnasium until she reached the football oval, finding another one of her old hangout spots under the bleachers where she must have spent time wagging school, but there were no other students there and she gave up after several minutes of sitting alone.

'I'm guessing from the way you responded to that smoke and every item of clothing in your closet that you are not the type of person that skips class, but where would I find the kids that do these days? There is one in particular that I need to find,' she said with a sinister edge that I didn't find all that comforting.

I have no idea, I thought, and it was true, I had been living here less than a year and had never noticed the kids that ditched classes.

'Sophie?' I heard someone calling my name as Mia walked past the lockers. Although I knew exactly who it was, I deliberately made my mind go blank so that Mia would be caught out not knowing her name. She tried to keep walking, but the voice called out again.

Turning in the direction of the voice the familiar figure caught up with us in a matter of seconds.

'Oh … hey there, I didn't hear you,' Mia said to Alice, who had caught up with us. Again, I made my mind focus on anything apart from Alice's name, I ran through the periodic table, considered the color of our science teacher's toupee, anything hoping that Mia would be caught somehow by Alice. And then it popped into my head, deliberate, one word, 'Allie'.

'Hey, I tried to call you last night. Was there any movement on the clock tower?'

'What do you mean?' Mia asked, sounding vague.

'Did you have another look up there? Find anything?' she looked around, making sure that no one was eavesdropping around us and leaned a little closer in to whisper, 'No spirits?'

Mia rolled her eyes and brushed Alice off. 'Is that all you think about? Really you need to focus on something else Allie. To be honest I have had enough of the ghost chat for the time being. Let's just have a break from all of that.' She turned on her heel and walked off before she could be caught out. But I knew deep down that Alice would be suspicious not only of my behavior but also by Mia calling her by the wrong name.

When we got back home after school Mia started rummaging around my bedroom, obviously looking for something. I was by no means the tidiest person, but she was quickly turning my room into a complete pigsty.

Stop that! Just tell me what you're looking for! I screamed internally.

She stood up and surveyed the mess that she had created.

'You got anything in this haunted house that would constitute a weapon?' she asked, and before I could make my thoughts go blank my mind went immediately to the gun that I had found in George's study.

'Perfect!' she declared excitedly, grabbing one of my handbags off the floor and heading straight to the study. The gun was still sitting in the cupboard where I left it, along with the box of bullets that were sitting next to the velvet-inlaid box of the gun.

What are you going to do with that? I asked in a mild panic. She loaded it and then tucked it into my handbag.

'Nothing you need to worry your pretty head about Princess Sophie,' she sneered. She headed back upstairs and put on a pair of pajamas over the top of some jeans and a white T-shirt and then made a big song and dance of saying goodnight to my parents. She yawned hugely and rubbed her eyes and even though I thought she was laying it on a little bit thick my parents didn't seem to notice, bidding Mia a good night.

Mia walked back towards the staircase but darted to the right and out of the house through the greenhouse. After ditching my pajamas next to the glasshouse door, she threw on my converse shoes and grabbed the handbag with the gun.

We walked for about a quarter of a mile before she jumped onto a bus and headed to a part of town that I had never been to before. I didn't recognize any of the shops, but we were definitely not in an upmarket part of the Hamptons. There was a tattoo parlor, a supermarket, and various restaurants and bars lining the footpath. As soon as she jumped off the bus she headed towards the supermarket.

What the hell was she planning? Was she going to use the gun to rob the supermarket, I wondered in a panic as I felt the weight of it in my bag. But she walked past the supermarket and into the bar next door. I swore at her; what could she be thinking? I could almost see the look on my parents' faces when they came to retrieve their daughter from the police station after I had been arrested for underage drinking. But there was no bouncer at the door and when we walked into the bar no one even looked up. I guess this was not a place that the police were concerned about, and I had to admit I could see why.

The place was a dump. Tables and chairs that looked like they had been collected from a garbage dump, the roof had exposed beams that looked like they could give way at any minute. The carpet was a dark patterned burgundy color, which had obviously been selected for its ability to hide stains but was failing miserably, probably due to the sheer amount of food and liquid that had been spilt on it.

Mia glanced over to the bar where the bartender was the only person in the room that seemed mildly interested in our arrival.

NO! NO! NO! NO! I screamed internally as Mia strolled over to the bar and ordered a whiskey. The overweight and, judging from the bags under his eyes, overworked bartender raised an eyebrow but took the cash that Mia had thrown down on the counter and poured the drink.

She threw it back in one shot and ordered a second. I could feel the liquor burning down my throat and into my stomach and I wondered whether she was getting the same buzz in my body that she would have got before she died. She took the second drink off the counter and walked around to the other side of the bar, obviously looking for someone. There were no other young people; it was mostly older gentlemen and one or two older women as well as an odd-looking couple who seemed to be on a date. I caught myself thinking how desperate they would have to be to come on a date to this dump of a place and then realized too late that Mia could hear what I was thinking.

'We can't all be dating little princelings that are inheriting their family money, can we?' she muttered into her glass as she poured the second drink into my body. I felt the burn again, but it was starting to take effect and I was already feeling a little foggy. Mia could obviously feel my body suffering under the alcohol too because a moment later she muttered, 'Wow I am not going to be able to put much of the good stuff in you am I, Miss Sobriety.'

She walked back to the bartender and whistled to get him to turn around as he put glasses onto the shelf. I was horrified and wondered whether he might turn around and punch me in response to Mia's rude whistle, but he just turned around slowly with the look of someone who had heard much worse.

'Help you?' he muttered.

'You know where Pete and his gang are hanging out these days?' I wondered who Pete was and why this man would know where he might be.

'Yeah,' he grunted, 'but you don't look like the type that should be seen around those low-life's, lady.' He looked at my clothes and Mia glanced down at what I was wearing too before glancing back up and sneering at him.

'Yeah, well thanks, but they ordered some Girl Guide cookies and I need to deliver them.'

He grunted a laugh. 'He rents a place out on Verona Street with a group of other deadbeats. Good luck with your cookies,' he said dryly and turned back to polishing the glasses that looked like they were still dirty.

We walked back out of the bar and started walking in what I assumed was the direction of Verona Street. Mia stopped and crossed the road when she noticed a twenty-four-hour tattoo parlor but had second thoughts when I told her I would likely pass out from the needles.

Next door there was a convenience store that also sold clothes and makeup. She bought a black T-shirt with a heavy metal band on the front, some black eyeliner and lipstick and used their bathroom to change out of the white shirt that I had on, leaving on my converse sneakers and jeans, which she had either deemed acceptable or too expensive to change.

As soon as we left the shop, she pulled out my phone and navigated to Verona Street. We walked along the street until she spotted a black Mustang parked in a driveway with several other cars. The Mustang had the number plate PTE 1. I rolled my eyes internally thinking what a stupid personalized plate and Mia muttered that PETE 1 was taken. I wondered who this guy was to Mia – a relative? A friend maybe, or a boyfriend.

The house itself was a surprisingly nice-looking two-story grey weatherboard with white windows and

I wondered who owned it and why they would rent it to a couple of kids who from the sounds of it were nothing but trouble.

The front door of the house was wide open, and my thoughts initially went to robbery until I realized there was a party in full swing. We walk into the kitchen where there was a group of people standing next to a keg of beer.

'Can I grab one of those?' Mia asked a guy manning the keg, who looked like he should be at university and not a party for eighteen-year-old seniors.

'Sure,' he looked me up and down and tried to put a serious face on, 'right after I get some ID.'

Mia flipped him the bird, 'Here's your ID.' He burst out laughing and handed me the drink.

'Do you guys know if Pete is here tonight?' Mia asked the group and a couple of the girls laughed.

'Are you sure you're looking for Pete?' A girl asked, as she checked out my outfit. It clearly got the thumbs down.

'You don't really look like his type,' another one of the girls said dryly. The girls had the same look as Mia in her driver's license. Black jeans and tops, fair skin and tattoos, bordering on goth. Obviously, Mia's ten-minute makeover on my conservative appearance had not worked.

'Unless there are a stack of tattoos hiding underneath those clothes?' another one of the girls laughed. Mia glanced around ignoring their snide remarks and I noticed one of the guys across the room was also checking me out. He had dark brown hair, piercing blue eyes and was good-looking. Like most of the other partygoers he had a tattoo creeping out from his top and down his arm. I wondered whether he was Pete, but Mia walked past him. I felt like I was sticking out for all the wrong reasons, and I was being noticed by a lot of people at the party, but Mia seemed completely unconcerned by this. She continued walking around the house from room to room with people doing shots, smoking and taking other recreational substances until she found someone whom I assumed to be Pete.

He looked like he had passed out on the couch, his head resting on the armrest. She nudged his foot until he lifted his head.

'Hey Dan, how's it going?'

He looked at me with bleary eyes and I wondered whether he was drunk or high or maybe both.

'Do I know you?' he asked, sounding confused and almost definitely stoned.

'Not really but I know you. I'm Sophie. Where's Pete?'

'Dunno. Probably in his room making sweet love with the latest lucky lady.' He stifled a giggle and scratched his head. 'You are really pretty. I feel like I would remember you. When did we meet?'

'Just before you smoked that last joint. Which one is Pete's room again?'

'Upstairs, the first one on the left. But I wouldn't go up there if I were you, he gets really grumpy when he is interrupted. Sophie?' but Mia had already walked away from poor stoned Dan and was making her way towards the stairs. She reached into my handbag that she brought with her and put her hand on the gun, sliding my hand over the trigger as she made her way up to the second story of the house. I was fairly certain at this point that Pete must be her ex and it seemed unlikely she had come to the party to just tell him how much she has missed him, and she was sorry for killing herself and leaving him heartbroken.

JESUS MIA WHAT ARE YOU ABOUT TO DO??? I screamed at her in my mind. *You can't go and kill someone while you are in my body — I will get sent to jail!* I was trying everything to convince her not to do it, but she kept moving one foot in front of the other, robotically, up the stairs and to the door that Dan had indicated was Pete's. He had obviously done something terrible to her. Maybe he had cheated on her and that was why she had jumped off a roof. Whatever happened between them before she died must be her unfinished business. I knew she needed to get closure somehow, but I continued to beg her not to resolve whatever it was while she was inside my body, leaving me to pay the consequences for it.

She opened the door quietly and it took less than a minute for my eyes to adjust to the darkness. As soon as she realized there were two people on the bed, passionately kissing and moaning, her resolve seemed to solidify. She leveled the gun in the direction of the bed and pulled the trigger.

CHAPTER

I heard a click and waited for the explosion, followed closely by the vicious recoil and screaming, but nothing happened.

Mia looked down at the gun just as the couple that had been rolling around the bed realized that they had company. She slid the gun back in the bag just as they started screaming at her to get out. It didn't look like either of them knew they could have just been killed. They both just looked irritated about being interrupted. Mia backed out the door mumbling, 'Sorry, wrong room.'

I wondered how my body was still staying upright while I was trapped inside it going berserk.

I'm guessing that was not Pete, right? So, you almost just shot two complete strangers while they were having sex – are you CRAZY???

But of course, she must be. She had almost thrown me off a roof, gone underage drinking in a bar and tried to kill someone with what was probably a weapon from the early 1900s that had fortunately malfunctioned.

What the hell did he do to you anyway? It can't be worth this!

'Murder Sophie, that's what,' she hissed. 'You just assume that I wandered over to your big ugly house and jumped off the roof. NO! You want to know what Pete did? He pushed me off that roof. So, you want to know what I'm doing here? I'm taking revenge, and since I need a human body to do that, you are what is called collateral damage.'

She moved across the hall and opened another door. It was the same scene but a different couple. The next two bedrooms revealed the same and the fifth was empty. I had been to a handful of parties in my life and none of them were like this. I was shocked by the drugs, underage drinking and sex that was going on, but not as shocked as I was by Mia's revelation.

He pushed you off the roof of my house? That's unbelievable! I was starting to get a better idea of why Mia was hell-bent on blowing her ex-boyfriend's brains out. I could feel myself becoming sympathetic to her plight, but I still didn't want to be complicit in her plan, and my mind scrambled for an alternative path that didn't involve a revolver.

Why can't you just go to the police?

'The police don't care about me. The case is closed; teen runaway takes her own life. Open and shut. They didn't even need to break a sweat, why would they want to go and open that can of worms?'

Mia walked back down the stairs after her failed murder attempt and did another lap around the living room, still, I assumed, looking for Pete. In the same vague way that I felt disconnected from my body I wondered idly whether the gun that Mia had tried to shoot would at some point blow up in my bag since it hadn't yet discharged.

I heard her chuckle in response to my thoughts.

She returned to the kitchen and poured herself another beer. As the alcohol worked its way through my system, I could feel my thoughts becoming numb and nonchalant to the prospect of going to jail based on another person's actions. In fact, under the influence of that much alcohol I started to wonder if I wouldn't do the same thing in her situation. I mean, what an asshole! Who pushes their girlfriend off a roof?! Wow, I thought dimly, who knew all it would take for me to turn into a murderer would be two shots of whiskey and a couple of beers.

'Why are you looking for Pete?' I heard someone behind me ask, interrupting my thoughts. Mia turned around to look in the direction of the question and I saw the good-looking guy who had been staring at me earlier leaning against a doorframe, sipping a drink from a red plastic cup and watching me carefully.

'None of your business,' Mia fired back rudely and turned her back to him, but I could tell that she also thought he was attractive by the way she didn't just walk away.

His voice when it came next was just next to my ear, so he had obviously moved a lot closer.

'You don't belong here little girl so whatever misplaced crush you think you have on Pete, I recommend you forget it and get the hell out of here before you get yourself into trouble.' His voice was insistent but not threatening and I wholeheartedly agreed with his opinion. I tried again to urge Mia to leave. Based on Mia's accusation earlier

Pete sounded dangerous. But almost as soon as I had that thought I remembered that Mia was carrying a gun in my handbag, making her equally dangerous. Whether or not it would fire was another matter.

Mia turned around to no doubt say something biting and sarcastic to the handsome stranger, but he was no longer standing behind me. Looking around for him Mia spotted someone else she knew in the lounge room of the house and moved quickly across the room towards whomever she had spotted.

'Hey PETE!' she called out as she walked towards the sofa, and I shrunk down in my mind, waiting for her to pull the gun out of my bag again, only this time there were dozens of witnesses.

Pete had greasy-looking dirty blond hair and a scar down the side of his cheek. His arms were covered with a sleeve of tattoos on each side, and I could see more tattoos on his chest. All I wanted to do was run but Mia held us both in place and glared at him.

He looked up from a conversation he had been in with a woman who was straddling his lap and glanced in the direction of the interruption with an irritated expression, but when he saw me a sleazy smirk came across his face and he licked his lip, flashing a tongue stud.

'And who might you be sweet thing?'

Sweet thing? Come on Mia! You seriously dated this guy? Get us out of here, I pleaded with her. His voice sounded innocent, but his eyes moved up and down my body oozing sleaze, which made me deeply uncomfortable.

'I'm a friend of Mia's,' Mia said in my voice, and all I wanted to do was dig a hole and hide in it. Pete's face turned sour, and he resumed petting the woman sitting on his lap.

'Man, that bitch is dead. Couldn't handle it when I broke up with her.'

There was complete silence apart from a couple of sniggers from the hangers-on sitting around Pete and I felt something in Mia snap. She lunged at Pete, pushing the girl aside, and started raining down blows on his face and body until I felt a strong pair of arms grab me and pull me off him. The arms wrapped around me and I felt the person who was pinning me breathing in my ear, telling me in a quiet voice to calm down.

The voice was familiar to me as well as Mia, and she immediately glanced down at the arm that was restraining me. I recognized the tattoo of the guy who had warned me to stay away from Pete. He was doing his best to diffuse the situation while restraining me. One arm was wrapped tightly around my body, holding down both of my arms, which seconds ago were being used to assault Pete, and he was holding the other arm out in front of us as Pete came roaring over to retaliate. He came within a couple of inches of me, and I could feel spit coming out of his mouth as he screamed, 'Who the hell do you think you are, you crazy bitch?'

'She's just a silly drunk girl, forget about it Pete,' the guy holding me said, calming Pete down. He quickly took me out of the room, pulling me up the stairs while

Mia fought against him, and then plonked me down in a bedroom upstairs that wasn't currently occupied and closed the door.

'Are you crazy? What was that about? He could have killed you!' the guy said in an agitated voice, releasing my arms. He poked his head out the door to check if we had been followed.

'He already has,' Mia mumbled as she started looking around the room. It looked like a guy's room. There was a blue duvet cover on the bed, a desk with some books sitting on it and a bookshelf full of a variety of different reading material from medical journals to Stephen King and Jeffrey Archer novels.

'I don't know who you are but that was a very bad idea,' he reiterated. His face was tough, but his soft eyes betrayed his concern.

Mia rolled her eyes. 'Please! He is all bark and no bite,' she said as she slotted one of the books back into the bookshelf. *Seriously Mia! You just told me that he pushed you off a roof!*

'Who are you?' he asked, his eyes narrowing.

'I'm a friend of Mia's.' Mia smiled serenely at him, but he seemed to have a keen eye for detail and was happy to call her on it.

'That's funny, I've never seen you at these parties before,' he stated, sounding suspicious.

She shrugged, 'Maybe you were drunk. Speaking of which, I would love another drink. I wonder if there's any booze in this bedroom ...' She started going through the drawers of the desk as he sat down on the bed and continued to appraise her suspiciously.

'This is my room, and I don't drink so you aren't going to have much luck in that department.'

'Well that explains why you're so boring.' Was she flirting with him? I wondered. She frowned at my thoughts and moved back towards the door to leave the room. He slid in front of the door to block her exit.

'Don't.' He put his hand over my hand that was on the doorknob.

'Ohh, I am touched, are you concerned about me Scott?'

'Scott?'

'Yes, Scott no friends, Scott no drinks, Scott no idea what you are talking about. Pick one,' she rudely responded, reaching again for the door handle, but the guy took both my hands in one of his and pinned me to the door.

He smiled at me, finding Mia's sarcasm amusing. 'Jack. My name is Jack. And I would rather my house not be an active crime scene after Pete kills you.' His voice was joking but his free hand was pressed firmly against the doorframe, and I got the sense that he was not going to let me out in a hurry. I could feel my body responding to Jack and realized with horror that Mia's flirting could lead to something more. I already had enough issues in the male department and was not keen to be involved in some sort of kinky ghostly threesome. Mia could obviously hear my thoughts and was amused by them. She leaned in towards Jack's arm that was pushed up against the door.

'Well, if you insist on keeping me hostage in here and you have no booze what are we going to do to keep ourselves occupied?' She smiled suggestively and moved my face so that it was within inches of his. When he began to lean closer, I wondered if he was going to kiss me. But when his lips were just inches from mine and I could feel his breath on my mouth his eyes looked into mine and he murmured, 'Five minutes ago you were trying to punch on with one of my house mates. You move on quickly don't you!' He chuckled as Mia pushed him away and began stalking around the room again like a caged tiger.

I wondered whether she might start breaking things in his room, so I started talking to her in my mind. *Calm down Mia. He didn't actually reject you and besides, you don't even know him.*

She had walked over to the window and was assessing the tree just outside, its thick branches reaching out to the windowsill. 'You seem to have a problem with me leaving via the front door but would you object if I left via an alternative method?'

Jack walked over to the window to stand next to me. He was standing so close I could feel the heat of his body. He eyed off the tree and then looked dubiously at me, sizing up whether I would make it to the bottom in one piece. Before he could respond we heard someone opening the bedroom door. Jack moved to stand in front of me in a protective way, but he needn't have bothered; it wasn't Pete standing outside the door but a couple giggling and kissing as they came into the room, obviously looking for some privacy. Wow, didn't these kids have anything else to do?!

Jack relaxed his stance from standing protectively in front of me and moved around behind me, putting his arms affectionately around my waist.

'This room is taken,' he informed the couple, who quickly stopped giggling and turned to look at us.

'Oh oops – sorry!' the girl said, the two of them backed out of the room quickly, closing the door behind them. Mia glanced at Jack questioningly. He removed his arms from my waist and smirked in the direction of the departed visitors.

'What was that?' Mia breathed out, staring at Jack's face.

His eyes met mine and he gave me a wink. 'They would have never left if they didn't think the room was being used for a good reason.'

Serious and threatening one minute and flirty and jokey the next – I couldn't quite figure this guy out and I was sure Mia probably felt the same way.

'Oh,' was all Mia could come out with, but I could tell she felt a little disappointed that was the reason he had made a move, again a little embarrassed. She turned to the window and aggressively started trying to unlock the bolt, clearly wanting to get out of Jack's room as quickly as possible. Maybe she was a little more embarrassed than I initially thought. Jack put his hands gently over mine and easily unlocked the window, easing it open. Mia practically threw my body out the window in her rush to get out of the room and away from her perceived humiliation, almost slipping as she climbed out onto the top limb.

Jack put his hand on my hand that was still on the windowsill and Mia paused her escape. 'Hey! Probably best to let go of your grudge and just forget Pete, Sophie.'

Mia looked at his hand and then up at his face. 'How do you know my name?'

'I heard you talking to Dan downstairs,' he smiled.

'You don't miss a thing, do you?' she said in an accusing voice and pulled my hand out from underneath him.

Jack leaned out the window, trying and failing to hide his amusement at my climbing technique. 'Also, it would probably be best if you don't come back here again. Pete is wasted so there is a chance he won't remember you or what happened in the morning.'

'Ouch. I wish I could say that I was offended that you don't want to see me again,' she said sarcastically.

'I didn't say I didn't want to see you,' he clarified, 'just that it might not be safe for you here after this evening's events.'

'Thanks for the clarification,' Mia said sarcastically again, rolling her eyes and then quickly refocusing on the tree as my left leg slipped down to the next branch. Given my lack of tree climbing experience I was surprised that we reached the bottom of the tree with only a couple of scratches. When Mia got closer to the ground, she jumped from one of the lower branches and then looked up at Jack's window with a defiant sneer. I thought he might have been back down at the party but when she looked up, he was still there, his face shrouded in shadows so I couldn't make out his expression. Mia laughed and then turned and walked away.

I wondered whether she was going to head back into town and look for more bars that were open but instead she headed back to my house. I thought about whether my parents would find out that I had been out half the night but when Mia snuck back into the house it was still and quiet and there was no one waiting for me in my room tapping their watch. I wasn't sure whether I wanted them to be waiting for me or not. Maybe they would be concerned that I was out so late and figure out that it was not me, but that seemed completely unlikely given they didn't know about the ghosts in the first place. More than anything though I was disappointed that Gus was not in my room because I knew he would know that Mia was not me and maybe he could somehow find a way to alert Alice.

CHAPTER

20

The next morning Mia continued the charade that she was attending school to my parents but then spent most of the day hanging out under the bleachers with a group of misfits that she had found, some of whom I recognized from the party the night before. They all seemed mostly harmless though, which I was relieved about. They included Kai, a soft spoken, graceful hippie and her boyfriend Toby, who seemed to be stoned most of the time and just lay on the grass with his head resting in her lap blowing smoke rings into the cloudless sky. Then there was Jonathan who seemed more of a preppy pretty boy. He didn't seem to have a problem with academics and had already been earmarked for a spot in his father's law firm after he earned his college degree at a local college, where he had already been offered a place and therefore was just marking time before he left school.

One of the girls who had been standing near the keg when Mia got a beer at the party was there. Her name was Evie and the other person I recognized was Dan, whom Mia had first approached when we got to the party to ask about Pete. There were others who wandered in and out of the group during the day, but I didn't recognize their names or faces from the previous night. It hadn't occurred to me that some of the people who had been at the party would go to my school and I had to admit to myself that Dan's face had not registered with me at all. I guess it was because I was always attending classes while they had all actively avoided going to class.

When Dan turned up, he gave me a friendly smile and a wave and called across the group, 'Hey Sophie!'

It surprised me because he had seemed so stoned at the party, I assumed for sure he would not remember me. It made me wonder whether Pete would recall Mia's attack on him.

'Hey Dan,' Mia replied.

After saying hi to the rest of the group and having a long discussion with Toby about a new marijuana dealer that he had been speaking to Dan came and sat down next to me.

'You coming to the party?' he asked.

Not another party! You cannot go back to the house where you almost shot two random strangers and then attacked your ex-boyfriend, who, incidentally, looks like a serial killing drug dealer!

'Is it at Pete's again?'

Dan nodded his head. 'Always.'

'I'm not sure I'm welcome back.'

'Nah, that's not the first time Pete has been attacked by a scorned woman and I'm sure it will not be the last,' he chuckled when Mia screwed up her face in response to being called a scorned woman. 'You should come,' he said a little too enthusiastically.

When we arrived home from school that afternoon Milo cowered behind my dad. Milo hadn't slept in my room since Mia had taken over, but no one seemed to have noticed except maybe Clara. Mia claimed there was a big assignment that she had to work on and headed up to the clock tower. I wondered what she was thinking about when she sat up there for the next hour watching the sun go down over the water. She obviously could hear my curiosity but must not have had the urge to fill me in.

During dinner my parents still didn't seem to be aware of any difference in my behavior, but I suspected that Clara was watching me a little more carefully than usual and Milo would still not come near me. My mom did look a little concerned when she asked about Charlie and Mia told them that it was over.

'It was fun while it lasted but I think we want different things,' Mia reassured them. I noticed my mom glance at my dad with a raised eyebrow, but he continued studying a guide for how to do your own plumbing, oblivious.

Despite my mental pleading Mia couldn't resist the lure of Pete's house and headed to the party that Dan had mentioned at school. Instead of walking through the front door this time she climbed the tree up to Jack's room. I was conflicted. On the one hand I was happy that she wasn't downstairs within sight of Pete but on the other I was fairly certain what she was doing could be considered breaking and entering, and along with the attempted murder she had already committed she seemed set on finding a way to get me arrested.

As Mia climbed into the window, I was relieved to see that no one was in there so technically she could lie and say she had just walked through the front door. Mia snickered as she assessed the room, clearly overhearing my thoughts.

My relief at not being caught climbing through the window lasted for all of forty-five seconds, which is how long it took for Mia to start going through Jack's things. *I am pretty sure that going through someone else's things is also illegal Mia!* I thought, but she ignored me.

'Everyone has something to hide Jack, let's see what you are hiding …' she mumbled to herself while sifting through his drawers. She lifted up notepads, half a chocolate bar and a handful of pens. Pulling out a set of drumsticks she eyed off the drumkit on the other side of the room. Reconsidering, she dropped them back into the drawer and pulled at the edge of a photo that was sitting under another notepad.

'Find what you were looking for?' The sound of Jack's voice was a surprise even to Mia and she dropped the photo of him she was holding. He walked over and picked it up, standing so close I could smell his breath. It smelt like a mixture of coffee and chewing gum. 'You came back,' he observed, looking down at the photo, which was of him standing next to an attractive girl. The emotions that clouded his face came and went so quickly I wondered whether I had imagined them.

Mia looked from the photo to Jack, a little taken aback by his statement.

'Yeah, I didn't get to kill Pete the other night, so I came back with a bag full of kitchen knives,' she joked, but Jack glanced anxiously at the bag she had slung over my shoulder. She opened the top of the handbag, challenging him to check for himself. He came closer and peered into the bag, his face moving closer to mine until we were almost touching. Mia closed her eyes anticipating his lips meeting mine but after what felt like several seconds she opened them again and saw he had moved over to sit down at his desk, pushing the photograph back into the drawer from where Mia had taken it.

'What are you doing in my room Sophie?'

'Trying to find out your dirty little secrets,' she replied, abandoning the desk and walking over to his bookshelf. She pulled out the first book that her fingers touched, which happened to be a book about anatomy.

'Yikes, I think I already found it. Do you have a fetish for killing people and chopping them into little pieces?'

'I was training to be a paramedic.'

'Really?' That surprised me as much as her. He didn't look how I would have expected a paramedic to look, and he lived in a house currently filled with potential patients.

'And what are your dirty little secrets?' he asked, looking amused.

'Oh, I'm an angel' she said sarcastically turning back to the book collection. I felt her comment was

directed more towards me than it was at Jack. He laughed again.

'Well, that is a dirty little secret to have in this house, but don't worry I won't tell anyone.' His mouth tugged up at the sides. 'You said last night that you were a friend of Mia's?'

'Yeah, so?' Mia mumbled, continuing to look through the book selection.

'I moved in here a couple of months after she died so I never met her.'

He hadn't asked a question, so Mia maintained her focus on the books and didn't say anything.

'What happened? Some of the people here said that she killed herself.'

Mia spun around and looked him in the eyes. 'No.'

'You sound fairly sure about that. How can you be so sure?'

Mia collected herself and turned back to the shelf of books. 'She just didn't seem like the type that's all.'

They both said nothing for a minute, and it felt like Jack was studying me from his position at the desk.

'So, you said you *were* training to be a paramedic. Does that mean that you didn't make it?' she deflected and glanced back to look at him.

I was surprised to see his eyes water and he looked away, standing up and walking over to the window. 'I qualified but something happened ... there was an accident, and after that I couldn't do it anymore.'

Mia hesitated but then walked up behind him and

touched his arm. I felt an electric current between our two bodies and Mia must have too because she removed my hand immediately.

'Hey, I'm sorry, I didn't mean to upset you,' she said, surprising me by sounding more gentle than I had suspected she was capable of.

He was silent for a minute and then turned back to look at me.

'It's in the past.' He said the words like he had truly made peace with it, but I wondered if he meant what he said.

'So, what do you do now that you're not saving lives?'

He seemed a little confused by the question, so Mia clarified, 'Now that you're not working as a paramedic?'

'Oh, I'll probably go back to it at some point. But at the moment I'm just working at a bar in town. And what do you do?' he asked turning the question around to focus on me.

Mia moved around the room glancing at his things and pretended to focus her attention on some books on his bedside table, picking one up and flicking through it, 'Oh you know, nothing much.'

He came over next to me and I could feel the heat radiating off his body.

'You don't like to talk about yourself much, do you?' From the sound of it neither of them liked talking about themselves particularly.

She turned around to look at him and sure enough he was less than two feet away, staring intently into my eyes like he was looking for the answers to his questions and he might be able to find them in the pools of green.

'Everyone likes to keep a little bit of mystery about themselves,' she stammered, clearly affected by his proximity.

Our eye contact was broken when the sound of laugher and people leaving the front of the house floated up through Jack's open window. Mia glanced down at my watch. It was close to midnight.

'I guess it is time for me to go,' she said reluctantly. She walked slowly over to the window and then stopped when she realized that she was still holding Jack's book. She turned and held it out for him to take.

'See you soon mystery girl,' Jack said touching my hand as he took the book back. Again, I felt a current pass between them, and he leaned towards me. I wondered whether he was going to kiss me, but again we heard people talking, this time in the hallway outside his room.

Mia quickly climbed onto the tree outside, and this time gracefully moved from limb to limb until she was at the bottom. She glanced up at the window and Jack's silhouette watched as we left.

When we returned to my house I thought about Gus and Charlie. I knew that Gus wouldn't be waiting for me, and Charlie was also giving me distance so I could make up my mind, or perhaps because they had enough of my splintered heart so neither of them would be able to help. I felt so trapped and Mia seemed to be having way too much fun in my body to give it up. If I was in control, there would be tears streaming down my face, but I wasn't.

'Don't worry princess, you are way too annoying, I will give your body back eventually,' Mia answered my thoughts.

When? I challenged her.

'When one of two things happen, either I murder Pete …'

Or? I wondered.

'Or I sleep with Jack,' she said gleefully.

I was horrified but given the option I would definitely go for the second one. I reasoned that no judge in the US was going to allow my defense that the victim's vengeful ex-girlfriend possessed me. At least Jack seemed like a nice person – I felt like I could trust him, and he seemed different from the other guys at the house. I didn't think that he was about to try to get into Mia's pants without getting to know her, and hopefully by then she would be sick of me, or someone would have figured out she wasn't me and removed her from my body.

CHAPTER

21

At school the next day I was hopeful that one of the options to get rid of Mia may come to fruition.

'Hey, can I speak to you?' I heard Charlie's voice next to me and Mia turned to see who had spoken. She was wagging classes again under the bleachers with all of the other slackers.

'Alone please,' he followed up when she said nothing.

Mia rolled her eyes. 'I'm sure whatever you have to say can be shared with all of my closest friends,' she gestured to the group. Dan was high and giggled like a five-year-old, Toby took another drag from his joint, and Jonathan looked nervously between Charlie and me.

'No Sophie, I need to speak to you alone.'

His voice was firm and compelling, and he reached his hand out to me. Mia appraised him for several seconds before rejecting his offer of assistance, instead pushing herself up and gesturing for him to lead the way.

Charlie led me away from the group to the nearby arts building, a beautiful old house that had been converted into a studio. His eyes searched my face for a full minute maybe waiting for me to speak first, but Mia was obstinately staying silent.

'Alice came to see me. She said you've been missing a lot of classes. Is this about us? And what are you doing hanging out with those … those people? Are you alright?'

'What's with the interrogation?' Mia said taking a step back from him. 'I am absolutely fine. Living my best life actually. And for you to think that this is about you is so arrogant.'

'No, I … we haven't spoken since that night when …'

'When you left me crying in a ball for an hour on my driveway?' Mia threw back at him.

'You were? I … I didn't know,' he said softly, his shoulders sagging. Having said her peace Mia started to walk away but turned back to look at Charlie to deliver one final blow.

'In case you thought otherwise I am doing absolutely fine without you. So, you can run back to Alice and tell her the same thing that I am going to tell you. Leave me the hell alone.' She spun around and stalked back to the group without looking back. Again, I felt torn. Half of me wanted to crawl out of my body and run back to Charlie and reassure him that it wasn't me who had said any of the words that had just come out of my mouth and the other half of me felt a little validated by what Mia had said to him.

Both he and Gus had left me heartbroken and alone with their joint ultimatums. I knew it was mostly my fault – me and my indecisive heart – and I knew that they deserved for me to make my mind up and not lead them both on, but I couldn't help but wonder if they hadn't pushed me away whether I would be trapped in my current situation.

Of one thing I felt certain: if Charlie hadn't moved on before now then he absolutely would move on after that conversation and I wasn't sure if my heart would handle it when I saw him, over at his house, in his room or at school with someone else.

Charlie obviously relayed the encounter back to Alice because the same afternoon she came to speak to me too.

'Sophie?' I heard her quiet voice behind me. She cleared her throat, mustering up some confidence. 'I need to talk to you.'

'About what in particular?' Mia asked, in a singsong voice, not letting her off easily.

'About you know what!' she looked at me meaningfully and then around at the group that I was sitting with.

'You can say it, we are all friends here,' Mia's voice sounded menacing, and she put on a sarcastic smile which Alice couldn't help but notice. She shook her head at me obviously trying to send me messages by the look on her face. I was reading them loud and clear, but Mia was enjoying her discomfort and had no intention of making it easy for her, as she had done for Charlie.

'Come on Sophie, why are you being so difficult? Why are you acting so weird and why are you missing all of your classes? The teachers have been asking me where you are, and I have been making up excuses, but I can't keep covering for you anymore.' Alice clearly had lost all patience and was doing her best to convince me to get back on the straight and narrow, but Mia had no doubt had the same discussion and similar scoldings many times before from teachers, well-meaning friends and probably her parents and she barely flinched. I felt my eyes narrow as Mia considered her response.

'You know what Alice. No one asked you to cover for me so why don't you go and stick your nosy nose somewhere where it is wanted.'

'But ...' Alice stopped and took one more look at me, as if pleading with me to reconsider, but of course I couldn't because it wasn't me calling the shots in my own body, it was Mia, and she wasn't going to do anything that would jeopardize her total control over me. After a long drawn-out minute she shook her head and walked away to jeers from my other slacker schoolmates.

Inside my body I was trying everything to show Alice that it wasn't me. In that moment, as Alice walked away, I hated Mia more than anyone I had ever disliked in my entire life. She was destroying my life piece-by-piece, person-by-person. I knew, without a doubt that even if Mia ever did leave me, she had done irreparable damage to almost all of my relationships. My parents were none the wiser so far, but Charlie and Alice had clearly reached breaking point. I knew I would probably act the same in their shoes, but it hurt a little to think that they believed that I would do a complete 180 and change so much in such a short space of time and with absolutely no reason. I wondered what they would put my character swing down to. More than likely it would be the aftershock of my life and death experience with Marcel or breaking up with Gus or Charlie, or all of the above. I was so frustrated I wanted to scream and cry and if Mia was still alive, kill her.

After watching Alice walk away without looking back Mia sat back down next to Dan and he put his arm around my shoulder a little too familiarly and pulled me into him.

'Don't worry Soph! You don't need her anymore, you have us!'

The thought of this made me even sadder. My sadness may have had an effect on Mia because the next thing I knew she had shrugged off his arm and turned to look at him seriously.

'Dan, what do you remember about Mia?'

'Mia?' he asked surprised at the change of topic. 'Why do you ask?'

'Well … I didn't know her that long before she died. But she seemed like a really great person,' she said, sounding bereft. I wondered what she was fishing for.

'Oh yeah, she was alright.' He took a long drag from his smoke and looked into the clouds that were approaching from the north.

Mia seemed irritated by the response, 'Alright?' she asked in a high-pitched voice, unable to mask her irritation. 'I thought she was a friend of yours. She told me a lot of nice things about you.'

'Yeah, we were friends, but I guess when she hooked

up with Pete it was like I ceased to exist. Just like nothing else mattered apart from Pete. He is a bit like that I guess, like really demanding, but we were friends, and I felt a little kicked to the curb, you know.'

I was surprised by his emotional intelligence. I guess I was generalizing but I thought a stoner like him would have the emotional density of a plank of wood. He turned to look at me and observed Mia deep in thought. She must have been considering his feedback on her behavior and I thought again of how toxic this person had been in her life.

'I didn't see you at her funeral,' he said quietly when Mia said nothing in response to his revelations.

'Her funeral?' she repeated sounding distracted.

'Yes, they had a service for her at Saint Andrew's.'

'Oh yeah? I didn't know that there had been anything for her. I guess her parents organized that?'

'No, actually I think it may have been her social worker. I didn't see her parents there.'

Mia turned to look at him, eyes wide in surprise. I admit I was surprised too; why did she have a social worker and why weren't her own parents at her funeral?

'Her parents didn't attend. Really? Who was there?'

'Just a couple of us from school and the school chaplain. Oh, and there was this really old lady who lived in the house where Mia jumped off the roof.' He cleared his throat and backtracked after realizing how harsh that had sounded. 'I mean where she died.'

Poppy! I thought. She had been at Mia's funeral.

The revelations kept coming. I suddenly felt sorry for Mia. From Dan's description it sounded like there had been less than ten people at the service. No wonder she was so sad, misguided and needy. I wondered again about her parents. Why hadn't they been there? I thought about the people who would grieve if I died and I had to admit it was not a cast of thousands, but it would be more than the half a dozen that had attended Mia's service.

'Hey, are you free tonight?'

Mia tried to shake whatever depressing thoughts were going through her head and focused on Dan's question.

'Of course, I'm free every night.'

'Some of us are going to Frankie's bar around 11 pm to watch some of our friends who are in a band. They're really good.'

'Sure. Count me in!'

Mia got up from the group in a swift, sudden movement, surprising Dan who seemed to be edging closer and closer.

'I'll see you tonight. Meet you at the park near Milson Street around 10.30,' she declared, and without waiting for a response she turned and walked back towards the school. She went straight to the library, ignoring looks from curious teachers who passed her in the hall, and into the computer section that was tucked up in the back-left corner.

She lowered my bag to the ground and clicked on the internet search bar, typing in 'Mia Thompson'. Underneath several images for different Mia Thompsons, a link for an author by the same name and a dancer from the Sydney ballet company, there was a link to a local article that had covered her death. As soon as she clicked on the link an image appeared on the screen of a young girl with jet-black hair wearing a black T-shirt. She was smiling but her eyes had the same haunted sadness. Her big brown eyes seemed to have seen too much, they looked flat, unhappy. The transcript read like any other small-town paper that had been asked to feature a small piece on a local tragedy. They didn't mention the suicide but in small writing down the bottom of the article it included a phone number for a local helpline where you could speak to councilors if you needed assistance. Anyone reading would have come to the same conclusion – suicide.

Underneath the call center details there was the name of a funeral company and the time and date of the small service that Dan must have been talking about. Mia wrote down the phone number and the other details and left the library to use my phone to call them.

A kindly-sounding woman called Rita answered the phone on the second ring. I wondered at the sort of calls she would have to deal with on a daily basis and built an image in my mind of an old, greying woman who had seen people on their worst days, dealing with the death of loved ones, and having to do her best to remain upbeat. The voice on the other end of the line, helpfully answering a barrage of questions from Mia, would never have suspected that the person she was really speaking to was, in fact, one of the dead people she had buried. I wondered if

Rita believed in ghosts, or if she had ever seen one. Would ghosts stick around funeral homes? I'm not sure why but I kind of doubted it.

'I wanted to see if you kept a register of guests that had attended each service,' Mia asked in a rushed voice, like she had to get the question out before Rita hung up the phone.

'Well yes, we always have a guest book. But it is up to the attendees if they want to sign it. Not everyone does you see. Some guests are so overwhelmed by their grief they don't even think about signing the book.'

'Of course. So, um, can you tell me if there was a guest book for Miss Mia Thompson's service. And if there was, are you able to tell me who signed the book.'

'Are you family dear?' I could feel the hand that was holding the phone tense and Mia took a deep breath and then let it out.

'Actually, I'm a lawyer. I'm the executor of Miss Thompson's estate and I wanted to get in touch with some of her friends that attended as she included a clause in her will that requires me to distribute some of her remaining worldly possessions specifically to those of her friends and family that attended the funeral. I wasn't told about the service as Mia's mother and father didn't attend.' Mia had lowered my voice and tried to sound official, but I was certain Rita was not going to buy it.

'Oh well in that case, just wait one moment please.' I could hear Rita working her way through a filing cabinet and a moment later she came back on the phone.

'Let's see now ...' there was a long pause as Mia held her breath. 'Yes, here it is. Who signed the book? I can see Dan Milton, James Harper, Elizabeth Anderson, who I think is a social worker and a Mrs Poppy Farrell.' She paused and I could hear the sound of her flicking through more pages and obviously finding no more names.

'Oh dear,' she said, sounding bereft and surprised. 'I wonder why there were only four people. Hang on a minute ... Mia ... Mia ... yes, I remember that service, it was so sad. I wondered whether her parents had also passed away because neither of them attended the service, but I think the old lady must have been her grandmother. Always nice to have some family in attendance isn't it.' Rita paused her barrage of verbal diarrhea and waited for Mia to say something to validate her comment, but Mia said nothing. I wondered what she was thinking. Maybe her parents were unwell and couldn't make it or maybe they were out of the country and couldn't get back in time. But all of the possible reasons I came up with sounded hollow and unlikely even in my mind. I wondered what excuses Mia had come up with and whether they made her feel better or worse. I knew with all of my heart that the only thing that would stop my parents from attending my funeral would be their own death.

'Hello? Ma'am? Are you still on the line?' Rita's cheerful voice broke into my thoughts and Mia's.

'What? Oh sorry, yes, I suppose that's right. Thank you so much for your assistance. I will make sure

I recommend your service for other clients,' Mia said in a vague, empty voice.

'Well, that is lovely, thank you so much for …' I heard Rita's voice cut off abruptly as Mia ended the call.

CHAPTER

22

After dinner that night Mia told my parents that she wasn't feeling very well and was going to bed early, before sneaking out of the house. She met Dan and the others halfway between the bar and my house. She obviously didn't want them knowing where I lived in case they knew it had been the house where she died.

She had gone to the local thrift store on the way home and picked up some second-hand ripped jeans, a white vintage Metallica concert T-shirt and a black leather jacket. She had stashed her new clothes and makeup in the glasshouse and once again had changed out of my pajamas before leaving out the back of the house and walking down along the beach. When she was out of range of the house, she had pulled out a mirror and the makeup and pulled my hair out of the messy bun she had put it in and then braided it so that it fell down onto my left shoulder. Mia was a bit of a psychopath, a poor student and from the sounds of it an average friend but she was really very good at putting together an outfit and makeup. She could be a stylist, I thought before remembering that she was no longer alive. I knew that

I looked good when we joined the group walking to the bar.

When Mia appeared in front of Dan out of the shadows, he had taken in my new look appreciatively, which made me feel a little uncomfortable. I was certain that Mia was not interested in him, but she didn't seem concerned by the ogling. The band we were going to see must be popular, I thought, when we arrived and there was a queue to get into the bar. I eyed the bouncer nervously but when we got to the front of the line, he exchanged a friendly fist bump with Dan and another guy we were with and the group walked in without a single person pulling out any kind of ID, real or otherwise.

Dan and Toby went to the bar to get drinks and Mia found a spot to stand, near the stage with Toby's girlfriend Kai.

'Have you seen this band before?' Mia asked Kai, conversationally.

'Oh yeah, they're awesome.'

'It looks like it,' Mia said gesturing to the room, which was packed. I noticed a group of girls standing at the front of the stage dressed in skimpy outfits like they were heading out to a nightclub not to a bar to watch an indie band.

'They look a little overdressed – or should I say underdressed,' Mia snorted. Kai looked up from her phone.

'Ha! Yeah, they would be here for the drummer,' Kai said laughing.

'Oh, is there a bit of eye candy in the band?'

'Yeah, he's really nice too. He's a friend of ours. His name is …'

The crowd started cheering as the band walked out making it hard to hear what Kai was saying. Mia was momentarily distracted by Dan and Toby who rejoined the group, handing her a drink that looked like a long island iced tea and tasted just as potent.

'WHAT WAS HIS NAME?' Mia yelled to Kai, straining hard again to hear her response.

'JACK!' she yelled back, nodding to the stage and my head snapped up as Mia searched for the drummer.

The lead singer was a really attractive girl with jet-black hair that matched her black outfit and tattoos. She was standing in the middle of the stage, talking to her guitarist who was strumming cords on his guitar. Mia craned her neck to see past them but her vision was still blocked until the singer pulled back enough that Mia could get a glimpse of the drummer's arm.

It was enough to confirm that the person holding the sticks was the Jack who was living in the party house with slimy Pete, Mia's ex-boyfriend. The tattoos moved as the hands holding the drumsticks began expertly beating out a tune. Mia turned to glance at the scantily clad women in the front row cheering enthusiastically for Jack and I felt my eyes roll. *Don't like the competition?* I teased Mia, and she quickly shifted her view back to the stage. The singer had moved to one side of the stage and the guitarist to the other so that there was now an uninterrupted view of the drummer.

Even I had to admit Jack looked extremely attractive sitting behind the drum kit, a plain black T-shirt hugging his muscles, and female groupies aside, the band seemed to have a loyal following in the bar. The crowd knew the words and were singing along.

Part way through the second song Jack glanced up and looked directly at me. I felt my heart flutter in my chest and Mia's intake of breath. Mia raised her glass to him in greeting. He looked surprised to see me and nodded his head back. Then he spotted who I was standing with and I had the distinct feeling he didn't approve of me being there with Dan. I noticed a couple of the girls from the front of the stage looking around to see who he was looking at. He finished the song still staring intently in my direction. As the song finished, he turned his attention back to the singer who was instructing them on the next song.

After an hour and a half and a couple of encores they finished their set and the band members dispersed through the crowd to speak to friends. Jack spoke to a couple of guys near the bar before walking obliviously past a couple of his female fans to make his way to our group.

'Awesome set Jack,' Kai said giving him a friendly peck on the side of the cheek. 'Thanks Kai,' he said, but he was looking at me and asked, 'What did you think Sophie?'

'Very unexpected.'

'Unexpected? That doesn't feel like a compliment.'

'No, it was great. You have a talent. Like I said the other night. Everyone has something that they are hiding, like your musical abilities.'

Mia took a deep drink from the long island iced tea and I felt myself feeling a little lightheaded. Kai and Toby headed to the bar to buy more drinks and I was left standing in an awkward triangle with Dan and Jack. Mia clearly wanted Dan to leave, Dan clearly wanted Jack to leave, and I had no idea what Jack wanted but he didn't seem to be interested in leaving the conversation.

Even though subtlety was clearly not a strength of Mia's, Dan was not going to budge and the conversation revolved awkwardly around Jack asking Mia a question and Mia enthusiastically answering and asking him a question back, only to have Dan chip in with his thoughts unprompted and unwelcomed. Finally, Jack excused himself. Mia immediately volunteered to walk back to his house with him. He smiled and shook his head, 'No need thanks Sophie, I drove here.'

'Oh, OK,' she sounded disappointed, but Dan looked undeterred. Dan went to speak, most likely to offer to take me home, but Jack got in before him.

'Can I give you a lift somewhere?'

'Absolutely,' Mia said at the same time as Dan said, 'That would be great.'

Jack looked from me to Dan and then back at me as he said, 'Actually I only have room for one person, sorry.'

Before Dan could bow out graciously Mia immediately pitched in with a rude, 'Well, I guess I'll see you at school tomorrow then Dan.' She waved goodbye to Kai and Toby and followed Jack out to the car park. I was relieved that she didn't look behind her because I didn't want to see Dan's reaction to Mia's brutal rejection.

As Mia pulled her jacket on, she looked around the car park for Jack's car but then realized he wasn't following her. She turned around to see him flipping the brake up on a black motorcycle and holding a helmet out to her to put on. *Of course, he drives a motorcycle,* I thought to myself. *Where did this guy come from?* He pulled on a leather jacket and started up the bike. The engine revved and Jack looked up at me expectantly, waiting to see whether I was game to get on.

Of course, Mia was. She was the least risk-averse person I had ever met. It was almost like she was drawn to anything within a 10-mile radius that was likely to kill me. She threw her leg over the back of the bike and wrapped her arms around Jack's midsection. My arms went around him and one of his hands momentarily went from the handlebars to touch my fingers. As our hands touched, I felt a shiver run down my back and Mia wrapped her arms tighter around him. His hand went back to the handlebar and he took off, throwing some of the dirt and pebbles that were sitting on the asphalt.

Instead of driving to Jack's we drove around for about half an hour and ended up on Coopers Beach. Jack helped me climb off the bike and then Mia followed him down to one of the oversized lifeguard viewing seats. We climbed up and sat down next to each other, listening to the sound of the water lapping across the sand. Both Mia and Jack seemed happy to sit together without speaking. After a while I wondered whether Jack had fallen asleep but when Mia glanced over his eyes were open and he was looking out at the dark water. He closed his eyes when she looked at him and they sat there absorbing the calm night.

Mia was the one to break the silence. 'It's so peaceful down here. Can I ask you a personal question? What are you thinking about over there?'

Jack opened his eyes and smiled, the sides of his eyes crinkled up like paper and he looked out again at the darkness of the water.

'Nothing actually. I come here every night after we've played a gig. I'm always on such a high and the sound of the water calms me down.' He looked up towards the stars, taking them in for a minute then closed his eyes again and Mia did the same. Jack was next to fill the silence and it gave me a bit of insight into what he had been thinking about.

'Can I ask you a personal question?'

'Sure,' Mia answered, my eyes remaining tightly closed.

'Why are you hanging around with Dan?'

My eyes opened in surprise. 'Why? Are you jealous?'

'No, you just seem like a really smart girl and to be honest he's a bit of a loser. Did you know that he's been arrested in the past for dealing drugs?' His eyes bore into mine like he was trying to communicate something important but couldn't say it out loud. It was a little disarming and Mia obviously felt it too because she shifted her body so that my knees were pulled up against my chest.

'If you don't approve of any of the stuff that goes on

211

at that house why do you live there?' Mia asked defensively.

'Good question,' he said staring again into the dark water, not providing any further insight.

'And how come you don't drink?' Mia continued to probe.

He dodged any further interrogation by pulling off his shoes, jeans and T-shirt and climbing down to the bottom of the lifeguard station, hanging the clothes up on the side, and then turned around and held his hand out for me. Mia stubbornly refused to climb down until he answered one of her questions. I was sure it was hard for her to resist given he was standing in front of her in nothing but his underwear. The muscles in his upper torso rippled as he held his arm up and Mia examined his tattoos. His left shoulder was dominated by a large eagle that curved over his bicep. On his right pec I could see a sun that had been partly covered, perhaps at a later stage, by an overlapping moon and further down his chest, were some words in Sanskrit that I couldn't read.

I wondered about the meaning of the words as they eyed each other off, seeing who would last the longest in their standoff, but cracks were beginning to show on both sides. She was trying not to smile and failing, and he took that as an invitation to try to remove my shoes and laughed when Mia squealed and pulled my feet out of his reach, waiting for him to answer the question.

'Come for a swim with me and I will answer a question,' he conceded with a sigh, holding his hand out to me again.

Mia removed my shoes and socks, stripping down to my underwear, and then climbed down to the bottom of the seat and waited expectantly, but Jack wasn't spilling the beans just yet. He took my hand and led Mia towards the water. As soon as my feet touched the cool water Mia let out a shocked squeal.

'Expecting it to be warmer?' Jack laughed, tugging my hand and pulling her out further. The water lapped up to my stomach and I felt Mia's intake of breath, but although I felt freezing, I could tell that Mia was not going to let Jack see any more signs of weakness.

He let go of my hand and splashed a little bit of water at me. Mia squealed again and pushed him into the deeper water. He pretended to fall backwards, disappearing under the surface. The water went still around my legs and Mia looked all around for where Jack had gone. After a minute even I was starting to get concerned. Two full minutes later I felt hands wrap around my waist from behind. Mia let out a loud scream as Jack pulled me towards him.

'Not funny!' Mia gasped, smacking him on his arm as goosebumps rose from the slight breeze in the night air hitting my arms where the cold water had just been.

Jack stifled his laughter and raised his right hand in the air. 'I promise I won't do it again. Scout's honor!' He smiled and dodged another one of Mia's playful swats.

'How did you even do that?' Mia asked, looking around at the cold, dark water, obviously wondering where he had managed to hide for two minutes.

'I trained to be a free diver. You have to be able to hold your breath for up to ten minutes.'

'How is that even physically possible and why would anyone want to hold their breath under water for ten minutes?' Mia asked, astonished.

'The ocean is so calm and peaceful. The creatures in it are so beautiful and you just have this sensation that you can't have on land. Weightlessness, freedom. I know it sounds ridiculous, right?'

Jack turned to look at me and I wanted to be able to glide under the water like a fish and feel the sensation of being free. I wondered whether Mia would make some kind of sarcastic remark, but she was clearly caught up in his spell too and managed to stammer out, 'Actually it sounds kind of incredible. Can you teach me how to free dive?'

He smiled at me and nodded his head.

Our bodies moved closer together in the water as we moved out deeper and Mia reached out to grab a hold of his arm to help her stay afloat. I wondered whether Jack would try to kiss Mia, but she began to shiver in response to the cold water. He took my hand off his body and pulled it around his neck so that I was lying across his back and towed me back into shore. We got out of the water and ran up the beach to our clothes.

'You are shaking like a leaf,' he said, rubbing his hands up and down my arms. 'I better get you home before you die of pneumonia.' Interesting choice of words, I thought as Mia pulled off my wet bra, standing there topless as Jack picked up our clothes. He cleared his throat awkwardly, averting his eyes as he sifted through the pile of clothes, dropping some of them as he tried to find a T-shirt for me to put on. I wished I could crawl into a hole and hide.

He passed over the dry T-shirt, which Mia pulled on, leaving the wet bottoms on and throwing the jeans on over the top. Jack tugged on his own clothes and then wrapped his hoodie around my shoulders and pulled me in to him, rubbing the sides of my body again to warm me up. Again, I wondered if he was going to kiss me, but Mia looked down at my feet and let out a sigh as she wiggled my toes in the sand. Jack glanced down curiously at my feet to gauge what it was that had Mia looking so happy.

'Um, what are you doing?' he asked in amusement.

'How great does the sand feel beneath your toes! I missed this.'

'What do you mean you missed it? We live next to some of the best beaches on the east coast! When have you had an opportunity to miss it?'

'Not that long ago I … was sick. And I wasn't able to get out and feel the sand for over a year. It's amazing the small things you appreciate once they're taken away.'

Jack nodded his head and then looked up at the stars. 'You asked me before why I don't drink.'

'Yes,' Mia said expectantly.

'I was in a car accident. The person who was behind the wheel of the car that ran into me was drunk.' In the light of the moon I could see Jack's eyes had welled up a little. Mia reached over to touch his arm to comfort him.

'I don't remember what happened, but I was told later that he drove through a red light. The next thing I knew I woke up in the hospital and was informed that I was paralyzed. I spent months learning to walk again. I can't complain though. At least I can walk now. The driver of the other car died on impact. The female passenger in his car is still in a wheelchair. And my girlfriend died.'

'The girl in the photo?' Mia asked, remembering the photo of the pretty girl she had picked up in his room.

Mia reached out to take Jack's hand. He turned to me, his eyes refocusing on my face, back in the present.

'All that training to save lives and I couldn't do anything to save her. That was three years ago.' He looked so broken, like it had only just happened. 'So that's why I don't drink.' He shrugged his shoulders like he was trying to shrug off his sadness.

We walked back to his motorbike, Jack's warm hand in mine.

'Where can I take you?' Jack asked, climbing onto the bike and handing me the helmet. Mia asked him to drop her off at the park around the block from my house. He asked if she was sure but backed off when she nodded. When we reached the park, Mia waited until Jack had left to walk back to my house and climb up to my room through the secret passage.

CHAPTER

23

Two nights later Mia headed back to Pete and Jack's party house. I had yet to figure out who else lived in the house as every time I had gone into one of the other rooms, accidentally or otherwise, there had been a different couple fooling around in the bedrooms.

As soon as we arrived, I could tell Mia was looking around for one person in particular. She stood and spoke to Kai for a while, but it seemed like she was only listening to half of what was being said and occasionally replying with 'Really?' or 'Oh, right'. Kai didn't seem to notice; I think she may have had too much to drink and was rambling. As soon as another person wandered up to the two of them Mia walked off in the middle of one of Kai's monologues, leaving the other person to listen to the rest. She moved from room to room, ignoring Dan's calls when he spotted her, and Pete leering at her as she walked past him. It had been a week since she had tried to attack Pete and it seemed like maybe Dan was right. He definitely seemed to remember me but alternated between eying me suggestively and ignoring me.

Just when I thought that Mia was going to give

up and leave, Jack walked through the front door. Mia grabbed a beer and made a beeline for him but before she got halfway across the room, she spotted a girl trailing behind him, touching the back of his grey hooded sweater.

She was tall and slender, with cascading shiny blonde hair hanging in perfect loose waves like she had walked off the set of a shampoo commercial. She was wearing a strapless dress with a cardigan and heels, which accentuated her tall, willowy frame. In short, she was very attractive, and it seemed like she was at the house with Jack, as his date. Mia stopped dead in her tracks, and I felt my mouth drop open as Mia looked at Jack in confusion and then back at the girl. I thought about being at the beach the other night and I was as surprised as she seemed to be, given the special moment they had shared. Maybe I got the wrong idea, but he had seemed different from the others.

Before Mia could recover her composure Jack noticed her standing in the middle of the room. He smiled at Mia and opened his mouth to say something but before he had a chance Mia turned on her heel, stalking through the kitchen, out the back door and into the garden. I could feel the nerves start to kick in and wondered what Mia would do in the face of rejection given she seemed like a very volatile person.

She stood on the grass as still as a statue, taking deep breaths in the cool evening air, looking at the sky to help fight back the tears that were threatening to spill. I heard the back door to the house open and I hoped that it was just a random person from the party walking outside for a smoke.

'Sophie.' *No such luck*, I thought as I recognized Jack's voice. 'What are you doing out here?'

Mia took a couple of deeper breaths before she turned around to look at Jack. His face was wary, like he was approaching the cave of a sleeping bear.

'Enjoying the fresh air,' Mia said sarcastically.

'OK,' he said slowly, still assessing her mood.

'What are *you* doing out here?'

'Checking to see if you're alright,' he said tentatively. 'You were there one minute and gone the next.'

'Why wouldn't I be alright?' she shot back aggressively, giving her true feelings away.

He shrugged his shoulders.

'OK well thanks for checking on me. Better run along back to that blonde stick insect before she follows one of your stoner housemates into one of their bedrooms.'

He frowned towards the house and started walking back towards the party. Mia turned back to look up at the sky, again fighting back tears.

'Sophie …' His voice sounded sad and I wondered what he was thinking.

'What?' Mia said betraying some of the emotion in my wavy voice and then cleared her throat. 'What?' she repeated, sounding more confident and abrupt.

He seemed to be deciding whether to say something or not. After a couple of minutes, I wondered if he had gone back into the house and I just hadn't heard him.

Mia's focus on the sky seemed to waver and I thought she might have turned around to check but then we heard him sigh.

'Never mind,' he said softly.

I heard the back door open and close, and Mia burst into tears. I actually felt sorry for her. *Let's go home Mia*, I thought, and for once she didn't do the opposite just to spite me.

At home Mia headed back to my room through the secret passageway so that she wouldn't be detected. My parents still seemed to be none the wiser even though Milo was still not sleeping in my room. Again, I felt the loneliness of Gus's absence. Mia and I both went to sleep feeling the overwhelming sensation of rejection.

CHAPTER

24

I wondered whether Mia would avoid Pete's house after seeing Jack with the other girl but when Dan told her about a party that Thursday night she went shopping for another outfit. This one, I was not so keen on. The top was a plunging black singlet top with thick straps that dipped down between my breasts pared with a short black skirt that could have doubled as a tube top. It was skimpy and left absolutely nothing to the imagination. She completed the look with some knee-high black boots and a fraction too much makeup, my hair out and flowing over my shoulders.

Not very subtle Mia! I thought, looking at myself in my reflection in the mirror and feeling absolutely horrified. All of the other clothes she had picked out had not really been my style but at least they hadn't made me look like one of the girls I'd seen at the front of Jack's concert.

'Don't worry Sophie, you can pull it off,' she sneered into the mirror and slipped out of the house via the secret passageways.

As soon as we arrived at the party Mia seemed content that her clothing selection was having the desired effect. Every guy in the house turned to look at her and more than one of them offered to fetch her a drink, which she happily accepted and quickly consumed – I could only imagine for a little Dutch courage when she saw Jack, but he was nowhere to be seen.

An hour and a half and too many drinks later I spotted Jack enter the room, the same blonde woman in tow. Uh oh! I thought to myself. Mia's carefully created demeanor slipped momentarily, and she took both of the shots that Dan had just offered her in the space of fifteen seconds.

Jack noticed me immediately, his eyes just about falling out of his head when he took in my outfit. I felt like his expression was equal parts desire and disapproval and he came straight over to me, pulling off his hoodie as he got closer.

'Sophie,' he said, a note of parent-like disapproval in his voice.

'Jack,' Mia said sarcastically, mirroring his tone.

'Put this on,' he said holding the sweater out for Mia to take. She threw back my head and laughed.

'Who are you? My mother?' she slapped his hand away and then pushed past him, walking into the room where the music was playing. She turned it up and climbed up onto the dining table where she started to do what could only be described as pole dancing without the pole. Pete, who was sitting on one of the couches in the same room pushed his girlfriend off his lap as he got up to stand around the table and cheer with the rest of the crowd that had started to gather. His girlfriend, who I had discovered was called Sasha, looking extremely irritated, walked over to one of the other guys in the room who had joined in cheering. She talked into the big guy's ear and angrily gestured towards me.

Jack stood leaning against the doorframe, just inside the room, muscled arms crossed across his body. His girlfriend walked up behind him, glanced at me, and then whispered something in his ear. He nodded, not taking his eyes off me, and she disappeared out of the room. Mia noticed this exchange and obviously decided she had nothing left to lose.

She started pulling off the singlet top and the crowd cheered louder. A couple of the other girls also climbed up onto the table and began dancing next to me. I was relieved that I was no longer the only person on the table making a spectacle, but it didn't help that Mia seemed to be the only one taking her clothes off. I was horrified that this room of complete strangers was potentially going to see me completely naked, and I mentally begged Mia to cut it out.

The next minute seemed to go in slow motion, but it probably didn't feel like that to anyone else in the room. I noticed Pete's leering face as he reached out and touched my leg and then glanced up and saw his girlfriend Sasha who looked livid behind him, Mia tried to push his hand away but the several shots that she had fed into my alcohol-intolerant body had just clicked in and I felt my body stumble and then fall towards the floor. My eyes closed before I could feel the weight of my body hit the carpet. I was falling, falling, falling but then I felt my body bouncing. Strong warm arms were carrying me upstairs and then tucking me into a bed.

The last thing I saw before my eyes closed again and I passed out was Jack's face looking at me with a concerned expression.

'What am I going to do with you Sophie?' he sighed.

'That's easy. Kiss me,' Mia said with a drunken pout. My eyes closed again, and I wasn't sure whether because she thought she was about to kiss Jack or because she was exhausted, and they didn't open again until I felt the morning sun on my face.

I heard the whistling of the birds and then felt the dryness of my mouth. It took me a minute to realize that I was in Jack's bedroom, in his bed wearing a T-shirt that was not mine and a pair of boxer shorts, my underwear thankfully still on underneath. I moaned, rolled over and lay there for several minutes, my head throbbing and my vision blurry as I tried to piece together what happened the night before.

I had flashbacks to Mia doing shots, sculling beers and finally, almost getting naked in front of a room full of cheering people, and my stomach lurched. I pushed myself up and ran to find the bathroom. It wasn't until after I had been sick in the toilet and was in the process of throwing cold water on my face that I realized I was in full control of my body. Me, not Mia, and I quickly look around the room that I was standing in, to see whether she was there with me but there was no one but my own ghostly-looking reflection.

I tiptoed out of the bathroom and walked downstairs, weaving my way through passed out people and discarded cups and bottles. In the lounge room I found myself a piece of paper and a pen and hastily scribbled out a note:

Jack, please don't ask me to explain and please never mention this note to me but you need to find Alice Duncan. Tell her that the clock tower at Sophie's house was not empty — the ghost of Mia Thompson was in there and has taken control of her body. I know this sounds crazy but PLEASE just talk to Alice.

I urgently need your help,

XO Sophie

I slipped back upstairs into Jack's room. Looking around for Mia I spotted her translucent form still lying on the bed where I had been just minutes before. After frantically looking around the room for the longest ten seconds of my life I decided on sticking the note inside one of Jack's books and then placed the book on the seat of his desk, hoping that he would try to sit on the seat and notice it out of place. Mia was still out as I lay back down on the bed and closed my eyes willing my mind to block out what I had just done but at the same time hoping that Jack would find my message ASAP.

During the past couple of days, I had the feeling that unless Mia was deliberately listening in to my thoughts or I was screaming them at her she tended to be so lost in her own thoughts that she had, to a certain extent, stopped hearing mine anyway.

Slowly I sensed Mia was coming to and I kept my

eyes firmly closed. I heard her gasp as it dawned on her that she had disengaged from my body and then I felt the familiar sensation of ice water running through my veins as she once again took control.

She started to push herself up to have a look around the room, possibly to make sure I hadn't been up before her, but almost at the same time the door handle turned and Jack's head appeared around the doorframe.

'Hey,' he said gently, coming into the room and closing the door behind him. I noticed he was holding a tray with some orange juice, ibuprofen and two pieces of toast. He placed the tray on the bed and sat down next to it.

'Hey yourself,' Mia said warily, pushing Jack's pillow up against the wall and leaning up against it.

I wondered whether Mia was embarrassed about her behavior the night before, and almost in answer to my thoughts she lowered her gaze to a loose thread on the duvet cover and started picking it with her fingers.

'I'm really sorry about last night, and the night before,' she said sheepishly. 'Did you and your girlfriend have to sleep somewhere else?'

'Excuse me?' he asked, sounding confused.

Mia looked up at him, also confused, 'You and your girlfriend – did you have to sleep somewhere else because I was sleeping in your bed?'

A smile crept across his face and I heard him chuckle quietly under his breath. 'Ohhhh, my girlfriend. You mean Abbey, the girl who has been here with me the past couple of nights?'

Mia nodded, still confused, as was I, but Jack was laughing in earnest now, like Mia had told a hilarious joke. He noticed the look of complete bewilderment and mild irritation on her face and stopped laughing.

'Last time I checked incest was illegal in the state of New York. She's not my girlfriend. She's my sister. I would have introduced you the other night but you left before I had a chance and then last night she was feeling a little bit jetlagged so around the time that you decided to give your impromptu striptease she headed back to her hotel to sleep. I slept on the couch downstairs.'

'Your sister,' Mia repeated with a wry smile and then frowned a little. 'I'm not sure she is going to want to meet me after last night.'

'I'm sure she has seen worse,' he said, turning away momentarily before turning back to me. 'Have something to eat,' he said gesturing towards the tray of food.

Mia swallowed the ibuprofen with a sip of orange juice and then started to nibble gingerly on the toast.

'Did I fall off the dining table? I seem to remember the falling part but not the crash landing.'

Jack walked to the cupboard, pulled off the T-shirt that he had slept in and grabbed a fresh long-sleeved top out of the cupboard. I watched the ripple of the muscles on his back and as he turned to look at me, I caught sight of a tattoo on his chest that I hadn't noticed before, a blue badge with some Roman numerals. Mia dragged her eyes away from his toned abs to look at his face. Fortunately, he hadn't realized that Mia was gawking at his body or, if he did, he wasn't giving anything away. He pulled on a fresh pair of jeans and some socks and came back to sit on the bed next to me.

'I caught you before you could hit the deck,' he said with a serious expression and Mia buried her face in one of the pillows. After taking several breaths I felt Jack gently tugging the pillow away. Mia looked everywhere apart from Jack's eyes.

'I'd better head off, I guess. You don't happen to know where my clothes are do you?' Mia asked, searching the bedroom for black fabric. Her eyes passed over the desk chair but didn't pause. Jack climbed off the bed again and pulled out a pair of black running leggings and a sweater that looked like it could have been his but had shrunk in the wash.

'I think it would be better if you wore these,' he said, holding back his laughter. 'You may receive a little too much unwanted attention in the clothes you were wearing last night.' He tried and failed to make his face look serious when he noticed that Mia was mildly irritated with his comment.

'I mean, you could catch a cold with the lack of fabric and what-not,' he continued teasing. Mia grabbed the clothing that he was holding out and without saying a word she pulled off the T-shirt that I had been sleeping in and the boxer shorts. She took her time to redress in the jumper and leggings while Jack tried and failed to look away, taking in my body in just my underwear.

Mia enjoyed him watching and she was obviously

delighted that Jack had clarified that the beautiful woman who had been around him for the past couple of days was not, in fact, his girlfriend but his sister. She slowly, deliberately pulled on the running pants and then, keeping eye contact with Jack she pulled on the sweatshirt one sleeve at a time and then tugged it over my head.

I was absolutely positive that Jack was about to make a move and from the sensations going through my body, Mia was also sure of it. I could see the desire in his eyes as he stood up but instead of coming over, he walked to sit in front of me on the corner of his bed, taking my hand in his.

'I need to talk to you Sophie.'

'About what?' Mia and I both knew this conversation had to be going only one way, but based on how close Jack and Mia had become I had to admit I was more than a little bit surprised; relieved but also surprised. I could tell he was really interested but his voice and his body were saying something else at the moment.

'I don't think you should come here anymore,' he said quietly, sounding sad.

'*What?*' Mia pulled my hand out of his and she took a step back, studying his face. 'It's because of last night, isn't it? Are you embarrassed by me? Is that it?'

'No, nothing like that. I like you. *Really* like you. A little too much. But I think you already know that. I don't want to upset you.'

She moved back towards him, holding his face, and studied him. His arms went automatically around my

229

body, and I could feel the warmth, but he was still holding me at a slight distance.

'Why are you pushing me away then? You're hiding something, I can tell.'

He stood up and walked towards the windows. When he spoke, his voice came out sounding strangled. 'You aren't safe here. The people that are here, that come to the house for the parties. I'm worried that one of them is going to hurt you.'

Mia was not convinced. She must have suffered a lot of rejection when she was alive because her walls went up immediately. She grabbed whatever she could find from her skimpy outfit the night before and stalked towards the door. At the doorway to his bedroom, she paused for a minute and turned back to look at him.

'You're hiding something from me. I don't know what it is, but I have friends here and I won't stay away just because you don't want me to discover whatever little secret it is that you're hiding.' And with that she turned and walked out the door.

By the time we arrived home, it was almost 8.30 am and there was no way someone was not going to notice Mia arriving at that time of day.

'Sophie?'

Finally! I thought to myself, she has been caught out! My parents had instilled a sense of self-respect and discipline in me that Mia had totally disregarded, going out every night and stealing back into my room in the middle of the night. But at last she was going to be caught out in the act. I almost wished she had been wearing the horrible outfit from the night before but from the look on my mother's face it didn't matter.

'Where have you been young lady?'

'What do you mean? I went for a run,' Mia said, gesturing to my clothing.

Nice try Mia, I thought, but I haven't been running since my primary school decided to make the whole school do several laps of our block in Brooklyn as an annual cross-country event. I finished second last in my house and hadn't been running since. My parents had been standing at the finish line, waving their little blue house flag as I crossed the finish line. I sniggered internally at what my mom was going to say to Mia next.

'I was not talking about this morning Sophie.' Her arms crossed her body and her face was taut. I almost felt guilty even though I had absolutely no control over what Mia had done.

'I went into your bedroom in the middle of the night and you weren't there. Your bed hadn't been slept in and it was exactly the same this morning when I went in there.'

'Ohhhh, I thought you were talking about this morning,' she said slowly, buying herself time to come up with a story. 'Last night I was sleeping over at Allie's house. We were working on an assignment, and you know how it is, it got late and her mom practically insisted I stay over, just to be safe you know. I didn't think you would mind, so long as I was safe.'

'Allie? Do you mean Alice?'

'It's a bit of a nickname I gave her – you know, Al, Allie, Alice.'

My mom didn't look convinced but seemed to give her the benefit of the doubt. 'Well, if you are going to do that in future you need to call or at least leave a message with Clara.' She looked like she was going to say something else for a minute, but she didn't and then her phone beeped to notify her of an incoming message. Mia took the opportunity to go upstairs to get dressed for school. I couldn't believe she had gotten away with it.

She threw on some of my clothes and rushed out the door. In her haste to get out of the house Mia collided with Thomas on the front steps of the house.

'Excuse me,' she mumbled trying to get around him, but he stayed where he was standing. I could tell from his face that he had something on his mind. He cleared his throat and looked down at his hands.

'Hi Sophie. Gus asked me to um ... check up on you and see how you were going.'

Mia took a minute to consider her response, obviously wanting to avoid further interrogation or investigation from Gus that might uncover her secret.

'I'm going OK thanks. I'm not sure what Gus has said to you, but I think that we did the right thing taking a break from speaking to each other.'

He looked a little uncomfortable at being the messenger. When he didn't immediately walk away, I wondered whether he had more that Gus had asked him to pass on, but he was finding it difficult to say. Mia looked down at my watch and let out a sound of surprise.

'Is that the time! I really appreciate you checking in, but I have to get to school. Thanks again.' She ducked around one side of him and skipped over to my car, throwing her bag in the window and taking off down the driveway, leaving Thomas standing on the front step watching.

It seemed to be a day for confrontations. As soon as we reached school Alice was waiting for me at the top of the stairs that led to the entryway.

'Sophie!' she called out as Mia approached and tried to weave her way around Alice. I wondered as quietly as I could whether Jack might have found my note and acted on it already. Mia was distracted from trying her best to avoid Alice, so she didn't seem to overhear my thoughts.

Mia almost got past her, but Alice reached a hand out and grabbed my arm tightly, which made Mia turn around and glare at her.

'What? Is there something that is so important that you have to physically assault me?'

She looked taken aback for a minute, which helped confirm to me that Jack had not received my note or, even worse, if he had, he had decided not to act on it.

'I wouldn't need to physically assault you if you didn't deliberately ignore me.'

Mia simply stood there looking obstinate and saying nothing. Alice accepted that she was going to get nothing, looked out at the car park and, taking a deep breath, she seemed to steal herself.

'I apologize for taking up your precious wagging time, but your mom called me this morning and if you are going to use me as an alibi you might want to run it past me next time.'

My mom obviously hadn't bought Mia's story this morning. I wondered what she thought I had been up to. Mia was going to have to be a little more careful if she was going to keep up her nocturnal activities.

Mia was taken aback for a moment but quickly recovered. 'Duly noted. Anything else?' she asked dismissively, and I felt Alice's opportunity to tell me what she really thought of my recent behavior evaporating. For a moment I thought she might walk away but she steeled herself and shook her head.

'You've changed. I thought you wanted to help the ghosts in your house to find peace. I wanted to help you. We were a team,' she said, her voice pleading. My eyes rolled as Mia groaned.

'Find peace? Who cares about the ghosts in the house? They can stay locked up for all I care.' She raised her voice a little and gestured to the people milling around us. 'Unless you want me to tell the rest of the school what it is you get up to on the weekends, I suggest you leave me alone. Maybe I'll start by telling my new friends about your hocus pocus,' Mia threatened. Alice's face went red. She was mad.

'What are you doing Sophie? Skipping classes, hanging out with those losers, lying to your parents and your friends? It's like you're a different person.'

'Maybe I am a different person or maybe, just maybe, I was never the person you thought I was in the first place.'

'What about Charlie and Gus?' she asked me quietly, knowing that it was a sensitive topic.

'What about them?' Mia asked, becoming impatient and irritated by Alice's line of questions.

Great question Alice, I thought. I wondered whether she suspected just a little bit that I wasn't completely me in that moment. Mia had cavalierly brushed off these two people whom I had obviously adored since childhood with a shake of my head and a sneer on my face. I wondered if Mia could tell she had gone too far, but she wasn't about to backpedal.

'For the last time. Leave me alone. Find someone else to preach to. You, Charlie, Gus and anyone else who would like to tell me how to live my life can take a long walk off my short, shitty jetty.' And with that she turned on her heel and left Alice standing there with the same look on her face as she had moments earlier, suspecting that something was not quite right.

25

For the next five days Mia didn't go to any of the parties at Jack's house and even attended some of my classes. I wondered whether the change of heart was from my mom's reprimand, Alice's confrontation or Jack's perceived rejection.

Each day when I woke early in the morning and Mia was not in control of my body or hearing my thoughts, I wondered whether Jack had discovered my note and whether he would contact Alice or consider it all a little too strange and just brush it off as drunken ramblings.

I knew Mia couldn't stay away from the parties forever though. Jack was like a magnet and Mia couldn't resist being drawn to him. I was sure that his concern for her in the face of whatever trouble he perceived probably just made the whole thing more appealing.

Sure enough, the next weekend she threw on some of my clothes, which were probably a compromise from what she wanted to wear but a damn sight better than the revealing outfit she had worn the last time she went to the house.

When I arrived, Dan was extremely happy to see me and some of the people that Mia regularly spoke to made a point of welcoming her back. I knew that she would be wary of Jack's reaction to her being there and when he first spotted me, he did a double take. He was standing in the kitchen talking to two guys I hadn't seen before, and he immediately assessed what I was wearing. I wondered whether it was out of concern that I might have been scantily clad again just to be provocative or whether he was thinking about what I had written in the letter and he was studying me to see whether I was crazy. His eyes were telling me again that he was happy to see me, but he gave a little shake of his head, telling me that he was annoyed that Mia had ignored his request to stay away from the house. After a minute he turned back to the conversation he had been in without coming over to say hello.

Since Jack was playing hard to get Mia obviously decided to flirt with every other male at the party with a heartbeat. I could tell from his face that Jack was getting more and more irritated with each touch, smile and flirtatious giggle and Mia knew it too.

When Mia leaned in suggestively to Dan, who was in his usual state looking mildly stoned, he took the less than subtle hint that Mia was giving him and began stroking my face, running his hands down my arms, his face creeping closer and closer to mine. It seemed Jack had finally had enough of watching Mia flirting.

'Excuse us for a minute,' Jack said to Dan, taking my hand and leading me into the garage. He cornered me beside a storage cupboard and strategically placed one of his arms to block Mia's escape. Not that she looked like she was trying to get away. His face was a mix between anger and frustration.

'What are you doing Sophie? You are going to get yourself in trouble!'

'Oh, I didn't think you cared as long as I wasn't turning your little palace into a crime scene,' she fired back sarcastically, throwing his words from the first night we met back in his face.

He rolled his eyes at her but before he could respond we heard voices coming towards the garage. Jack quickly opened one of the cupboard doors and pushed me into it, climbing in next to me so we were jammed right up against one another. I wondered again whether he had contacted Alice. In the panic of climbing into the cupboard Mia didn't seem to hear my thoughts and I stopped thinking about the letter immediately in case she happened to tune in. He left the door slightly ajar, peering out to see who the unwelcome visitors were, the crack of light illuminating his face in the darkness.

'What the hell are you doing?' Mia protested but stopped when Jack put his hand over my mouth and gestured for her to be quiet. The warning look on his face alone would have stopped me, and I urged Mia to be quiet.

The voices became louder until I realized they were inside the garage where we were hiding. My eyes widened when Mia heard one of the people mention my name and she looked at Jack in alarm. He nodded his head, confirming that he had heard it too and put his hand to his mouth again to silence her.

'Why does she keep coming back here?' I recognized the whiny voice that belonged to Pete's girlfriend, Sasha.

I didn't recognize the male voice that responded but it was likely one of Pete's hangers-on. 'Don't worry about her Sash, she seems to be into everyone else apart from Pete. Didn't you see her just before latching onto Dan? He looked like he had hit the jackpot.' The guy snorted with laughter.

'Yes, but the problem, you idiot, is that Pete is taking notice of her, and I don't like it. I want her gone; do you get me? Like never coming back to this house. All you have to do is rough her up a little.' She continued to whine like she was a child having a tantrum.

'What do you mean? Like smack her around? Or something more?' he said in a more menacing tone.

'Whatever you want to do. I don't care. Just make sure she never comes back here. Do you get my drift?'

'Yeah.'

I heard the sound of heels on the concrete floor moving away from where we were standing and then the door from the garage to the house being opened and closed. Jack shifted his arm slightly and I realized that Mia had been digging my fingers into his skin. She pulled back and put my hands over my face and I felt several tears silently running down my cheeks.

Jack gently stroked the sides of my face and then pulled me into his chest and held me as my body shuddered while Mia quietly sobbed. I was horrified at the thought of one of the big meatheads trying to sexually assault me and the fact that Mia seemed genuinely scared by the threat made me even more concerned. I wonder exactly which of the big, creepy-looking guys had been chosen as Sasha's messenger.

Jack gently pulled my ponytail back so that I was looking into his face and leaned down planting a kiss on my forehead 'I'll protect you.'

Mia hugged him to her, and I felt his arms around my back returning the hug. My heart fluttered at the return of affection. Mia leaned back and looked up, moving my hands to his waist. He continued to stare intently into my eyes, not taking his arms away from my back as Mia moved my face closer and closer to his until our lips touched. It may have been the craziness of the situation, but Jack didn't try to stop Mia. She pressed my lips to his with more intensity and he responded, his hands pulling me closer into him, deepening the kiss. I could feel his heart beating wildly and his breathing becoming louder.

Mia broke it off first and whispered quietly, 'Can we maybe get out of this closet?'

Jack looked torn between taking me up to his room and finding a quick escape for me, from the garage and far away from this house.

'Wait here, OK? I'm going to make sure it's safe.'

He snuck a glance out of the cupboard to check that Sasha and her goon had both left. He motioned to me to stay in the cupboard while he went out to look. After several minutes of listening to my heart beating and trying to calm my rapid breathing, I heard the garage door open again and footsteps coming towards the cupboard. The door opened but it wasn't Jack standing on the other side of the door, it was Dan.

'Hey there Alice in Wonderland,' he giggled, and Mia looked at him in surprise, clearly wondering what the hell he was talking about. His face clouded over, and he looked up at the roof as though the answer he was looking for was up there. 'Oh no, that's right, it was *The Lion the Witch and the Wardrobe*.'

I was still confused, and so I assumed was Mia. She pushed past him and climbed out of the cupboard, looking around.

'Where's Jack?'

Having let go of whatever fairytale story involving a girl in a cupboard he was trying to conjure up he refocused his glazed eyes back on me and remembered what he was supposed to be doing.

'Oh yeah. You need to come with me.' He led me over to a door that led from the garage around to the side of the house and then to the tree that led up to Jack's window. 'Jack asked me to bring you here, but I'm not sure why. It feels a little cold out here, if you want to come inside with me, I could warm you up.' Dan wrapped one of his arms around my shoulders, but Mia shrugged it off, letting him down gently.

'Thanks Dan but I just want to sit outside alone for a few minutes because I'm not feeling that great. I'll come back inside in a minute, OK?'

He smiled and nodded, reminding me of a dopey

but lovable dog, so loyal and trusting, gentle and kind. I almost felt bad for him, but Mia obviously didn't. She hardly waited until he was out of sight before she threw her leg over the bottom branch of the tree and quickly climbed each limb until she was outside Jack's window.

She carefully peered inside, smiling shyly as she looked across his bed and around the room, but it was empty, and the window was locked shut. There was no book sitting on the desk chair and I wondered whether he had found the note inside yet.

Mia waited in the tree for what seemed like an hour, checking her phone and looking into the window every couple of minutes, but after another couple appeared at the door, neither of whom was Jack, she climbed back down the tree and did a lap around the house trying to find Jack inside. When she got back to the front door I thought she was going to storm into the house but after staring at the door she glanced at my watch, noticed the time and instead headed back to my house.

I noted that she was extra careful to make sure no one was lurking around waiting to spring her arriving home in the middle of the night before she climbed through the secret passage and into my bedroom. What she hadn't noticed, and neither had I at the time, was the motorbike rider sitting at the top of the driveway, watching me weave between the trees that led down to my house under the cover of darkness.

CHAPTER

26

The next night, after heading up to bed around 10pm, Mia waited for my parents to go to bed and then threw on a black hooded sweatshirt and a pair of dark denim jeans. I knew she would want to speak to Jack to find out what had happened to him the night before and I had to admit I was curious myself.

She took my bike from the side of the house and peddled quickly over to his house, dropping the bike behind a bush close by. It was the first time I had been to the house without a party. It looked so different without all of the lights on, music blaring and loud drunken voices. You could almost mistake it for a regular family house.

The lights were off in most of the rooms, but I could see the living room light was on and the TV was going. There were four people watching TV and Mia squinted to make out the back of their heads. I was sure the one on the left was Pete, his distinctive dirty-colored hair spiking out from his head as he reclined on the couch, a pillow propping him up to watch something that looked like football. The two in the middle I wasn't sure about but the one on the opposite couch to Pete, who was occupying a two-seater couch to himself, was definitely Jack.

Mia paused for a moment and then walked around the side of the house and climbed up the tree to Jack's window. I had expected the window to be stuck fast like it was the night before, but it opened easily, and Mia quietly swung a leg over the sill and slid into Jack's room. The light was off in the bedroom, but my eyes had adjusted to the darkness and could see that there was no one inside.

She walked around the room, as she had done the first time we had been in there, noting things as she went, smelling his cologne, looking through his books and peering into his wardrobe. His jeans and sweaters all lay in tidy piles on his cupboard shelves and his shirts and jackets all hung neatly from hangers. I was a little surprised at how neat everything was. As an only child I hadn't spent much time in guys' bedrooms but even Charlie, whose house had to be the cleanest one I had ever been in, did not have his room as tidy as Jack's.

I heard voices mumbling in the hallway and Mia quickly pulled her shoes, jeans and hooded sweater off and climbed into his bed in just my underwear. The door opened and for a moment I was terrified that it might not have been Jack coming into the room. I breathed a sigh of relief when I recognized the dark-blue hooded sweatshirt he had been wearing downstairs. He silently closed the bedroom door, walked towards the bed and turned on the bedside-table light.

I had expected for him to be startled to see me in his bed, but he just glanced at me like he knew I was going to

be there and simply raised an eyebrow. 'Did you get lost on the way home to your own bed?'

'No, I just like the look of yours more.' Mia stuck my tongue out at him and made herself even more comfortable in the bed, burrowing into his pillow. The bed smelt like his aftershave and whatever shampoo he used. I had smelt the same scents when we were stuck together in the cupboard in the garage the night before.

Jack walked over to the cupboard that Mia had just been snooping through, pulled off his top and was looking through to find a T-shirt. Mia's control of my body was absolute as even though I knew I was completely in love with Charlie and Gus, I felt myself being drawn to Jack. I wondered whether it was because of Mia or because, like Mia, I could tell that, even though the crowd he hung out with seemed mostly like deadbeats, Jack was a good guy. He was an amazing drummer, seemed like a really smart person and, most importantly, also appeared to be genuine, caring and thoughtful, which was rare among guys in general but particularly, it seemed, his friendship group. I hadn't seen him with any other girls apart from his sister even though some of the girls the other night at the bar were throwing themselves at him.

Maybe he's gay, I thought, watching the way his muscles rippled as he pulled a T-shirt over his head. He turned back to look at me lying in his bed and ran his fingers through his hair. As soon as he raised his hand to his face, I noticed the bruises and red, angry welts. Mia noticed too and quickly glanced at the other hand, which had matching scars.

Mia sat up, the covers dropping around me, and reached out to take one of his hands, inadvertently revealing what she was wearing, or rather her lack of clothing.

I abandoned the idea he was gay the moment that he looked at my body in my underwear. His eyes widened and he bit his lip as he took in my body. I noticed his lip was also swollen like he had been hit in the face.

'What happened to your hands and your lip?' Mia reached out and put a finger gently on his lip and his eyes moved to look into mine. 'And what happened to you last night? Why did you send Dan to come and get me out of the cupboard and take me to the tree outside your window? I waited there for ages for you to come but you never did.'

After staring at me for what felt like forever, he stepped closer, easing me down onto the bed and pulling the duvet back over me, lying down next to me but on top of the duvet, which acted as a barrier between us. I could tell Mia was as confused as me because a second ago, he had desire written all over his face. I thought back to the night before and the way that he had kissed me in the garage. Mia was obviously thinking about the same thing.

'I needed to make sure you were safe. I asked Dan to take you to Oak Tree Park, near your house, where I dropped you the other night, so you would be safely away from here when I confronted the guy that Sasha had asked to hurt you. But Dan must have been too out of it. He took you to an actual oak tree next to our house.' Jack rolled his eyes and Mia gently touched the back of his hands that had obviously been used to send a message to Sasha's thug.

'Were you hurt?'

'No. You don't need to worry about me, I can handle myself.' Judging from the tone of his voice I didn't doubt that.

'I waited for you for ages, then some random couple came into your room and ...' Mia suddenly looked at the sheets.

'The sheets have been washed,' Jack said chuckling, and then reached out his hand and smoothed the furrow between my eyebrows, which were knitted together.

Mia leaned into his hand, which had lingered on my face, and looked up at him with big doe eyes. She moved a little closer and looked up again to gauge whether he would reject her advances. He didn't move away. The duvet slipped down a little from the top half of my body and I saw Jack looking down at my cleavage. He bit his swollen bottom lip again while looking at my mouth and then closed the gap between us and I felt his lips press against mine as my eyes closed.

'Sophie,' Jack moaned in pleasure and his mouth pushed more urgently against mine. When my lips parted I felt his tongue run across mine and his hands move down my back and across my thighs. Mia took this as an invitation to climb out from underneath the duvet and onto his lap, straddling him as he lay back against the pillows.

After several minutes he pushed me back just slightly and mumbled, 'Sophie, we can't.' Mia pressed my lips harder against his and pushed my hips into his and I heard him moan again and felt his body responding to mine.

She moved my face back very slightly and suggestively whispered, 'Why can't we?' then slid my hand down his chest and onto his inner thigh. As soon as my hand got too close, he grabbed both my hands and pulled them together into one of his and flipped me onto my back where his body pinned me down, stopping Mia from rocking any more against his body.

'You don't want me?' she asked, sounding raw, and I wondered what she would do if he rejected her. 'You wanted me last night in the garage cupboard. And you do want me tonight. I can tell.'

'Of course I want you. Look at you! You're gorgeous and so smart and funny and all I want to do is … but we can't. I need to protect you and you're not safe here.'

'But last night you stopped Sasha's friend from hurting me. He won't try to hurt me again. You said that you would protect me.'

She was starting to break emotionally, I could feel it. He looked piercingly into my eyes, as if he was trying really hard to convey his message.

'He is only the tip of the iceberg Sophie. You are in danger here. I know this doesn't make any sense, but I can't tell you any more than that. I can't tell you why and I don't want to hurt you. You deserve an amazing guy. Someone who can give you everything, and all of himself and the truth, and I can't give that to you right now.'

Mia tried to get my hands free, and I couldn't tell

whether it was to pull him back to her or to slap him across the face. I suspected Jack was thinking the same as his grip was strong and he wasn't giving in to her.

'Let me go,' she demanded in an emotional but determined voice after conceding defeat and ceasing to struggle. He waited for a moment, assessing her mood, but as soon as he let my hands go, she hit him in the arm and jumped out of the bed as if she has been electrocuted. She pulled my clothes back on, muttering angrily as she got dressed.

She took one more look over at him and I wondered what she was going to say. He was sitting at the edge of his bed, watching me carefully, and I wondered what he was thinking.

I hated to admit it but out of the whole time Mia had been in control of my body I had not wanted to know more what she was thinking than at this moment. I tried desperately to hear her thoughts.

My mouth opened for Mia to say whatever she was thinking but instead I felt an overwhelming sensation of sadness and tears pooled at the corners of my eyes, lingering there for a moment before streaming down my face. Jack looked torn between maintaining his stance that he couldn't be with her and pulling her back into bed with him.

The latter won out and he stood up, reaching his arms out for her to walk into. 'Don't cry Sophie. Come here.'

Mia too seemed to swing between her desire for him and her offense at his perceived rejection. Unfortunately for

both Jack and me the latter was driving her. She shook her head, seemingly clearing her desire for him, and turned to the window, ripped it open and almost fell the two stories to the ground below in her rush to get away from him.

'Sophie, wait! Please, come back,' I heard him whisper urgently into the darkness. He started to climb out onto the top limb of the tree but although he was strong, Mia was used to climbing up and down the tree now and was down and into the dark night within seconds.

CHAPTER

27

I wondered if she was going to head straight back to my house but instead, she walked the streets for a while before returning to the bar that she went to the first night she had taken control of my body. On the surface she appeared calm, but I knew that something in her spirit had shifted, and she was moving towards becoming unhinged. Again, none of the patrons seemed to be concerned by my obvious underage status and I suspected even if I had stood on the top of the bar and held up my ID proving my lack of qualification there would still be no objection to my presence.

After glancing around the room Mia ordered two beers at the bar and took them over to one of the male patrons, sitting alone clutching a handful of betting slips and watching one of the TV screens intently. He barely glanced in my direction as Mia sat down and pushed one of the beers across the table towards him.

His face was weathered and leathery, eyelids half-closed with fatigue, and alcohol consumption masking his bloodshot eyes. There was a distinct odor that seemed to be leeching out of his skin, like he had pickled his insides from too much alcohol. His appearance suggested he was in his seventies, but I suspected he was actually a lot younger. Mia glanced down at the handful of tickets as he placed each one on the table, without taking his eyes away from the screen. She sat calmly as if she had observed this ritual before and knew when he could and couldn't be disturbed. She looked back up at the screen, checking the location of the current race and then looked down again at the ticket with the same location listed in small, black print on the docket. She glanced at the screen again and shook her head. Taking a big gulp of her beer she looked again at his face, sizing him up for something. I took it that the horse he had backed was not doing well and judging from Mia's behavior and the amount of alcohol he had consumed this was not a good thing.

When the race on the screen finished, he banged his fist angrily on the table, rattling the numerous empty beer glasses, and then scrunched up the betting slip closest to him. Only then did he notice the young girl sitting to his right who had bought his next drink. I wondered who he was, quietly praying that he wasn't some random stranger that Mia was going to try to sleep with, given she had just been rejected by Jack.

But the way that she was acting, knowing his behavior, organizing a drink for him and staying silent until he had enough time to absorb the sting of his gambling loss told me she knew him well and theirs was not a romantic relationship. In fact, from the way that she was treating him, like a small child, I would guess that somewhere along the years their roles had been reversed and he was her …

'Dad,' she blurted out, obviously forgetting that she was in a stranger's body.

'What's that?' he grunted, not hearing her properly anyway.

'No luck on the race,' she said, elevating her voice.

'Well thank you miss fucking obvious,' he said loudly, causing a couple of the guys hovering over the pool table to turn around and look. Mia gave them a wave and a pained smile to assure them that everything was fine and eyed off her father who had turned his attention back to the remaining tickets on the table.

'What do you want here missy?' he said gruffly.

'I wanted to ask you about your daughter Mia.'

'Are you one of them reporters? I will tell you whatever you wanna hear if you pony up the cash. She was my only child, and we were so devastated when she grew wings and went up into heaven.' He put on a half-smile flashing decaying teeth, which made everything that he had just said sound empty and insincere. His eyes searched mine hungrily to determine whether I was good for any money. Maybe he was in trouble with the bookies, I thought sadly.

'I'm not a reporter Mr Thompson.'

His lopsided smile faded quickly from his face and was replaced with an angry scowl. 'Well then, whoever you are, the truth is she was a good-for-nothing waste of space and she did everyone a favor by taking her own life.'

Every word out of his mouth was like a slap in the face and Mia just sat there taking every hateful word. I thought he was finished because his eyes moved back up towards the screens above us for the next race but when Mia stood to leave, she had yet to endure his parting blow. He turned and looked right at me, a cruel sneer on his face, 'And there is no way she walked through the pearly gates of heaven neither. She would have gone straight to hell.' He gestured to the ground beneath us in case I somehow could have misinterpreted his meaning.

I felt my body struggling to breathe properly, but Mia managed to blurt out, 'I guess I'll see you down there.'

'Eh? What's that?'

'Sorry to have bothered you,' she mumbled. She made it to the door of the bar before the tears started running down my face. She was so overwhelmed by her misery that she didn't notice the black motorbike that trailed her all the way back to my house and sat at the top of the driveway watching Mia until we disappeared into the darkness.

CHAPTER

28

The next morning when I woke up, I could again control my body for a few minutes before Mia took over. I took the opportunity to walk over to the window and sit at the window seat, looking out over the water. Out of the corner of my eye I saw movement in Charlie's house, and I glanced over to see him moving around his bedroom.

He looked like he had just come out of the shower, with just a towel around his waist. I wondered whether he had been running down at the beach. I resisted the urge to get his attention, pull open the window and tell him everything that had happened and beg for him to help me. From the mood that Mia was in it was likely that she could go on a rampage if I tried to escape her clutches. I felt like the whole experience was coming to a head and I wasn't sure whether I was going to be alive or in prison or worse by the time she had finished with me. Maybe it was worth using my precious minutes to simply yell to Charlie 'I love you'. But by the time I had thought it over he had left his room.

As Mia slowly woke, I watched her ghostly figure take in her surroundings and then jerk upright as she realized she was not in my body. She scanned around the room until her eyes fell on me reclined on a pillow, looking out over the water from the window seat.

'When are you going to give this up Mia?'

'Not today princess,' she said walking towards me. 'We have another excursion to go on.'

There was no one around when Mia walked downstairs and stopped only briefly to grab a croissant and a piece of fruit. There was a note on the kitchen counter from my parents saying that they would be visiting a couple of suppliers in the city and staying with friends for the night. They would be back early the next morning.

Clara walked into the kitchen, holding a bouquet of flowers and a vase, with Milo following closely behind her.

'Good morning,' she said, her eyes narrowed, and I wondered what she was thinking. Mia must also have been conscious of her scrutiny because she smiled politely at her, picked up the dog lead and called to Milo to go for a walk. Milo ignored her and stayed in his position at Clara's feet. She reached around Clara's legs trying to grab the dog but after a couple of failed attempts he growled at her and then sunk his teeth into my hand.

'Ouch!' Mia stood up and rubbed the back of my hand where there were small indentations in my skin.

'I've already taken him for a walk,' Clara said, observing the dog's reaction and picking up the upset puppy. I wondered what Mia would have done to him had Clara not been there. Mia shrugged and picked up the keys to my car, leaving without saying goodbye.

She must have changed her mind about driving because she walked straight past my car sitting in the drive and down the road to the bus stop where she waited until the bus came and took us to the part of town that we had been in the night before at the bar.

The houses in this part of town were mostly run down or cheaply built and she stopped outside a ramshackle double-fronted brick house that had definitely seen better days. Most of the paint had come off the front fence, which looked like it had once been white pickets, and every second picket had fallen off or was hanging at an angle. The pathway to the front door was partially covered by overgrown shrubs and the garden beds either side of the pathway had long ago been choked by weeds. As I walked up the pathway, I noticed one of the windows on the right-hand side of the doorway had been smashed and a piece of cardboard stuck up to try to stop the drafts from coming into the house. Reaching out to ring the doorbell I noticed below the bell a sign that read 'Jesus lives here'.

Who actually lives here Mia? I thought to myself, but before she could answer me a woman who looked like she was in her sixties opened the door in a faded pink nightgown and slippers. Her hair was an ashy grey color with streaks of black telling a story of a youth long forgotten. She took a long draw from the cigarette hanging between her lips, probably wondering what I had come to sell. By the looks of the front yard visitors were not a common occurrence.

'Hello Mrs Thompson, my name is Sophie. Would it be OK if I came in for a minute?' I realized it must have been Mia's mom. She couldn't have been more than forty but, like Mia's dad, she looked at least two decades older. Her eyes looked wary, but she must have been put at ease by my age and non-threatening appearance.

'What do you want?' she asked, her voice raspy.

'I just wanted to speak to you for a moment. I'm … I was a friend of Mia's,' Mia said quietly, carefully watching her mother's face for any signs of emotion. She simply grunted and moved back into the house, leaving the door open for me to follow her in. I walked through the entry and cast my eyes over the house. It looked in worse condition than Storybook House when we first moved in, and I wondered when it was cleaned last because there was a strange odor coming from the kitchen.

The carpet looked like it was from the 1960s, a mottled brown color that was coming away from the walls and curling up at the edges to reveal black colored linoleum underneath. The walls didn't seem to have been painted since the house was built and there were several cracks in the living room ceiling where I followed Mrs Thompson. She plonked herself down on a pleather couch that was ripped, the stuffing popping out as she sat down and lit another cigarette.

'Why do you want to talk about that good-for-nothing bitch?' she grunted after taking a long pull from her smoke. My mind was reeling at the thought that a person's mother could call her own daughter that, but my voice came out clear and calm, so I assumed Mia was not overly concerned by her mother's language or at least it was something that she had heard before.

'I've been thinking about her recently and I wanted to check on you and see how you were going.'

She made a noise between a cough and a snort, which I thought was her way of crying, until I noticed her mouth turn up at the edges and realized she was laughing. 'Well, aren't you just a good Samaritan. No need to be concerned about me. That girl was nothing but trouble from the day she was born. Better off without her. Never knowing where she was or what kinda trouble she was in.' She shook her head again like she was purging her mind of bad thoughts and took another long pull on her cigarette, picking a bit of tobacco off her lip before she finished with a flourish. '"Good riddance to bad rubbish" that is what they should have put on her tombstone.'

I could feel the tears prickling at the edge of my eyes and I was unsure whether they were from Mia or myself. How could this woman be so hateful about her own child, I wondered, and felt even more grateful for my own loving parents. Mia leaped up off the couch towards the wraith sitting in front of me and I wondered if she was going to hit her. Mrs Thompson obviously had the same thought because she shrunk back into the couch with a terrified look on her face. A minute earlier she had seemed so cavalier, so confident but now she just looked like an old, sad woman. Mia seemed to make the same assessment because after a long, hateful look at her mother she turned and walked out of the house, not bothering to say anything or close the door behind her.

As Mia strode back down the walkway towards the street Mrs Thompson called out from the door, 'Hey! Hey you!' Mia stopped midway to the gate and paused, still facing the gate, and I thought she was going to just ignore the woman and keep walking, but she turned, slowly, cautiously.

Mrs Thompson was standing behind the screen door, hiding just out of view, and I had to squint into the sun to make out her features. What could she possibly want to say that she hadn't already? Maybe she regretted her horrible words and she wanted to take them back. Mia walked tentatively back towards the door and the woman's long, bony arm shot out and dropped a bag of things on the front porch.

'I cleared out Mia's room. None of her other friends came here so I had no one else to give these to. If you don't want them, do us both a favor and just throw them out.' As I reached down and picked up the shopping bag with all the known possessions of Mia Thompson sitting on the top step of this miserable-looking house, where I was certain Jesus did not reside, I felt a small gust of air and then heard the door where Mia's mom had been standing only seconds ago slammed in my face. I was curious to know what was in the bag, but Mia had other ideas. She threw the bag over her shoulder and walked down the street towards the main road.

I could tell that she was upset, and I felt like even though I still couldn't hear her thoughts I was starting to be able to sense her feelings more. After ten minutes of kicking rocks down the street she started talking out loud, confirming my suspicions.

'You think I'm a monster,' Mia laughed without humor. 'You want to know how to make a monster Sophie?' she asked in a bitter, angry snarl. 'The ingredients are simple. You take any ordinary little baby, place her with two undeserving, nasty people who also happen to hate each other, let her simmer for fifteen or so years in a household of violence and neglect and then mix her with a turd of a boyfriend who throws her off a fucking roof. You wanted to know why I am what I am – now you have your answer. Pure unadulterated hatred.'

My thoughts were whirling but amidst all of the fear, anger and sadness I felt another emotion that seemed to outweigh all of the others. Pity. Even though Mia had used me unashamedly to try to exact her revenge, even though she had been rude to my friends and clearly had no regard for me or my feelings I felt pity for her.

You're not a monster Mia. A monster is not capable of love, but you are. I can feel how much you love Jack. But she didn't seem to hear me, or perhaps she did but she ignored me and continued on with her rant.

'What a waste of a life. Do you ever wonder why God makes perfectly wonderful people barren and then gives the gift of a child to people like that?'

We were still walking and after fifteen more minutes I realized she was not heading in the direction of my house. I wondered where she was taking us now. We finally stopped walking outside a sprawling brick building with a sign out the front that said, 'Bayside Retirement Community. Caring for the elderly for over 65 years'.

She walked through the sliding front doors, straight past the front desk, which appeared to be presently unmanned, punched in a code on the security monitor to the right and wandered down the linoleum hallway. She had obviously been there before, and I wondered whether we were coming to visit an elderly relative or a friend. I also thought about my friends at school and wished I was with them, and that this was just a bad dream. I wondered how many stops we were going to take that day on Mia's trip down memory lane and how it would end. Were we about to walk into another unpleasant confrontation?

The building had definitely seen better days, but it seemed to be well maintained and not at all what I had expected of the inside of a nursing home, having never been in one before. The walls were covered in a muted beige-and-pink floral wallpaper and the ceiling and floors were various shades of beige. It felt like the colors were designed to lull anyone walking the halls into a false sense of calm. There were names on each of the doors off to my left and right – Susan Stamford, Eloise Watts, Robert Lee – Mia kept going until we stopped outside a door with a label that said 'Ruby Thompson'. I nervously hoped that the reception that we were about to receive was nothing like the one that Mia's mother gave us.

When Mia knocked on the door I wondered if

maybe Ruby wasn't in the room or was sleeping because there was no response. Mia impatiently tapped a little louder and Ruby's neighbor from across the hall poked her head out of her door.

'Who are you?' she demanded, in a curt fashion.

Mia seemed to evaluate her for a minute to decide whether or not to be rude in return. 'Candy striper,' she said smiling sweetly, but my voice had a definite undertone of sarcasm.

The lady over the hall, Jill Burrows according to the name on the door, looked me over and said, 'You don't look like no candy striper. Where's your uniform?'

'I just finished my shift and they asked me to pop my head in to visit one last person.' I could feel Mia was running out of patience. 'Do you know where Ruby is or not?'

Her lips puckered like she was sucking on a lemon, and I braced myself for the worst. Either she was going to tell Mia that Ruby had died, or she was going to slam the door in my face.

'Every afternoon she goes and sits in the rose garden and tells them roses stories. She's as nutty as a fruit cake that one.' Before Mia could thank her, she had closed her door again.

Mia made her way back along the hallway looking for the door to the rose garden. When she reached the exit door, I noticed a small but elegant woman with greying hair walking through the rose bushes. Mia took a breath and headed out into the garden, slowly walking towards the woman.

Even though the weather was mild she wore a heavy-looking woolen cardigan. Her face was carved with lines and her wispy hair was pulled into a bun at the nape of her neck. She was holding her hand up to each of the roses and mumbling something over and over to each one, then gently letting them fall back into place.

'Nan?' Mia said, breaking the silence and still of the garden air.

She slowly turned her body ninety degrees and looked warily in our direction. 'Pardon? Did you say ham? Is it already time for lunch? But it is not yet eleven.'

Mia took a minute to remember that she was in another person's body and took a few more steps towards her grandmother. She reached out her hand to gently touch one of the rose bushes and her grandmother watched her apprehensively.

'No, sorry, I'm not here about lunch. I actually wanted to ask you about your family.'

'My family?' she asked, looking surprised. 'Well, my son was just here the other day.'

I thought of the angry drunk in the pub the night before and I felt Mia mirroring my thoughts.

'Really? And how is he going?' Mia asked, a dubious note in her voice.

'Oh, he is good. Yes, very good.' She leaned into me a little conspiratorially, 'I think he might have a lady friend.'

'A lady friend?' Mia asked, unsure. Again, I thought of Mia's dad, and besides the commitment he seemed to share with the television and those ticket stubs I thought it was unlikely he would have any other serious relationships.

'Yes, her name is Sarah, he told me, and she is the same age as him.'

I could sense Mia was getting a little agitated and I wondered why.

'And how old is that?' she asked her grandmother.

'Twenty-six. I think he might even ask her to marry him. Wouldn't that be lovely! I haven't been to a wedding in years! They must have a fruitcake at their wedding, and flowers, yes lots of flowers. White roses, yes … white, a symbol of purity and future promises …' she continued muttering to the roses and appeared to completely forget that I was standing there.

Mia stood there for a minute and then turned on her heel and walked back through the door from the garden, down the beige hallway and out the front door.

'FUCK!' she swore as she made her way back along the street and down to the harbor. She stood at the edge of the bay and threw stones into the water as hard as she could, watching each one sink.

Did your grandma have memory loss before you died? I asked Mia in my mind. I could fell hot tears rolling down my face.

'Yes, that is why my dad put her in that place, but she always remembered me. She was the only one that ever gave a damn about me and now her memory stops before I even existed.'

I'm really sorry Mia.

'You're sorry? You are sorry? What do you feel sorry

about?' I could tell she was getting upset and I didn't want to make it worse, so I thought nothing.

She stood there for several more minutes, throwing stone after stone into the water until she couldn't see from the hot tears in my eyes and then she sat on the soft sand. The water lapping over my feet may have had a calming effect on her because the tears began to slow. It made me think of the night that she went swimming with Jack. As soon as the memory came to me, she leapt up. I realized that I had probably upset her calm and cursed that I had accidentally interrupted her peace. I wondered whether she would now go off the deep end completely. I didn't have to wait very long to find out.

CHAPTER

29

After doing a quick trip past the liquor store, where Mia managed to shoplift a bottle of vodka undetected, we walked down the road for another mile or so past where the shops ended and into an area where the blocks of land were larger, and there seemed to be a couple of small farms. We reached a set of large wrought-iron gates marking the entrance to Everlasting Grace cemetery.

Mia pulled a printout of a newspaper clipping out of my pocket and I recognized it as the obituary piece that the local newspaper had run where Mia had found the details of the funeral parlor she had contacted.

As she walked into the cemetery, I sensed that we had reached our next and possibly final stop on Mia's trip down memory lane.

She wandered up and down each row of grey headstones, some with ornate plaques and decorations marking the names and ages of the deceased that lay beneath them and most of them decorated with assorted shades of flowers in varying degrees of decay. By the time we reached the back of the graveyard the headstones had become blander and simpler. I sensed that the real estate in this part of the cemetery had been donated to those without the financial means to afford to pay for the pleasure of everlasting rest at 'Everlasting Grace' themselves.

She stopped when she found the headstone that was marked for Miss Mia Thompson. There were no flowers on this gravesite, no small teddies that had been left by adoring parents for their lost little girl, no poems or words of love, and despite my hatred for Mia and her holding me captive against my will, again I felt an overwhelming sadness and pity for her.

I was unsure whether she was listening to my thoughts, or she was suffering the turmoil of her own, but I felt the sensation of my eyes welling up with tears and Mia collapsed to the ground, lying my head against the cold stone where she stayed, weeping uncontrollably for a full fifteen minutes.

When it seemed like she had run out of tears or the energy to cry them she turned her back to her gravestone and then sat on it. Pulling the vodka out of the bag of things her mother had dumped on me at her house, she took several quick swigs from the bottle, stopping only once I felt my body becoming numb.

She then looked inside the shopping bag at her final remaining possessions. There was a photo frame with a picture of Mia and Pete, a diary, a photo album that I could see contained photos of Mia as a small child. She flicked through until her eyes started to well over again and she slammed the album shut.

The last thing left in the bag was what looked like a plastic sandwich bag marked with the familiar logo of the police. Inside there was an evidence slip and a ticket with Mia's mother's signature on it confirming that she had received the contents.

This must have been what was left of what Mia had been wearing when she died, I thought, and a chill ran up my spine. There was a Minnie Mouse watch with a black band, a ring with a dark-green stone in the center and a phone with a crack in the top right-hand corner. Mia tried to turn the phone on, but it had long since run out of battery. She put the contents back in the bag and stood up, taking another sip of the vodka and then spat it onto the gravestone.

'What a waste of life! Look at this thing would you Sophie! No flowers, no photo or words about me on the stone. It's like I never even existed. At least when you die there will be people who care. People who love you. People that will mourn that you no longer live and breathe and walk among them. What do I have? Nothing and no one.' Her sadness had dissipated, replaced with bitterness and anger.

I care about you Mia. I thought in my mind, trying my best to placate her, to make her feel better, but it did the opposite. My words just seem to inflame her anger.

'You care about me?' she snorted aggressively. 'No Sophie you feel sorry for me – that is not the same thing. You have no idea how it feels to be me.' She went quiet for several minutes and I wondered what she was thinking.

'No, you have no idea do you. But I can change that.' With that she grabbed the bag and the bottle and left the cemetery, heading back in the direction of my house.

CHAPTER

30

She didn't speak to me the whole way back to the house and I could feel my anxiety rising with each minute. What had she meant when she said I would know how it feels to be her?

When she reached my house, my fears were realized when she headed directly to the clock tower. She pulled out the bottle of vodka, leaving the rest of her bag of memories inside the small room and for the second time she climbed over the balcony railing, this time sitting down on one of the pitched roof tiles that sat above the little windows. The sky was getting dark as the sun slipped behind the horizon, and I noticed for the first time that night that there was a full moon. As she worked her way through a third of the bottle, she started venting some of the anger that she had been building during our trip home.

'You are just like all of them. The teachers, the social workers. They all felt sorry for me but none of them ever did anything to actually help me. You know how many times that child services were called out to my house in my life? Thirty-seven. And that is only the ones that I remember.'

Tell me how to help you then, I pleaded with her in my mind.

'I don't want you to help me. I have had enough of people wanting to help me. I admit it Sophie, I envy you, I really do. You have two people who love you, who are willing to fight for you. You know Charlie still obviously loves you even though you kissed Gus in front of his face. And Gus … he is clearly stuck on this earth not being able to leave because he can't leave YOU. It's pathetic. Maybe I should do them both a favor and make the decision for you. If you are a ghost, then there isn't really a choice is there.'

She nudged closer to the edge of the tiles, and I could feel my body tilting from the alcohol.

Mia please! Please don't do this! I begged her.

'Sophie please don't.' Mia spun around at the sound of Jack's voice repeating the words that I had just said in my mind. She clasped the vodka bottle harder and for a minute I thought she was going to throw it at him, but instead she moved it to her lips and took another swig. I wondered how much more alcohol my body could take before I just fell off the roof without her having to throw me off.

'Go away Jack,' she spat, and turned back to look out at the moon.

I was hyper aware of where he was standing and knew she had the ability to throw my body off the roof before he would be able to reach us.

'Please just let me help you,' he begged. 'I'll do

anything. If you want me to punish Pete, I'll do it. You want me to punch him in the face just say the word. Better yet, just give me time and I'll find a way to send him to jail. I know for a fact that the police are trying to put him away for drug dealing. Please, just tell me what you need to help you find your peace.'

'Find my peace! Find my peace!' she repeated in a drunken, mocking voice. 'Since when did you become a yogi!' She spun back around and in that moment she seemed completely sober, my back was as straight as a rod and both Mia and I worked out at the same time that somehow Alice had spoken to him.

'Where is that sneaky little witch?' Mia scanned the roof and Alice appeared from behind the doorway. 'There you are. Figured it out, did you?' Mia said and laughed without any humor. 'What gave me away? Was it when I called you Allie?'

'No,' Alice said quietly, 'it was Sophie's dog. He loves Sophie and Clara told me he wouldn't go near her. She told me that Milo bit Sophie.'

Mia took another swig of vodka and muttered, 'Figures' to no one in particular.

'So, you think there is some miracle way that you are going to rid Sophie of me? Is that it? You want me to find peace? Well, isn't that an interesting concept. I tried to find peace *Alice*, but it doesn't seem to want to find me. I went over to my killer's house and tried to kill him, that didn't work. I thought I would try to speak to my parents because even though they treated me like dirt while I was alive, surely they would be sad their only child had died, but they are not. And I even went to see my Nan because god knows I thought she might have been the only person on earth that might have possibly ever loved me, but she *doesn't even remember me!*' She flung my arms out in a shrug and lost her grip on the bottle of vodka, which seemed to hover in midair before it fell to the ground smashing on the pebbles in the drive. It was a horrifying glimpse into what would happen if Mia decided to push me off this roof and I whimpered internally.

'Don't worry Sophie, you will hardly feel a thing,' Mia said quietly. 'It is almost like flying, if only for a few seconds.'

She started to move closer to the edge of the roof and I closed my mind, bracing for the impact of the gravel on my body and wishing that I could be with Charlie one more time before I was thrown to my death. In that moment I wondered whether I had my answer of who I loved more between Charlie and Gus. The desire to be able to touch and kiss Charlie was overwhelming, the center of my being.

'Love? That's it isn't it?' Mia turned back around to look at Jack, whose face had lit up in a smile. How could he possibly be smiling at someone who was about to take someone else's life the way it was suspected that she took her own? He reached his hands out to her, but she shrunk back, moving closer to the edge, almost losing her footing. She looked back up at his face, and while he had lowered his hands, he was nodding like he had it all worked out.

'Your unfinished business is that you never found love. You felt that no one ever truly loved you. But I do. I love you.'

She took a step towards him and then stopped, shaking her head, 'No, you love Sophie. You would never have looked twice at me if I wasn't in her body.'

Jack shook his head, frustrated because he didn't seem to be able to get through to her. 'I know I can't prove to you that I will still love you, but I have never really met Sophie. Someone's appearance is only a tiny part of them. I was never talking to Sophie I was talking to you. I love your sense of humor, your stubbornness, your fire. I might be attracted to Sophie physically, sure. But I love Mia's personality.'

'Then why do you keep pushing me away?'

'I have a good reason for that. Come off the edge of the roof and I will explain everything to you. I promise.'

She looked into his eyes, his face looked sincere and genuine, and she shifted her weight to move towards him. I breathed a sigh of relief but in the same moment one of the tiles that she was standing on made a cracking noise and I felt my feet slip out from underneath me.

'No!' I heard Jack scream as I slid uncontrollably down the roof towards certain death. Mia scrambled, grabbing onto anything and everything. Just as I was sure the roof was about to disappear from underneath me my hands got a grip on one of the roof tiles. Mia looked up as Jack threw himself over the railing and eased down to where Mia was clutching the roof for dear life.

'Grab onto my hand,' he called, holding out his arm. Mia risked a look behind. It looked like we were two feet away from the edge. She tried to get a foot hold, but my foot slipped back again, and she nearly lost her hold on the tile. She looked back at Jack again. His face was a mask of concern and desperation. I should have felt more scared but to be honest I could sense the desire, the need for Mia to know what Jack was going to tell her. I was no longer afraid that she would intentionally let go of the roof. She took a deep breath and reached my left hand that was not gripping the tile to Jack. He reached out and grabbed my hand, easing the two of us slowly up the roof. After a couple of terrifying small backward slips, we made it to the railing, and my body relaxed.

As soon as my heart had slowed fractionally Mia turned to Jack and pressed him for answers. 'I'm off the edge of the roof now,' she announced, 'so spill.' We were still on the wrong side of the railing, but she was not going to budge any further until Jack gave her answers, despite the fear she had shown moments earlier.

I could see in his face that he knew this too and, as frustrating as this was, he seemed to accept it. He took a deep breath, launching into his explanation, shocking both of us.

'I'm an undercover police officer. I was recruited to investigate your slippery ex-boyfriend Pete for drug dealing, car theft and underage sex offenses.'

Even though I had sensed Pete was a dirt-bag from the beginning, and I knew that he had pushed Mia off the exact roof that I was standing on, I was surprised by the depth of his criminal activities, and I could tell that Mia was too.

'And the reason why you wouldn't sleep with me was …'

'I didn't want to start a relationship with you based on a lie.' His shoulders sagged. 'Every time you thought I had rejected you all I wanted to do was be with you and every time I drove you into the arms of someone else I hated myself. I nearly quit this job because I wanted to walk away but I couldn't walk away from you, and I knew if I left you would drown in their toxic poison.'

'Prove it,' she demanded. Jack's expression of relief turned to one of confusion. He reached into his jacket and pulled out his police ID, which Mia pushed away.

'I don't care about the badge. Prove that you love me.'

Jack looked at Alice and she nodded her head. He smiled and reached his hand out to pull my face to his.

At first all I could feel was Jack's soft lips on mine, his tongue, the fire in my body as Mia pulled him closer, kissed him more passionately than she had before and him responding, his arms tightening around my body and his breath sounding ragged.

The next thing I knew I felt a tugging sensation like I was being pulled in two different directions and then my stomach lurched, and I felt like I was going to be sick, but my body felt so warm, like I was sitting in a bath. What was happening to me? I broke away from Jack and looked down at my legs and then at each of my arms. It took me a few seconds to realize that my body was moving on my command. My head whipped up and I felt Alice's hands fixing a necklace around my neck. The necklace that Alice had found in the safe and had given me for my birthday. She must have found it again. The stone on the amulet felt so cold against my skin. I touched it and turned it over in my hands.

Glancing up I could see the spirit of Mia Thompson standing no more than four feet away. She looked just as confused as me as to how she had been removed from my body.

'I assume that you didn't just remove yourself voluntarily?' I asked Mia cautiously in case she tried to get straight back in, which is of course was exactly what she tried to do. She moved quickly over to me, and I could see she was trying but it clearly wasn't working. *It must be the necklace that Alice put on me*, I thought to myself and touched the cold stone again. I looked over at Alice who looked livid.

'I learnt a thing or two from a witch that Sophie and I met a few months ago.'

Diana, Alice had to be talking about Diana. She must have found Diana's journals with her spells in them.

Mia looked at me with a mask of uncertainty and then back at Alice, obviously unsure of her next move. 'Of course, there were some very handy ones about removing a spirit from a possessed person and how to ensure that person can never be possessed again. Oh, and then there was an interesting one about sending a spirit to hell. Would you like to hear that one Mia?'

Mia looked as though she was going to be sick. I thought back to how sad she had been at her parents' house; how angry she had been at Pete her ex-boyfriend; and how hurt she was when she realized her grandma couldn't remember who she was. Then I thought of the overwhelming feeling of love and desire that she had felt for Jack and I looked at his face.

He looked like he was experiencing mixed emotions. He obviously felt guilty about his part in helping Alice tonight and possibly grief at losing Mia. I truly felt how much he loved her and from being possessed by her I knew how much she loved him. I looked up at the full moon and a plan emerged in my mind that might just solve everyone's problems.

'Wait,' I said but it came out as a timid mumble, and I was sure that no one had heard me. Alice was still glaring at Mia, Mia was looking around for an exit, and Jack was looking at Mia with a desperate look on his face.

'Wait!' I said again, but louder so that everyone turned to look at me.

'I think I have a solution that will make everyone happy, but it's almost midnight, so we're going to have to do it soon.'

31

'No Sophie.' Alice knew what I was going to say, and I could tell from her face she didn't like it at all.

'Please Alice. Mia has been in my head; I know that she can find peace and move on. I feel like there is just one thing she needs.' I turned to look at Mia, 'I know what you need Mia. Jack was right. All you have ever needed was love and it is standing here on the roof of my house. Jack loves you; I know he does. There is a way that you can be together, but just for tonight.'

Mia looked longingly at Jack, and he smiled encouragingly at her.

'OK, let's do this,' I said before anyone could point out how insane my life had become. I was going to turn a key in a clock so that the spirit that had possessed my body and tried to ruin my life before she almost tried to end it could be intimate with a man who had fallen in love with her while she was in my body.

I walked back into the house and into my room to retrieve the key. Mia and Jack followed me to my room and Alice waited outside, protesting.

Turning it in the clock over my fireplace I watched

as Mia's body was restored to its non-translucent self. She looked just as I had imagined she would. Her hair was jet black and cut short with a blunt fringe, her arms decorated with various tattoos, the most prominent was what looked like a guardian angel on her top right bicep, and she wore a black Guns N' Roses singlet with ripped black jeans and Timberland boots. Just like in her license photo I noticed that underneath the black makeup she was really pretty. I wondered why she seemed entirely devoid of self-esteem but then thought back to her dirt-bag of a boyfriend, alcoholic father, a bitter and cruel mother and dysfunctional group of friends. I glanced over at Jack. He looked like he was meeting a blind date for the first time after speaking to them for years over the phone.

'Hi Mia,' a shy smile made its way across his face and he reached out his hand to hold hers. She nervously reached her other hand out to touch his face and, when it did, she glanced in my direction in complete shock and then focused again on Jack.

'How long did you say this will last?' she asked me, not letting go of Jack's hand or looking away from his face.

'Only an hour. I will have to turn the clock back at 1 am.' Mia didn't waste another second speaking to me. She turned back to Jack and pulled his head down to hers, kissing him passionately. I took this as my cue, leaving them in my room and closing the door behind me. Giving them a bit of privacy, I headed downstairs to ensure none of the ghosts in the downstairs rooms left the house. But it seemed like they couldn't. This was only the second time since we had moved into the house that the clock had been turned one turn too far, all the spirits becoming full bodied again, and I didn't want to take any chances.

I was met at the bottom of the stairs by a very timid looking Alice. I immediately went to her and wrapped my arms around her in a tight embrace.

'I'm sorry for everything that Mia said to you while she was in my body Alice. You need to know that I was trapped inside screaming at her to stop.'

'I'm so very sorry Sophie that I didn't realize it wasn't you from day one,' she murmured into my shoulder.

'Don't be. How could you have known? Thank you for saving me! If you hadn't been here tonight …'

'Actually, I had a bit of help …' She looked behind me up the stairs where Gus, Clara and Charlie were all standing. Milo came bowling between the three of them and jumped up my legs until I reached down and picked him up, and he licked the side of my face.

'Hey little guy. Did you miss me?' It felt so nice to feel his soft fur between my fingers that I indulged him for another thirty seconds before I put him down and ruffled his soft head, refocusing my attention back to the human population standing on the steps.

'Thank you, Clara,' I walked up the stairs and gave her a big hug. 'I knew that you would smell a rat and thank god you did! Roland will be non-spirit-like at the moment if you want to steal some kisses,' I said and winked at her. She touched her hand to the side of my face and smiled kindly at me.

'It is nice to have you back Miss Sophie,' she said and then walked quickly back up the stairs.

I smiled as I watched her walking away and then turned to look at Gus, who was also not currently translucent. He briefly eyed off Charlie and obviously decided to jump in first, reaching out his arms and pulling me into them, his lips resting on the top of my forehead. I breathed in his smell. I was so relieved to have complete control over my body again I forgot that Charlie was standing right next to us and ran my fingers down Gus's back, feeling his body shiver in response to my touch.

'I'm sorry I wasn't there for you,' Gus whispered, his breath tickling the top of my face. 'If I hadn't forced you into making a decision I would have been there with you at night and I would have known she wasn't you. I would have been able to figure it out. I would have been able to stop her.'

I leaned back and looked into his face, raising my eyebrows.

'And how would you have done that smarty pants?'

He smoothed out the furrow between my brows and touched his lips gently again to the top of my head.

'I don't know. But I would have found a way.'

Charlie cleared his throat, and I eased my way out of Gus's tight embrace to walk over to him.

'When I thought that Mia was going to jump off the roof, I kept thinking about you and how I would never be able to hug you again,' I said, my breath catching as tears formed in my eyes and I let out a sob. He pulled me into him in a tight embrace.

I knew that Charlie and Gus would be comparing how I behaved with each of them, but I didn't care. I was just so happy that I was alive and now had the luxury of being able to control my body. I snuggled into Charlie's dark-blue sweater. I felt his intake of breath and he hugged me tighter to him, running one of his hands up and down my back and through my hair.

'I'm so sorry I didn't suspect that something was off when I saw you at school. After what you ... she said about me leaving you crying I thought you must hate me. All I could think about was that I wanted to be with you for so long and by pushing you away I had just ruined the only chance I had with you. Even when we found out that it wasn't you, I found it hard to believe. I mean, I'm still getting my head around the other additional residents in your house,' he said gesturing to Gus, who rolled his eyes at Charlie's comment.

I pulled back without letting go of Charlie and he kept a protective arm around me.

'What *did* happen?' I asked turning to look at Alice. 'And how did you figure out how to get her out of my body?'

'I lied a little upstairs to Mia. Clara and Milo did play a part in it but really it was all you. Jack came to school and found me after he found your note. He made up some story about being a cousin and some sort of family emergency. The principal was a little suspicious,

I suspect because of his tattoos, so she made Jack wait in the office while she took me out of class. I had no idea who he was – I don't have any cousins – but as soon as he said your name, I told the principal it was OK, and we went somewhere private.

'Jack was great. I could tell that he felt uncomfortable and odd about what he was telling me – well done on the note by the way. I had suspected that day that you … or rather she, had told me to leave her alone, and then Clara told me about Milo's strange reactions to you, but the note cemented it. I think you put just the right amount of detail to get the point across without alarming him too much. The pieces started to fall into place once he showed me the note. The way that you had been so rude to everyone, skipping classes, everything. To be honest I felt so foolish that I hadn't figured it out sooner.'

I reached out and touched her arm. 'How could you have known Alice, really, don't be so hard on yourself.'

'But I could have. I knew there was something about the clock tower that I didn't like. I could feel it under my skin. And then when you were completely offhanded and dismissive … even cruel, each time I spoke to you and walked away feeling hurt, thinking that wasn't you, you wouldn't talk to me that way, and I was right. I just never put it together!' Fresh tears sprang to her eyes, and she looked down at the ground.

'Please Alice, you can't beat yourself up about it forever. I won't let you.' I removed myself from Charlie's embrace and hugged her again. 'If you had said to me some of the hurtful things that Mia said to you, I would probably never speak to you again.'

She looked up into my eyes and I nodded my head.

'So, where did you find Diana's belongings?'

Gus took over the story. 'After Jack contacted Alice, she came to see me in Dad's house. The two of us searched every single hiding place we could until we found Diana's trunk. It was in a storage cupboard in the servants' quarters upstairs. It looked like they put it in there when she left and it hadn't been moved since. We found other stuff too – a box in the basement that has some really old diaries, and you're going to love this, we found the outside exit points for two of the tunnels that lead out of the house that we saw on the blueprints you found. Dad thinks they may have been connected to alcohol smuggling during Prohibition and one of them leads to a graveyard in the garden.'

'You're kidding!'

'Pretty cool right.'

'Where is the entry into the house?' I asked curiously, at the same time thinking about whether George's diaries would help me pinpoint his location when he died.

'We don't know. We were too busy looking for the box, so we haven't found the entry points yet. But there are at least two pathways out of the house.'

'I'm surprised Mia didn't find them. She used every secret passage to get out and go partying most nights at Jack's house.'

Just as I mentioned his name Jack's face appeared at the top of the stairs, closely followed by Mia.

'Well that was quick,' I said without thinking. 'You have only been up there ten minutes.' I immediately chided myself.

Jack laughed and Mia scrunched up her face at me. 'We've been *talking* and I need your help again. I know how to get my revenge on Pete.'

I looked at Alice who shook her head vehemently and mouthed the word 'no'. Mia and her little revenge plots never ended well, and I suspected I wasn't going to like whatever she had been cooking up any more than the last one.

'Do you think that's the best idea, Mia? Remember that last little revenge plan came undone rather rapidly after you tried to kill two strangers with a turn-of-the-century firearm while they were having sex and you were in my body!' Alice, Gus and Charlie all looked at me in shock and alarm.

'Oh yeah, I'm totally serious,' I said answering all of their expressions.

'This is different. And it's brilliant if I do say so myself,' Mia said, sounding determined. I looked up at Jack. Given he was a police officer, and he was unlikely to do anything homicidal, I suspected I would feel slightly more comfortable with whatever Mia had cooked up if he agreed to it.

'And you are on board with this plan?' I asked Jack.

'Yeah, I think it might actually work.' He looked at Mia in admiration and she smiled back at him.

Gus, Alice and Charlie were now all shaking their

heads. I didn't like it any more than they did but I decided to at least hear what the plan involved.

I shrugged my shoulders. It looked like I wasn't allowed to disembark the crazy train just yet. 'What do I have to do?'

CHAPTER

32

Mia spoke quickly – we were going to have to move fast if we were going to be able to put Mia's plan to work. By the end of her five-minute run-down we all knew what we had to do and had conceded that if her plan worked it would actually resolve a couple of matters.

Jack and I left the house immediately, heading over to his house to round up our victim. The plan hinged on Pete being at his house and us being able to get him back to my house and quickly. I thanked the stars that my parents were away from the house that night. Even though the plan seemed foolproof it made it easier that they were not around to be caught up in the mess if anything went wrong.

As we rode over to Jack's on the back of his motorbike, I was struck by how strange it was to be around him when I was in control of my body and not Mia. When I climbed onto the back of the bike with him, I instinctively wrapped my arms around his body and had to remind myself to loosen my grip a little. He was obviously feeling it too; he put his hand on the top of mine affectionately and then quickly removed it when he remembered I wasn't Mia.

Here was another new normal to navigate I thought to myself, but I relished the freedom of being able to think thoughts without worrying about someone else using them against me.

When we reached Jack's house, I was relieved to see there was a party in full swing. It was the usual cluster of people hanging out, drinking and smoking. As we walked through the rooms, trying not to make it obvious that we were looking for one person in particular, people called my name and waved to me. I tried to be as Mia as I could in my body, which felt even stranger than Mia trying to be me with me trapped in my body. Finally, we found a small group sitting in the back yard around a fire. Pete was sitting in the middle of the semicircle, smoking what smelt like marijuana. I shot Jack a look and he nodded, heading over to distract Pete's girlfriend Sasha.

My turn, I thought, feeling immediately nervous about what I was about to do. I walked over and took the seat next to Pete. He turned to leer at me. Yuck! I thought, but at least if he found me mildly attractive my role in this little charade might be easier to achieve. I made sure no one else was listening, lent in close and whispered in his ear.

'Hey Pete, I've been wanting to speak to you. I saw how you were looking at me the other night when I was taking my clothes off and I wanted to see if you were interested in a private show?' I said suggestively. I wondered whether I was laying it on a little too thickly, but he looked at me hungrily suggesting he was falling for the ruse hook, line and sinker.

He glanced around the group sitting around the fire, obviously checking to make sure Sasha wasn't watching. Jack had worked his magic and she was nowhere to be seen. I wondered what he had said to get her away from the group. I knew I had to get Pete out of the house before she came back.

'Meet me in my room in five minutes,' Pete said, standing up to go.

I pulled him back down and whispered in his ear, trying to be seductive like Mia but probably failing spectacularly. 'Actually, I know a place that's really private so there won't be any risk of us being interrupted by your girlfriend. Interested?' He looked a little unsure, so I put my hand on the top of his thigh and gave a gentle squeeze. Any doubt was immediately cast aside as he whispered into my ear to meet him around the front of the house then he stood up and left. I watched him go and checked that we hadn't been overheard before following. I walked through the front of the house, nodding to Jack as I walked past.

When I walked out the front door, I saw Pete going around to the driver's side of his car. I had only just escaped certain death from Mia trying to push me off the top of the house; I wasn't about to die in a car accident. I leaned against his body and took the keys from him making sure I did it seductively so that he didn't think I was being patronizing.

'Please can I drive? Your car is so cool,' I said looking up at him with big doe eyes. Maybe I had learnt more from Mia than I would like to admit.

'Sure baby, whatever you want.' He hurried around to the passenger door and I rolled my eyes. Baby! Did he even know my name? What a jerk! I thought.

I climbed into the driver's seat, turned on the engine and backed carefully out of the driveway. As soon as we were on the road and I was sure Sasha hadn't seen us I felt more relaxed. A mile or two down the road I spotted Jack's black motorbike in the rearview mirror and felt even better.

I pulled into the car park next to the beach a quarter mile away from the house. I thought it would be better to approach the house from the beach to ensure Pete didn't suspect where we were going until it was too late for him to back out. As we walked along the beach Pete's arm was wrapped around my back and his hand kept sliding down to rest on my backside. It took all my energy not to throw his hand off me.

As we neared the house, I pulled out a blindfold we had dug out for this moment. 'No peeking!' I said, turning my attention back to the matter at hand and again trying my best to sound seductive.

I walked quietly across the front lawn and led him into the secret passageway entrance that Mia had used a dozen times during her late-night party trips in my body. Once we were in the passage, I was comfortable that he didn't know where he was. I took him up to the top of the house, again making him close his eyes when we got to the passageway that led to the clock tower room.

I nervously looked at my watch; it was 12.45 am and I thought about whether Alice, Gus, Charlie and Jack

would all be in place in the clock tower. As I pushed open the door, I took my hands off Pete's face and made a ta-dah sound to indicate he should open his eyes.

He opened his eyes and looked around him, his eyes slowly adjusting to the darkness of the room, with small cracks of light from the moon slicing through the arms of the clock face. When his eyes finally had a chance to take in the room, I noticed his face blanch and he started shaking his head.

'No, no, I can't be here. Why did you bring me here?' He looked at me accusingly.

I feigned confusion, 'What do you mean?'

'Who told you about this place? Why did you bring me here?' he repeated again, his eyes darting around the room like something was going to jump from the shadows and attack him.

Perfect! I thought to myself, he was acting exactly as Mia predicted. I did my best to channel the vaguest person that I had ever met, a yoga teacher who had taken us as juniors at my school in Brooklyn. She had stood at the front of the room, facing away from the class speaking in a light, airy voice like a little garden fairy. Half the students had walked out during the class, and she didn't notice until the end when she turned around. She had checked the class list that she had ticked off for attendance at the start of the hour and looked back at the handful of people left, shrugged her shoulders and smiled, then dismissed us.

'What do you mean? I heard about this place from some of my friends. They said it's really romantic. I even found this blanket that we can lie on.' I spread out the blanket that Mia and Pete had used to make love on before he had pushed her off the roof. His eyes took in the blanket and I saw shock and horror pass across his face. I heard the door to the clock tower from the house quietly, magically lock behind me. Alice was doing her role on the other side of the door, and I knew it was time to push him right over the edge mentally. I felt safer knowing that Charlie and Gus were both standing outside on the rooftop should anything go wrong.

'You don't look so good Pete. Maybe you need to go outside and get some fresh air.' Pete nodded his head, so I walked over to the door that led to the balcony and opened it.

Standing in the doorway, blocking the way outside, was Mia.

CHAPTER

33

'JESUS CHRIST!' Pete screamed.

Mia stepped into the room and Pete dove for the door that we had come through, but Alice had it locked up tight. He threw himself against the door again and again trying to break it down, but as I knew from experience, there was no person living or dead that was going to be able to get through that door.

'Good to see some things never change,' Mia said, looking me up and down.

'It's not real, it's not real,' he chanted to himself, his eyes telling him differently.

'Pete? Are you OK? What's wrong?' I asked, feigning confusion.

'What?!' he looked from me to Mia and then back again. 'You can't see her?'

I shook my head. 'See who? Who can you see?' I pretended to look out the door into the night sky to see what he was so scared about. I turned back to look at him as Mia walked past me and into the room. She slowly, tortuously walked towards him. He shrank back against the door that he had just been throwing himself against and put his hand over his head.

'You're not real. This isn't real!!' He shook his head, trying to rid himself of the image of Mia.

'Pete?' Mia and I both said at the same time.

'What do you want?' he moaned.

'Are you OK?' I asked at the same time as Mia lent down next to his face and hissed 'Confess.'

'No,' he said, shaking his head, still shrunk down against the door. I wondered whether he was answering Mia or me. Probably both.

'Confess,' she said again, reaching out and touching him with her long fingers. He jumped up, horrified that she could touch him, and backed into one of the corners of the room. I was still standing in the doorway, blocking the exit to the balcony, but I wondered if I would be able to stand my ground should he try to escape out the door and jump off the balcony.

Mia followed him to the corner of the room. As soon as he turned around to try to look for another exit, she slapped him in the face. I tried my best not to cringe. I knew it came nowhere near getting complete revenge for him having murdered her, but she had a satisfied smile on her face. There was no way he could deny that she was real now.

'Do you remember that night Pete? I was so in love with you, and I wanted our first time together to be special.' She looked wistfully towards the arms of the clock that blocked the light of the moon from completely illuminating the room. Pete had started to whimper. 'You know I didn't tell you this that night, but I thought I would want to remember that night forever.' She laughed with no humor. 'My forever wasn't very long though, was it! *You* took my forever from me.' Her voice broke a little and I saw a tear run down the side of her face. I worried whether she was going to be able to push him far enough or whether her emotions might get the better of her, but her glazed eyes cleared, and her face turned back to stone.

'Even so,' she continued, her voice now tinged with ice. 'I didn't know that so I thought I might take a little video of our special time together.' She pulled something out from her back pocket and leaned down, so the object was dangling next to his face. He glanced up to look at what she was holding. The police evidence bag with Mia's phone inside that I had been given by her mother. Was she serious? I wondered. She had videotaped the whole thing?

'Do you know what they call this Pete? This is what they like to refer to as the nail in your coffin, or maybe the syringe in your arm.' I was fairly sure that the state of New York no longer had the death penalty, but it was unlikely that Pete was aware of that. Mia pointed at the black throw rug on the floor, the one that had the white stains on it.

'That rug has biological fluid on it from both you and me and was found in this room. The vodka bottle we drank that night also had both of our fingerprints all over it. Either you hand yourself in or ...' she lowered her face down next to his, 'I will haunt you until the day, you, die.' She said each word slowly.

'Seriously Pete, what's wrong? What can I do to help you?' I asked Pete, still pretending not to know why he was hiding in the corner of the room. He looked up at Mia looming above him and then at all of the evidence scattered around the room and in her hand. For a moment I worried that he was going to try to take the evidence and make a run for it but then he turned to look me in the eye.

'Police,' he stammered. 'I need the police.'

'Police? What for?' I acted surprised.

He cleared his throat. 'I have to tell them that I … that I … killed someone.'

'Seriously? Did you just say you killed someone? Who did you kill?' I said in horror for the benefit of my phone, which I had on record.

'My girlfriend Mia. Last year we came to this exact house. She wanted to find somewhere romantic that we could be together. I brought her here. I had been here before, drinking with a friend. I was high and … we were standing on the edge, and she was so fragile … I knew I had her life in my hands and I just reached out and … I thought no one would ever know. But she is here still. She is standing right there, and she won't let me be unless I confess.' He looked like he was going to start bawling. 'She said she will haunt me until the day I die.'

'OK, OK. I'll call the police.' I made a show of calling the police on my mobile phone but really, I was speaking to Jack. Jack had organized for his squad to come and take Pete's confession. They were already waiting at the top of my driveway he told me at the other end of the phone.

'Are you OK?' Jack asked, his voice laced with concern.

'Yes,' I replied, trying to keep my voice even and confident.

Pete stood slowly from his crouched position on the floor to look into Mia's face. She stood her ground.

He looked scared and uncertain. 'Are you … alive?' she shook her head.

'No, you took that from me, remember?'

'That's why I can see you, but she can't,' he said gesturing to me on my phone.

'Yes. I'm part of your conscious. You did a terrible thing and now you need to be punished for it.'

He nodded, accepting his fate. I didn't know whether to laugh or cry.

'So that is it then? Once I've done my time, I'll never see you again?' he asked sounding desperate for that to be the case.

'Ohhhh don't seem so disappointed,' she said, eyebrow raised at his lack of compassion about his responsibility for her death. She walked to the doorway I was standing next to that led to the rooftop terrace. I did the best I could to avoid looking at Mia, to maintain the illusion that Pete was the only one who could see her. 'I'll be watching you Pete. Don't make me come back.'

He stared at her standing there in the doorway and I pretended to look out the doorway like there was no one there. As she walked around the corner and out of sight, I could see the lights of the police car flashing at the top of the drive, and I heard the door click on the other side of the room leading back inside the house as Alice unsealed it again. It was time to wrap this up.

I cleared my throat. 'Pete?'

He turned to me with a look of shock on his face. I wasn't sure whether it was because he had forgotten that I was there or whether it was just dawning on him that he wasn't asleep and in the middle of a nightmare.

I gestured towards the door to the house. 'They're here. Are you ready?'

He shook his head and for a moment I panicked, thinking that now Mia had gone he was going to back out, but he gestured towards the door that moments before he had been attacking. 'That door is locked.'

I walked across the room in a couple of strides and twisted the handle. It moved easily in my hands and the door opened. Pete's eyes were popping out of his head as he followed me through the doorway, glancing behind and twisting the door handle on his way out to try to understand why just minutes ago he couldn't get out.

He walked in a zombie-like trance as I led him through the secret passageways and out to the front driveway. The police were waiting at the top of the drive and they immediately took him into custody and drove away. As the car pulled away, I watched his face. He was staring out the window to the house that loomed up behind me, his face stricken. Turning to look behind me I realized that he had been looking at the top of the house, at the small balcony that ran around the outside of the clock tower, where Mia stood with her hands crossed over her body. True to her promise she was still watching him.

The night air was cool but when I shivered slightly, I doubted that it had anything to do with the temperature. Mia could be very scary when she wanted to be. I jumped when I felt a hand on my back. Jack had been watching as Pete was taken into custody. Behind him was a woman that I recognized as the person he had introduced as his sister.

'Sophie this is Detective Abbey Fraser,' I reached out and shook her hand, smiling wearily. 'I'm going to take a wild stab in the dark and guess that you are not Jack's sister?'

She laughed and shook her head. 'I don't know how you did it but thank you for your help Sophie.'

'Sure,' I nodded, glancing at Jack who smiled at me. I could definitely see the appeal for Mia – he was really attractive in a bad boy kind of way. A little ironic now I thought about it; out of all the bad guys at Pete's party house I had felt like he was a really good guy. Turned out I was spot on, given he was actually a police officer. I thought back to Mia's little striptease on the table and Jack saying his sister had definitely seen worse.

'And um, I wanted to say, the other night at Jack's house when I was taking off my clothes on the table that wasn't really me. I mean it was me, but it was …'

'No need to explain. We've all been there! I have a tattoo on my calf of a dolphin that I don't remember getting. Too much alcohol gets everyone! But maybe try to lay off it until you're older ... and it's legal. See you later Sophie.'

Abbey waved goodbye and Jack laughed at me as we started walking back towards the house. My cheeks blushed red when I thought back to that night and all of the intimate things that Mia had done with Jack while in control of my body. I didn't know how to act around him now that it was really me and I didn't behave at all like the person that he had come to know.

'When did you find the note?'

'Not until yesterday actually. I'm sorry I didn't find it sooner. When I read it ... I didn't know what to think ... I don't, or I didn't believe in spirits. But I thought I'd better find Alice just in case there was something in it.'

'I guess you're going to have to find a new housemate,' I said, glancing at Jack out of the corner of my eye.

'Yeah, well I'm probably going to have to move out of that house anyway. My objective was to bust Pete for drug dealing but with you and Mia's help we've managed to exceed all expectations. He will be away for a long time for murdering her. Who knows though, they might get me to stay for a bit longer and try to bust up some of the rest of the drug ring.' He glanced up to the top of the house, but Mia wasn't standing on the balcony anymore.

I looked down at my watch. It was eight minutes to one. I needed to turn back the clock in my bedroom that had allowed Mia and Jack to have some time together. She had used almost all of her time to help put Pete in jail and I wondered how she was going to feel about that.

'I'm sorry but I need to turn back the clock now Jack. Mia will be a ghost again.'

He nodded his head and I wondered whether he had already figured that out. 'She's probably waiting for you in my room.'

We quietly moved through the secret passageways and back into my room where Mia was indeed waiting. I put the key in the back of the clock and waited for a moment with my back to Jack and Mia to try to give them a bit of privacy, but I could still hear what they were saying to each other.

'I think it's time for me to go now. Thank you for showing me what it's like to be loved Jack.'

'I'm really going to miss you Mia,' Jack choked out.

I knew I would regret saying what I had in my mind, but I thought that I would say it anyway. I turned around to see them embracing.

'I don't really know how this whole spirit thing works but I'm pretty sure if you decided to stick around you could,' I said gently.

Mia looked at me and wiped away a tear. 'After everything I've put you through you want me to stick around?' she asked dubiously. Alice, Gus and Charlie had walked into the room moments before and were also looking at me in disbelief.

'Well, I don't want you possessing my body again, or anyone else's for that matter, but you can stay in our haunted house if you want to. There are a few other spirits floating around.'

Mia glanced at Jack and he smiled. Mia returned his smile and kissed him lightly on the lips. 'Thank you, Sophie. I don't deserve your kindness.'

'You can say that again,' Alice grumbled quietly, still not forgiving Mia. Mia turned to look at Alice, Charlie and Gus. 'I'm truly sorry for the things that I said to you while in Sophie's body. I said and did everything to avoid having to give Sophie her body back and you have all still helped me regardless.' Gus and Charlie nodded their heads in forgiveness. Gus nudged Alice and she shrugged her shoulders. She wasn't going to forgive that easily. Mia seemed to understand and didn't push her.

'But honestly, I think I'm ready to go. I feel light now, like I've been able to remove a heavy weight that had been hanging around my neck. I'm not sure whether it was closure from seeing Pete being hauled off by the police or whether I feel whole from finding love with Jack, but I'm happy. Really happy.' She turned to look at Jack. 'I'm sorry I can't stay but I think it would be better for you to be able to move on if I wasn't here anyway.'

Always blunt and to the point, up to the very end I thought, smiling inside, but her comment made me think of Gus and whether he was staying just to be with me.

Before I could help myself, I glanced up at Gus who was watching my reaction to Mia's comment.

'It's time for me to turn the clock,' I said quietly and Mia and Gus both nodded their acceptance. When I looked back at the group two of them had faded into a translucent glow.

Mia turned to look at Jack one last time. 'I love you,' she smiled at him, and he smiled back.

'And I love you. I won't forget. I promise,' he said holding his hand up to his heart. She nodded her head, there was a white glow, then she was gone.

CHAPTER

34

'I think it's time for me to go too,' Jack said, still staring at the spot where Mia had been.

'Me too,' Charlie agreed softly.

I was more than happy for the three guys that I had effectively been seeing all within the space of a few months to go their separate ways before they started comparing notes.

'I'll walk you guys out. Do you want to stay?' I asked Alice and she nodded her head wearily. I was so happy to be back in control of my body and that I hadn't lost all my friends from Mia's actions. I reached out and hugged her again. I pulled the trundle bed, which was already made up, out from under mine.

'There are spare PJs in the bottom drawer. I'll be back soon. Keep Alice company, can you?' I asked Gus as I was walking into the secret passage leading from my room with Charlie and Jack following closely behind me.

We walked out the passageway that Mia had taken advantage of many times during the course of my captivity. It emerged from a trapdoor next to the glasshouse. I sucked in the cool night air feeling a mixture of exhaustion and relief.

'What will happen with Pete?' I asked turning to look at Jack.

'They've taken him down to the local station. The officers there will take a full confession. From there he will be held in custody and arraigned at court in the next few weeks. Because it's a serious charge, they'll set a high bail, which he won't be able to pay. After he is formally charged, he will be sent to a prison nearby. Given he is over eighteen he will be tried as an adult so he will likely go to Attica.'

I nodded, thinking about how his fellow prisoners would receive his smug, arrogant personality. I suspected he would need to hide that side of himself in order to survive the experience.

I held out Mia's phone in the police evidence bag for him to take, along with the blanket and vodka bottle that I'd found in the clock tower and put in a plastic zip-lock bag.

'I guess you'll need to take these in case he backs out of confessing when the cold reality of jail time hits him. Did she really take a video of them the night that she died?'

'Yeah, that's what she told me. When the police collected the original evidence, they mustn't have found the video. She gave me her pin code so 'll hand it back over to the lab to charge up and analyze. We have the backup of the recording you made of Pete's confession tonight too, if we need it.' He smiled but his eyes looked sad.

'Are you going to be alright?' I asked him. He had really only just met Mia, and she had clearly left her mark

on him. I wondered how much he had fallen in love with Mia and how much he had been in love with me, and I suspected it was a combination of the two of us, which would probably be a little confusing for him.

'Sure, I'll be OK. It's not the first time I've lost someone that I love. Maybe I'm cursed to be alone.'

I remembered the story that he had told Mia on the beach about losing his girlfriend years ago to a drunk driver.

'Are you alright?' he asked, reaching out and touching my arm gently. I immediately glanced over to see how Charlie felt about Jack touching me, but he had wandered in the direction of the beach to give us some privacy and I found myself feeling a little relieved. After all Jack had done a lot more than just touch my arm; we had made out in a cupboard and in his bed and he had seen me in nothing more than my underwear.

'Yeah, it'll take me a little while, but I'll be OK. Thank you for trusting that my note wasn't a joke. I don't know what I would have done if she had … if she had …' the reality of the evening's activity hit me, and I felt hot tears running down my cheeks. Jack stepped closer and pulled me into his chest.

'Hey, it'll be OK. Shushhhh,' he whispered into my ear and gently rubbed circles around my back. I could see Charlie wandering back up the beach towards us and I leaned back to give Jack a weak but reassuring smile.

'I'm so tired, I think I just need to rest.' He nodded and took a step back as Charlie reached us and eyed off

Jack and his tattoos as if taking him in for the first time.

'You OK Sophie?' he asked warily.

'Yep,' I said quickly, wiping away the tears.

'Let me know if you need anything, OK?' Jack said picking up on Charlie's protective vibe. He gave me one last hug and turned to walk around the house and back to his motorbike. Before he got to the side of the house I called out as quietly as I could, 'Jack?'

He heard me and turned around, his face half in the shadow of the house.

'Yeah?'

'Do you mind if I come and watch the band sometime?'

The half of his face that I could see lit up with a smile and he nodded his head enthusiastically. 'Of course! I'll send you through the details of our next gig.' I smiled as he disappeared around the side of the house.

I turned back to Charlie, who looked a little surprised. Most likely he was concerned that I was interested in maintaining a connection with Jack, who would be forever associated with a night full of trauma. He quickly rearranged his features into a concerned expression.

'Are you feeling alright?'

'Yes. I think I just need to rest.'

'OK,' he said gently. 'I'll head home and let you get to bed.'

Before we parted ways, I needed to know something that I had wanted to ask since I regained control over my body. 'So … no new girlfriend then?'

He chuckled softly and shook his head. 'Who am I going to date that is as interesting as you?'

'Good point.'

He looked out to the light of the full moon, shining a walkway across the water and then he studied my face. 'Take some time to make your mind up but you should know I will always be here for you Sophie.'

He stood there for a minute looking awkwardly like he wanted to kiss me but it might be overstepping, so he reached out and took my hands instead. I was desperate to kiss him, but I knew that it wasn't fair to him or Gus. They needed me to make up my mind and stick to my decision. I settled on a compromise and took his face in my hands, gently lowering it so that I could kiss him on his forehead.

'Thank you for your help tonight. Can I call you tomorrow?'

'Of course,' he said. He kissed me on the side of my cheek and hovered there for a moment, tempting me to pull his lips to mine, but the moment passed and he stepped away, jogging down to the beach and back around to his house. I looked up to my window and saw Gus standing in the window, obviously watching the farewell between me and Charlie.

Sighing I headed back into the house through the passageway and back up to my bedroom. When I got there Alice was snuggled into the trundle bed, already sleeping quietly. I was relieved that I didn't have to do a full debrief with her tonight. Just seeing her sleeping so peacefully made me yearn to be snuggled down under my duvet with my head on my pillow. Gus was lying on my bed and patted the spot next to him. I raised my eyebrows and he put his hands up in the air like he was being held up at a bank.

'I won't touch you, I promise. I will still await your decision but from now on I will be here protecting you from crazy spirits, OK?'

'Isn't that what this is for?' I teased, holding up the amulet that Alice had placed around my neck.

'Just consider me an additional watchdog.'

I rolled my eyes and lay down on the bed fully clothed, pulling the duvet over me. The feeling of bliss was just as I had anticipated, and I let out a contented sigh.

'This has been the longest night of my life,' I mumbled, already feeling the wave of sleep washing over me. I was vaguely aware that I had left the light on but seconds later the light went off. My eyes shot open, concerned about who had switched the light off, but the only person I could see was Gus. He walked back around the outside of my bed to lie back down again and put his finger to his lips in a sign that I should be silent.

'It's OK, that was me.'

I eyed him warily. 'You're getting pretty good at that aren't you?'

'You don't know the half of it!'

'So … different spirits have different abilities? Like Diana being able to throw things and Mia being able to control my body.' I shivered involuntarily at the thought.

'I look forward to hearing about your adventures

while possessed,' he said jokingly until I gave him a scathing look.

'I don't think you will enjoy it actually. The short version is that she spent most of the time trying to destroy my liver drinking copious amounts of alcohol, did a strip-tease at a party, tried her best to rob me of my virginity and then almost threw me off the roof.'

'OK, you're right. Had I known any of that I would have absolutely not let you help her tonight.'

I nodded. 'In the end I realized she was just a sad and lonely girl but I'm still relieved that she's gone,' I conceded, yawning loudly, and Gus touched me lightly on the cheek.

'Get some sleep Sophie. We can talk more tomorrow.'

I closed my eyes and fell instantly into a deep, dreamless sleep.

The next morning, I awoke feeling reborn. When I went down to breakfast Charlie was sitting in the kitchen talking to my parents who had arrived home early from their overnight trip. It seemed that Charlie and Gus were both going to be there, watching out for me.

My parents glanced up when I walked into the room and greeted me warmly, as they had the past few weeks blissfully unaware that it had not really been their daughter they had been speaking to. When I sat down at the table Milo curled into a happy ball at my feet. Charlie smiled at me sheepishly, which made me feel like running over and climbing into his arms. I felt a sense of happiness being somewhere that I belonged, and an overwhelming feeling of freedom and control now that I had my body back, but I also felt a tugging feeling of sadness, thinking about Mia's life.

Sitting in my warm kitchen with people who loved me was the opposite of how she had known life. I thought about her parents' reactions when we had gone to speak to them, of her grandmother's loss of memory and finally of her visiting the site of her own burial. The whole experience was horribly confronting, and I had to wonder whether anyone could be driven to homicidal acts if they had gone through the same situation as Mia.

I knew that she had done the wrong thing, but I wasn't certain that I wouldn't do the same as her, if I had been dealt the same cards in life. The whole experience had been hard on me and I decided, while I was sitting in the kitchen with my parents and Charlie, that I had to find a way to put what had happened in the past. Thinking back over that last day that Mia had spent in control of my body, I knew there was something I could do to get closure.

CHAPTER

35

A few days later, for the second time, I stood at the large iron gates that marked the entrance to the Everlasting Grace cemetery. The sight of the graveyard gave me goosebumps and I instinctively folded my arms across my chest. .

I hadn't realized that while Mia was in control of my body it had also dulled my senses and I was now hyper aware of everything around me. I jumped when a funeral car pulled up quietly behind me and the driver slammed his door as he got out of his car to open the gates.

I smiled politely at the man and helped him open up the gates so that the car could drive through, the sight of the black shiny coffin inside doing nothing to calm my nerves. I took a deep breath and began my walk through the rows and rows of grey headstones up to the back of the cemetery. It was a beautiful sunny day and as I walked, I spotted other people visiting the cemetery.

A middle-aged woman was standing beside the grave of a loved one, maybe her husband or a child lost too soon. She touched her hand to her lips and then touched the stone in front of her. Further into the cemetery two men embraced in front of a stone that had a small cherub sitting at the top of it and a family nearby wept over a large family plot.

I wondered whether any of their relatives were still here, trapped in limbo, waiting for someone to help them find their peace. Or whether, like Mia now, they had found it and were no longer tethered to our world.

As I reached the back row I was overwhelmed with a feeling of sadness. I didn't know why. It wasn't as though I really knew Mia and for the short time that I had known her she had been fairly horrible to me. But experiencing the world that she had been surrounded by before her death made me feel so sorry for her. Neither of her parents had loved her and her own boyfriend had pushed her off a roof.

I reached the plot that marked her final resting place and was again struck by the absence of any proper mementos on the plots around Mia's, and indeed her own. I knelt down, brushing the dust and dirt off the top of the cold stone, and laid the dried flowers that I had bought from the florist down the road on top. I then pulled out a small silver plaque that I had made at the local hardware store and some superglue, sticking the plaque onto the stone under the inscription of her name. I stood up and surveyed my handiwork. It still didn't compare to the large, ornately engraved plaques down the front of the cemetery but it looked much better than it had done, and I was happy that Mia didn't just have to rely on those who had mistreated her in life to remember her in death.

'I hope you are resting peacefully now Mia,' I said

and, borrowing a move from the lady whom I'd seen mourning her loved one, I kissed my hand and touched the cold stone one last time.

'Mia Thompson 02/12/2002 – 07/05/2019 May she rest in peace with love.'

I spun around at the sound of the voice behind me reading out the plaque that I had just stuck on Mia's gravestone. It was Jack. I suddenly felt a little embarrassed and silly. Here was this guy who was in love with Mia and yet I was so presumptuous to think I should be the one sticking the message up on the stone just because she had invaded my body for a few weeks.

I also still felt a little strange around him given we had inadvertently been in a relationship, and he had seen me almost naked multiple times. I gestured to the plaque that he had just read while my cheeks flamed red with embarrassment.

'Hey Jack. I'm sorry, I shouldn't have stuck it up there without asking you but the last time I was here it seemed so cold and heartless and I didn't know if you or anyone else knew about this place let alone would ever come here.'

'You don't need to apologize. I think it's perfect. I brought her a little something too.' He held up a small bear the size of my thumb that was made out of pewter holding an amethyst crystal love heart and a piece of paper.

'You've been here before?' I asked, surprised that he had also come bearing gifts. He nodded and placed the small bear on the grave. I held out the superglue. I didn't think anyone would mind if we stuck it down, but I worried that if we didn't some vandals might come through and take it. He thanked me, applying some of the glue to the bottom of the trinket and then pushing it down firmly onto the stone underneath my plaque.

He then opened the piece of paper and I saw that it started with 'Dear Mia'. It was a letter that he had written to her.

'I'll leave you to it,' I said, thinking that he might want some personal time to read the letter, but instead he touched my arm and asked if I would stay. I nodded and put my hand on his back as he turned to face the gravestone.

'Dear Mia, I'm not sure if there is a way that you will hear this, but I'm going to tell you anyway because if you can hear me somewhere, I know that it will make you happy. I wanted you to know that Pete confessed to your murder and he will most likely be sent to Attica prison for a minimum of 25 years. It is not exactly a life for a life but at least he will be punished. I started working undercover at Pete's house only two months after you died last year,' he held back a sob and took a deep breath. 'I really wish that we had met at my house while you were living, because I feel like we were destined to meet each other and maybe if we had met then you wouldn't have died. I promise you that whenever I think of you, and it will be often, instead of making me sad that I lost you, I will smile and be forever grateful that I was able to meet you.' He stifled another sob and tucked the letter back into his pocket. I soundlessly wiped the tears that were streaming down my face and when he turned to me, I wrapped my arms around him, hugging him tightly while his body shuddered with sobs.

Once his tears subsided, I pulled back and looked at his face. I ran the back of my hand over his face to wipe the lines of tears that marked his cheeks and he smiled gratefully.

We walked back down the hill together and Jack reached out and took my hand as naturally as it would have been for him to hold my hand when Mia was living in my body rent free. As soon as he thought about it, he let go of my hand. I looked up at him and he looked a little embarrassed.

'Sorry, I didn't think. It's just it might take me a while to reprogram my brain from Mia's Sophie. Sorry. Is that weird for you?'

'It was weird for me at the start. Everything that she was experiencing, her feelings for you, the way that she felt when she kissed you while she was in my body, I felt it. I sometimes wondered whether the feelings were because of her or whether they would have been there regardless of her.'

We reached the gate and he stopped walking and turned to me. 'Are you saying that you have feelings for me Sophie?' he teased.

I laughed and looked away but then looked back into his eyes with a serious expression. 'Honestly, I'm sure it was probably a mixture of both. I am and always will be so grateful that you watched over me – over her, over us both really. I'm not sure where I would be if you hadn't, and I would love to be able to stay friends. But as far as romantic relationships go, I have my hands full at the moment.'

He smiled at my choice of words. 'I thought I had picked up on that a little at your house the other night. The guy that lives next door and the ghost?'

'Picked up on that did you?'

He looked off into the distance recalling a memory, 'I could tell neither of them were all that keen on Mia's plan to use you as bait to coax Pete back to the house. It was pretty obvious they were both trying their best to protect you. I can understand that.'

I nodded and walked towards the gate to leave the cemetery, Jack following closely behind. When we walked out of the gates, he looked around for my car, but I had caught the bus, just as Mia had done that day she had brought me out here, in a way retracing our footsteps.

'Let me take you home.'

It was probably best if I used the walk to clear my head, but I was feeling an overwhelming sense of exhaustion, so I nodded my head and walked towards his motorcycle.

'Do you remember where I live? You've only been there once.'

'Actually, I've been there quite a few times,' he said and laughed when I turned around to look at him in surprise.

'What? When?'

'When Mia was in your body. I started following her

home to your place some nights when I was worried that she might have got herself, or you as it turned out, into trouble.'

I was overcome with a desire to hug him again, but I thought it was best not to confuse the situation any more than it already was, so I just put my hand on his arm. 'Thank you.'

'Anytime,' he said, his face flushed, and he handed me the helmet from his bike. I climbed onto the back once he was already on. He squeezed my hand then started the ignition and sped off towards my house.

When we reached my street, he pulled over at the top of my driveway and I climbed off, pulling off the helmet and handing it to him to put on.

'Thanks again, for everything,' I said, giving him a kiss on the side of his cheek.

'Anytime,' he said, sounding a little sad.

I started to walk away, and I heard the engine start before it cut off again.

'Sophie?' I turned around.

'See you soon.'

'See you soon,' I promised him, and he smiled before starting the bike again and leaving.

CHAPTER

36

The letter arrived on a Tuesday, stamped from Washington, and the front was addressed very professionally to Miss S. Weston. On the back of the envelope was a wax seal with the American eagle. Despite my curiosity I resisted ripping the letter open and instead eased the seam on the back until I could pull the letter out gently and carefully. I unfurled the letter that was folded in three and scanned my eyes down to the bottom of the page to find out who the mysterious letter was from. I could see the American naval crest and the title was Sergeant Andrew Ferguson, Veterans Affairs.

I couldn't believe it; someone had written back to me regarding Poppy's husband. I ran up to Poppy's room, taking the stairs two at a time, and burst in without knocking. I was disappointed not to see her in her chair, but she came around the corner just as I was about to retreat from the room.

'Sophie?' she said in a surprised voice. 'Is everything alright?'

'Poppy, I received a letter. I think it's about your husband.'

She rushed across the room and looked down at the letter, 'What does it say? Can you read it to me?' she asked urgently, her eyes trying to scan the page, but they had welled up.

It was only at that point I wondered to myself whether I should have read it first. What if it was bad news? I didn't want to upset her further. It was too late now so I walked over to her window seat and began to read it to her.

Dear Sophie,

I received your enquiry in regard to Lieutenant George Farrell and I wanted to write to you in person to advise what I understand from his case.

As you are aware Lieutenant Farrell was sent to the battle of Normandy. He was to land on the beach at a section the US forces were targeting, codenamed Omaha.

What you didn't know was, in the months leading up to the invasion, the Allied forces had conducted a military deception, which was codenamed Operation Barrier, whereby misinformation had been fed to the German forces. This misinformation was key to the battle as the German forces deployed troops in another area in anticipation of an attack in a different location.

From my understanding Lieutenant Farrell was born and spent a number of years in Germany as a young boy and was fluent in both English and German, a skill that we took advantage of, and he was deployed to act as a double agent.

Lieutenant Farrell was a key participant in feeding this miscommunication to the German forces and without his courage

and commitment to the US armed forces the Allied forces would not have been as successful as we were in the Battle of Normandy.

From the minimal information that I have it was suspected that Lieutenant Farrell was captured during the battle and taken into Nazi custody. We do not know the whereabouts of his remains but believe him to have passed away while in enemy custody.

If you are still in touch with his widow, I wish to send my condolences and pay my respects to her husband who is one of the finest wartime heroes I have researched in my time here at Veterans Affairs.

Kind regards,

Sgt Ferguson

I sat back on the seat and let out a whistle. Looking up at Poppy's face I could see that she was emotional from the letter. The cloud hanging over her head seemed to have cleared ever so slightly. I was sure that she still wanted to know what had happened to him but for now this would be enough. Just to have George's integrity questioned had laid the seeds of doubt in her mind and here was the proof that her conviction of his innocence and integrity was validated. It seemed he had been inserted into the Nazi party by the American Army and from the sounds of it he was a key chess piece in the game of war that the Germans had played and lost, and he had paid for the victory with his life.

'He was never working for the Germans.' Her expression was one of pure vindication.

'From the sounds of this letter he was doing everything in his power to sabotage the Germans.'

She looked out at the water and then at me with a pleading look on her face. 'I know I have asked a lot of you Sophie, but can you please try to get in touch with this sergeant to uncover the location of his captivity? Or any other details that you can uncover?'

'Sure,' I said. What harm could it do? It was only a letter and it wouldn't take me long.

When I went back to my room and had a chance to think about it I remembered that not only did I have to try to figure out what had happened to George I also had three more rooms in the house left to clear, preferably before paying customers started to stay in the house, the school's production of *Romeo & Juliet* was going to be held in the sunken theater in less than a month, and I had new tunnels to explore that sounded like they went under the house. I saw a movement out of the corner of my eye and glanced over to see Charlie walking around his room. More important than any of these things I had two amazing guys that I loved who wanted to be with me and I needed to make a decision that would inevitably hurt one of them.

'Hi Sophie.' I turned around to see Gus propped up by the pillows on my bedhead.

I looked back to Charlie's room. He spotted me and smiled then waved at me. My heart skipped a beat. This was going to be difficult.

ACKNOWLEDGEMENTS

Thank you to my biggest supporters, my family. My husband Sam, my son Will, and Sophie, my daughter/dedicated marketing superstar! You have all been wonderful champions of my first book, encouraging anyone and everyone to have a read and I am so grateful for your support.

Thank you also to my extended family, particularly my generous and wonderful parents and parents-in-law. There are a large number of 60-plus-year-old readers that this book was not targeted at who have gone out and bought the book because of all of you. I appreciate so much your belief in me and your enthusiasm! A big shout out to those readers too! I am so grateful for all of the wonderful messages that I have received from you.

Thank you to my book family at New Holland, Fiona Schultz and Arlene Gippert and editor extraordinaire, Liz Hardy.

Thank you also to my fellow writer and one of my closest friends, Skye. You helped make the book better than it would have been if I didn't have your screenshots and notes to guide me.

I listened to a podcast recently where three writers

were talking about how you measure the success of a book. When I wrote the first book in the series, success for me was to get the book published. This measure of success evolved, and I now know that success for me was having one person read the book and tell me that they liked it.

So, I want to say thank you to all of the awesome readers that have come up to me or sent me messages to say how much they liked the first book. You have made me feel like the book was a success. I want you to know that I appreciate your words more than you could ever know and I hope that you enjoy this book just as much.

First published in 2023 by New Holland Publishers
Sydney

Level 1, 178 Fox Valley Road, Wahroonga, NSW 2076, Australia
newhollandpublishers.com

A record of this book is available from the National Library of Australia.

ISBN 9781760795139

Group Managing Director: Fiona Schultz
Project Editor: Liz Hardy
Designer: Yolanda La Gorcé, Andrew Davies
Production Director: Arlene Gippert

Printed in Australia by IVE Group

10 9 8 7 6 5 4 3 2 1

Keep up with New Holland Publishers:
f NewHollandPublishers
@newhollandpublishers

US $14.99